Twisting Trails

North Star Kids of the Fur Trade Era

**CALUMET
EDITIONS**

Minneapolis

SECOND EDITION December 2022

Twisting Trails: North Star Kids of the Fur Trade Era
Copyright © 2021 by Michael Barnes.

10 9 8 7 6 5 4 3 2
ISBN: 978-1-959770-52-7

Cover and interior design: Gary Lindberg

Cover painting: "Shooting the Rapids" by Frances Anne Hopkins,
Library and Archives Canada, C-02774k

For Kelly

Table of Contents

Twisting Trails

North Star Kids of the Fur Trade Era

Michael Barnes

**CALUMET
EDITIONS**
Minneapolis

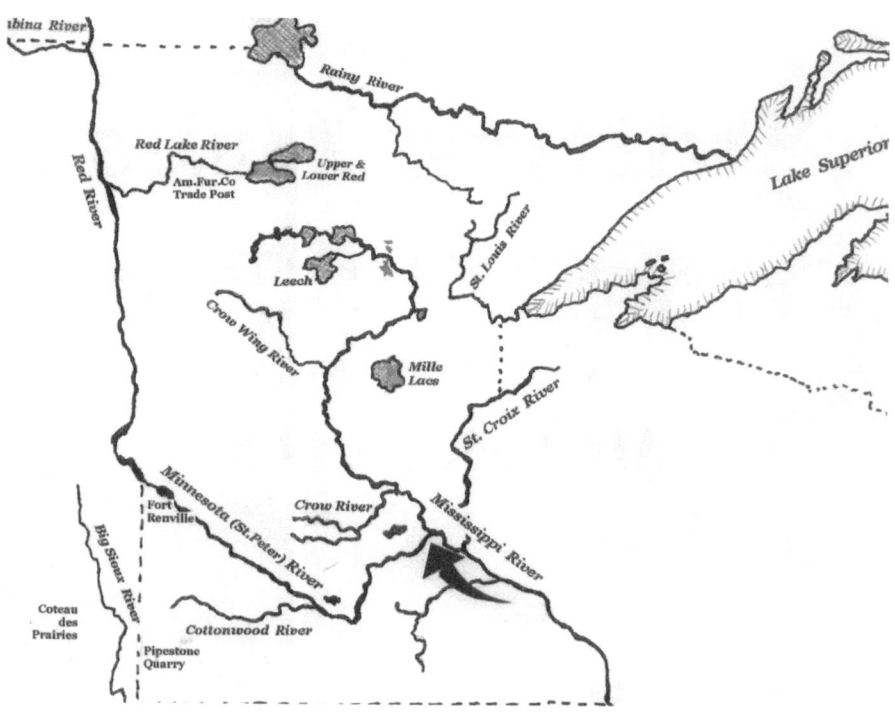

Chapter 1
1831 – Fort Snelling

Alexander Whitney's eyes grew wide as he gazed upward from the Mississippi River to the limestone walls of Fort Snelling. This eighteen-year-old soldier and everyone else on board the steamboat knew where to look. When they turned toward the afternoon sun, the steamboat skipper announced the final five miles of their upstream journey. There, just after the Minnesota River flowed into the Mississippi from the southwest, Fort Snelling loomed on a bluff ninety feet above.

In spite of the skipper's forewarning, his view of the fort's impressive ramparts overwhelmed Alex. "Citadel in the Wilderness!" he blurted to himself, repeating the nickname this young fort had earned. Officially, Fort Snelling was named after Colonel Josiah Snelling, who supervised construction and commanded the fort from 1820 until 1828.

Now in 1831, this was to be the first assignment of Alexander Whitney's military career. The father he never knew had been an army officer killed in the War of 1812. Alex's mother raised him by herself back home in Detroit. Both of them had worked to provide food, clothing, and a roof over their heads. Alex knew from an early age that he would join the army when he was old enough to enlist. In part, he yearned to carry on his father's tradition. In part, he was eager to become independent, no longer a financial burden for his mother. Alex was an ambitious, adventurous young man. This was

1

the beginning of his life's adventure, and he was determined to earn a high rank as an army officer.

He was ready. Alex's tall, slender body was well muscled for the rigors of army life. Though no stripes of rank adorned his sleeves, he wore the army uniform more neatly than the average enlisted man did. His shiny dark hair was trimmed and clean, as his mother preferred. She had enrolled young Alex in school, so he could read and write, another exception from the typical soldier. Education sparked his natural curiosity, and he was a keen observer of surrounding events.

Alex watched the skipper expertly maneuver the steamboat toward a half-dozen soldiers assembled onshore. A young lieutenant crisply commanding this group captured his attention. "Lieutenant Eastman!" the steamboat skipper shouted. "Good to see you again!"

Alex pitched in to help unload the cargo of supplies. When the skipper stepped ashore, he handed Eastman the monthly bundle of mail and said, "Lieutenant, allow me to introduce your new recruit, Alexander Whitney."

Alex remembered to salute and then shook Eastman's hand, relieved to see a smile spread across the young officer's face. At twenty-three, Seth Eastman was only five years older than Alex but had earned his lieutenant bars at West Point. He was a fit and trim officer with a neat goatee surrounding his smile.

"Young Whitney is quite a hunter!" the skipper told Eastman. "He kept our cook well-supplied with wild game all the way from St. Louis. Ducks, partridge, rabbits—whatever could be found within walking distance of our evening ports, fell to his marksmanship!"

The smile on the lieutenant's face grew wider.

* * *

The next morning at sunrise, all of Fort Snelling's army personnel rallied for roll call and to raise the colors. As the bugler played reveille, three soldiers quickly hoisted the US banner up the flagpole atop the fort's western tower. Twenty-four white stars were sewn into the blue corner of this flag, one for each American state. None of those states existed west of the Mississippi River, where Fort Snelling was built on ground identified as Unorganized United States Territory.

The muffled sounds of morning included the shuffling of stockinged feet on the barrack floor and mumbled morning greetings between soldiers, fabric rustling as soldiers made their bunk beds and dressed. Doors creaked open and leather boots scuffed across the boardwalk onto the parade ground dirt. The morning bugle pierced Alex's ears with sudden, metallic and loud reveille. Looking beyond the flag into the morning sky, Alex was struck by a stark contrast between the hard-edged, stonewalled fort and its surroundings. The walls separated the military control, established routines and rank within from the natural world extending for hundreds of miles in every direction. "Citadel in the wilderness," he murmured. "Yes, it is."

After Lieutenant Eastman dismissed the troops, he approached Alex. "Meet me back here after breakfast," he said. "I'll give you a tour of the fort."

Alex snapped a salute. "Yes, sir."

The garrison of more than one hundred enlisted men breakfasted on tasteless cornmeal gruel. However, across the parade ground the dozen or so officers dined on a tasty meal of potatoes, beans and squash from the fort's well-tended gardens and wild game hunted in the adjoining river valleys.

Alex stared down some twenty feet into the darkness of the well at the western corner of the parade ground, so Lieutenant Eastman's arrival surprised him.

"Limestone," Eastman said. "The entire bluff upon which this fort stands is limestone. Water seeps into the well between the layers of sedimentary rock. When Colonel Snelling arrived here eleven years ago, he decided to build the fort out of stones cut from the bluffs themselves."

Speechless, Alex pivoted completely around and beheld the ten-foot limestone walls.

"Snelling designed the diamond shape of the fort to fit the bluff," Eastman continued. "Each wall is 400 feet long. The northern

3

ramparts overlook both rivers, and the towers at each corner are filled with firing positions to overlap the defenses of each wall. This is the chapel." The lieutenant pointed immediately south from the well. "Beyond that is the gatehouse where you entered the fort yesterday. Our jail and guardhouse are beside the gate, along the wall. On the other side of the gate are the wood and metal shops as well as the fort's warehouse."

"I was in the warehouse yesterday, sir," Alex said. "Helped carry some of the cargo from the steamboat."

"Here's the hospital," Eastman motioned in front of the warehouse. Then, turning directly toward the morning sun, he raised his hand to shade his eyes. "Those are the officers' quarters, and that," he pointed to the far eastern corner of the fort, "is Commander Taylor's house."

"My father served proudly for Taylor nearly twenty years ago," Alex said. Colonel Zachary Taylor had been a major in the War of 1812. Then and since, Taylor had proven himself a capable leader in both war and peace. "The house looks like a mansion!"

"He's earned it," Eastman said. "And his family fills it up. The Colonel and Mrs. Taylor have three girls and a boy, the youngest. Their oldest daughter Ann is recently married to our fort surgeon, and they live in the house too."

Turning full circle, the sun now at their backs, Eastman and Alex scanned the long low barracks that housed enlisted soldiers.

"Come with me." The lieutenant began striding toward the west tower, past the sutler's store and the fort's armory. Alex followed Eastman into the tower and climbed the interior stone steps. A little sunlight filtered in through the narrow, vertical gaps of gun portals that allowed rifles to be fired from inside the walls. Eastman walked to the outer, western-most rim of the three-story tower's rooftop. Alex paused beside a twelve-pound cannon standing next to the flagpole, which had been the focus of this morning's muster.

"Our best drinking water comes from Coldwater Spring," said Eastman. "Not that well inside the fort." He motioned with his right arm along the Mississippi River. "The spring is about a mile upstream, on this side of the river. Crews haul barrels of fresh water to the fort in horse-drawn wagons. Our primary mission at Fort Snelling is to protect the fur trade."

Alex nodded. He knew well the prosperity of the fur business. Fortunes in animal pelts had been exported through the Great Lakes, past his hometown Detroit.

"There are two big threats," Eastman continued. "First, British-Canadian fur traders are still trespassing into the United States, trying to trade with Indian tribes in our territory. Second, we must keep peace between the Dakota and Ojibwe tribes, who are traditional enemies."

"Indians at war with Indians?" Alex asked.

Pointing toward the western plains, Eastman explained, "The Dakota people are horsemen, whose lands stretch south and west from the Minnesota River valley. The name Minnesota comes from Dakota words that mean cloud-colored or sky-tinted water." He leaned to look over the tower's edge. "Ojibwe are woodland people. They live along the lakes and streams inside the Mississippi River basin. The name Mississippi originates from Ojibwe words that mean Great River."

Alex studied Eastman's face in the silence that followed. He seemed to have forgotten that they stood there together. At last, Eastman continued. "There are bountiful hunting grounds between those two rivers. Warriors from both sides invariably cross paths, trying to provide meat for their villages."

"When hunters meet, they both have weapons?"

"That's right." Eastman hesitated and looked at Alex, "Speaking of weapons, I've been told you're pretty good with a gun."

"It's a fowling piece," Alex responded. "A double-barrel shotgun that belonged to my father. Folks back home say he was the best duck and partridge hunter in Detroit."

"So, marksmanship runs in your family," Eastman grinned. "Mine too." His grin broadened into a smile. "How about a shooting contest? If I win, you can take me on a bird-hunting trip. If you win, I'll take you hunting." Both young men laughed and shared a handshake.

* * *

Soldiers stood elbow-to-elbow atop Fort Snelling's west tower, jostling each other for better vantage points. More lined out the main gate, standing in the morning shade of the garrison's wall.

"Private Whitney and Lieutenant Eastman will be shooting straight away from us, with the sun behind 'em," said one excited soldier. Another confessed, "I've got a week's pay bet on this contest!"

Soon, the shooting competitors themselves came striding out from the gate, each cradling a shotgun comfortably across a forearm. Shouts of encouragement burst forth from the onlookers. Officers cheered for Lieutenant Eastman. The more numerous enlisted men loudly supported Alex. Neither Eastman nor Alex had a bet on this contest, and both were smiling broadly. Each young man was confident in his marksmanship and believed their friendship would extend through tomorrow, when they would be hunting partners searching for quail and partridge.

Flanked by a pair of soldiers, each carrying a canvas bag, Colonel Taylor arrived next. The commander joined Eastman and Alex while the soldiers peeled apart approximately ten paces to the right and left.

Taylor shook hands with each shooter, then turned back toward the men along the fort walls and raised his arm for quiet. "Good morning," he announced. "Welcome to this shooting contest which will determine Fort Snelling's shotgun marksmanship champion for the year 1831."

He waited for the enthusiastic shouts and applause to subside. "Each man will take ten shots, shooting alternately, left and right. The targets are stones made from baked river clay…" he nodded to the flanking soldiers, and they each produced a fist-sized rock from his canvas bag, "…which will be thrown by Sergeant Lewis and Corporal O'Rourke."

Colonel Taylor produced a silver dollar from his pocket and offered heads or tails to Alex, who chose heads. When the flip landed in his favor, Alex gave the first shot to Seth. "Good luck to you both!" the commander proclaimed. Then he backed up to watch with everyone else.

Eastman stepped forward and looked to Sergeant Lewis on his left. He shouldered his shotgun. "I'm ready."

The sergeant drew back his arm and hurled the first clay rock forward. *Boom!* Clay shards scattered into a puff of dust.

"Whoo hoo!" shouted the admiring crowd.

"Good shot," said Alex while he slid one shell into the barrel of his father's vintage fowling piece. Eastman nodded and watched the fluid movement of Alex's hands on his lovingly worn firearm.

Alex lifted the gun. "Ready."

Sergeant Lewis threw the stone. *Boom!* Then silence as the rock's arc curved down to thud untouched onto the ground.

The onlookers were also silent. Only Alex could hear the quiet voice near his side, "The sergeant's throw was weak. It looped down just as your shot passed above." Alex knew Eastman was correct. He also knew the comment was not to tease, but to help. Had the target been a partridge flushing to fly away, it would have continued to rise and connect with Alex's shot. He nodded, partly in appreciation of Eastman's sportsmanlike advice, but also to himself, vowing to correct his mistake.

Lieutenant Eastman stepped to the firing line again, this time turning to the right where Corporal O'Rourke was bouncing a clay stone in his hand. Eastman repositioned his feet and lifted the shotgun to his shoulder. "Ready." But the corporal, instead of tossing the rock immediately, swung his arms and then strode forward, unleashing a powerful throw. The unexpected timing and velocity of O'Rourke's launch caught Eastman off guard. He missed. "Behind it," he muttered. "My timing was off."

"You'll hit the next one," Alex assured him as he stepped forward and turned toward the corporal who produced another stone from his canvas bag. Alex paused a moment to visualize O'Rourke's first toss and prepared for his unorthodox throwing action.

"Ready." The corporal's gyrations produced another powerful throw, and Alex timed his shot perfectly.

The clay shattered. The enlisted men cheered wildly. Alternating back to the left, Eastman readied himself for the next toss from Sergeant Lewis. This one he blasted into dust. When Alex stepped up, he was ready for the sergeant's slower, looping throw and hit it perfectly. The two friends continued taking turns and broke every target, one after the other. At last, they came down to the final shots. Both Seth and Alex had hit eight of nine targets. Corporal O'Rourke held the last pair of stones.

"One more, lieutenant!" came a shout from the tower. "You can do it, private!" yelled another, and then the entire crowd was cheering. The uproar did not subside until the two smiling marksmen turned and waved to quiet the throng.

Eastman swiveled back to the firing line. He maneuvered himself into position, shouldered his shotgun, and calmly said, "Ready." The corporal's body coiled and uncoiled, hurling his rock toward the horizon. *Boom!* Pieces of the clay clattered onto the hard ground. "Hurrah!" shouted the officers, and Eastman saluted in acknowledgment.

O'Rourke juggled the final rock, passing it nervously between his hands. The contest hinged on this final target. Alex could tie it up with a hit or lose with a miss. Alex was nervous but did not let it show. He casually loaded the tenth shell and cocked his firearm. With a nod to the corporal, the gun came up smoothly and nestled against his shoulder. "Ready." O'Rourke pumped his arms, rocked forward and launched the stone. *Boom! Poof!* The soldiers crowded forward to surround both marksmen with congratulatory shouts and slaps on the back.

"Wait a minute!" yelled Sergeant Lewis, "We have to break the tie!" As the uproar subsided, heads turned one by one to Colonel Taylor. The commander held up both hands for quiet and paused a moment to collect his thoughts. Privately, he was glad the contest had ended in a tie because he was worried about hard feelings between soldiers over gambling debts.

"The way these men shoot," Taylor declared, "this contest could last all morning without a miss. Lieutenant Eastman is leading an expedition to St. Anthony Falls today, and Private Whitney is assigned to his detail. They need to get underway."

Some of the men began to grumble, leading the colonel to announce, "In honor of the tremendous marksmanship displayed by these men, an extra ration of beer will be served to every soldier after supper tonight! Three cheers for Eastman and Whitney! Hip hip…"

"Hooray!" shouted the men. "Hip-hip hooray!" They threw their hats into the air. "Hip-hip hooray!" Hoisting Seth and Alex on their shoulders, they paraded back into the fort through the main gate.

Josiah Snelling (1782 –1828)

Born in Boston, Snelling joined the Massachusetts militia at twenty-one years of age. He gained fame for bravery during the War of 1812, resulting in repeated promotions and command of Fort Harrison (Indiana).[1]

Colonel Snelling was appointed to build Fort St. Anthony on the unorganized territory of the Upper Mississippi River in 1820. This land had been part of the United States for only seventeen years, since the Louisiana Purchase.[2]

Snelling relocated the fort to the bluff overlooking the confluence of the Mississippi and Minnesota rivers (then known as St. Peters River). He helped design the diamond shape of the fort "to adapt to the shape of the ground," then supervised its construction, using locally excavated limestone blocks.[3]

Construction lasted six years, during which time the fort became self-sufficient, with its own sawmill to produce lumber, gristmill to provide flour, and a farm raising crops and livestock. In 1824, the fort was renamed in his honor.[4]

Unfortunately, an illness Snelling contracted during the War of 1812 re-emerged in 1826, eventually forcing him to relinquish command. He died in 1828 at the age of forty-six.[5]

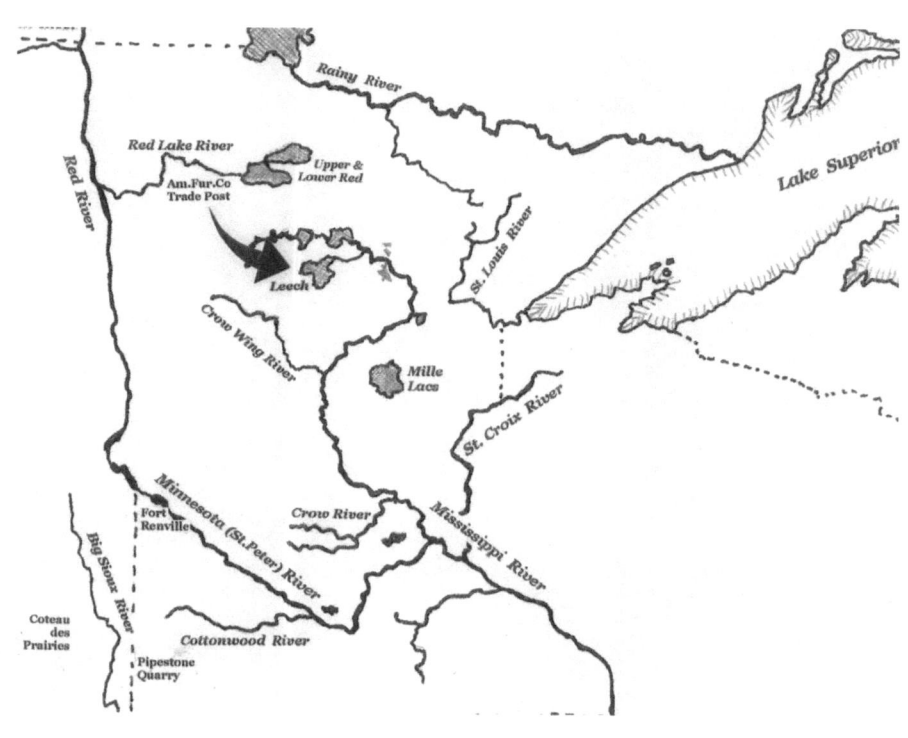

Chapter 2

1831 – Maple Sugar Camp

Angelique Reaume was a mess. The muddy ground of a late winter thaw had soaked into her moccasins and spattered her clothes. Sap from dripping maple trees covered her hands and coated her black hair where she had tried to tuck the wild strands behind her ears. The bright cool of the day and the exertion of running through the hardwood forest ruddied her cheeks. Her face beamed in a smile.

Angelique was thirteen years old. In her Métis family, that meant she was old enough to share in the chores of the maple sugar camp. The older women chose which trees to tap and where to pound spouts into the trunks, from which the maple sap would drip. Angelique and some of her female cousins were expected to watch over the birchbark buckets collecting the sap. The girls would carry the filled buckets to the fires where women boiled and stirred the sap into syrup. Most of the liquid evaporated, so it took thirty buckets of maple sap to produce one bucket of thick, tasty syrup and forty buckets to produce chunks of maple sugar.

Maple season was a festive time. The dripping sap and melting snow signaled winter's end. But the joyful expression on Angelique's face was familiar. Everyone knew her to be a cheerful girl who focused on the happiness in every task, every day, and every person. She especially loved her family, including her parents and younger brother and sister who lived along the Red Lake River and her grandparents, aunts, uncles, and cousins who lived near Leech Lake.

Angelique's parents came from different cultures. Her father, Jean Baptiste Reaume, was born into a French family near Montreal, the Canadian city on the St. Lawrence River. As a voyageur—a fur trader—he traveled throughout the northern Minnesota forest to trap animals for their fur and trade with Native American people for more furs. That is how he met Angelique's mother, White Loon. She grew up near Leech Lake in the Pillager Band of Ojibwe people. After their marriage, Jean Baptiste and White Loon established a home on the Red Lake River.

Many Métis families, with French voyageur fathers and Native American mothers, made the Red River Valley that stretched northward to Winnipeg their home.

Angelique's ten-year-old brother Lucien was at home with their father, working with the furs they had trapped through the winter. Depending on the time of year, her father and brother did the trapping, hunting, fishing and built things. Angelique and her mother attended the maple sugar camp in late winter and harvested wild rice in late summer; they also planted vegetables in the spring and harvested those in the fall. At seven years of age, Angelique's little sister Gabrielle was just beginning to help. Considered too young to be traveling through the woods, the little girl remained with her mother and aunts, gathering firewood to keep the kettles boiling.

"Be careful not to spill," cautioned White Loon while Angelique and her cousins poured sap from their buckets into the boiling cauldron. Her mother's voice was serious, but the merriment in White Loon's face betrayed her delight. Indeed, she was happy to see the camaraderie among her daughter and nieces, indicating a job well done.

Then, noticing Angelique's muddy clothes and rosy nose, White Loon's expression switched to concern. "Maybe you girls should warm up here by the fires," she suggested. Her sisters, also tending the fires, nodded in agreement. However, they were too late. The laughing cousins were already racing back into the trees, flailing their birchbark buckets as they ran. "Perhaps Grandmother can slow them down," White Loon muttered, turning sideways toward Gabrielle, who giggled and gave a doubtful shrug.

Angelique's grandmother was moving among the maples, monitoring the dripping sap. She had selected larger, more mature trees with expansive branches because she knew they would yield more and sweeter sap. Cold nights slowed the flow, but Grandmother's buckets were filling quickly today, especially from trees protected from the chilly breeze or exposed to bright sunshine. Instead of encouraging the girls to take a break, Grandmother urged them to move faster. Filled buckets stood on the ground beside replacement buckets, already collecting more sap.

"Angelique!" Grandmother called, motioning the girl toward her while waving other granddaughters on to different groves of trees. "This maple is flowing fast today," she said, pointing with both hands to spouts on several nearby tree trunks. "I have brought these two extra buckets for you. Fill them with the combined contents from all the maple trees in this cluster. Replace the empty buckets and carry the two full ones back to your mother."

"Yes, Grandmother," Angelique nodded while the old woman hurried away to direct the other girls. Angelique glowed with pride; the brief exchange was proof of Grandmother's confidence in her abilities. The older woman was held in great esteem within their village. Her son and White Loon's brother was Flat Mouth, leader of their Pillager Band. He was famous and much respected throughout the entire Ojibwe nation.

Angelique noted that although Grandmother's hair might be graying, the woman still moved gracefully between the trees, though perhaps more carefully than she had in earlier years. Her plain deerskin clothing was meant for work and not decorated with colorful beads or brightly dyed porcupine quills, as were her dresses for special occasions. She wore a long skirt over warm leggings that reached from knees to ankles, just to the top of her winter moccasins. Over her tight-fitting coat, she had draped a woolen blanket; no doubt acquired in trade. *I wonder,* thought Angelique, *if the trader was my father!*

Manufactured merchandise such as woolen blankets and metal tools were typical exchange goods in the fur trade. Voyageurs like her father, Jean Baptiste Reaume, transported these supplies from factories in European and American cities to Native Americans. Angelique adored her father and imagined him and his merry, bearded face with her brother back home beside the Red Lake River.

Plop. Another drop of sap landed in a nearby bucket, disrupting her daydreams. Angelique looked into the birchbark container to find it more than half-filled. She replaced that basket and scurried to another big maple tree trunk to check the spout. Split spruce roots laced each of her birch buckets together and looped above the tops to form flexible handles. She judged them to be sturdy and guessed she need not worry about filling each of them near the brims.

Soon her second bucket was full, and Angelique carefully bent to grasp the handles of both containers, one in each hand. Feeling their weight when she stood up, they were not too heavy, but sap sloshed near the tops of the buckets, so her first few steps were slow and cautious. Gradually she settled into a swifter, gliding rhythm. She glanced back and forth between the ground and her buckets, looking for a smooth, uncluttered path while eyeing the swaying sap inside her swinging buckets.

Beside the path ahead, she noticed a huge maple, tapped with buckets around the trunk. Passing by the tree, she peeked at the buckets to see how full they were. *Bump! Thump! Whump!* Angelique sprawled headlong onto the ground, her buckets sloshing across mud and snow. Looking after the empty containers with shock and despair, she heard a giggle from behind. Whirling on her hip, she looked into the smirking face of her cousin Wind on the Water, who was still holding the end of a long stick over which Angelique had just tripped.

"You're so clumsy!" Wind on the Water laughed.

Angelique's dark eyes glinted, and she leaped on top of the older, larger girl in an instant, flailing blows with both hands. Wind on the Water curled into a ball and covered her face with both forearms. When Angelique's frenzy subsided and the battering stopped, Wind on the Water scrambled around the big maple and peered fearfully from behind it. Angelique gathered her scattered buckets and silently turned back without even looking at her tormentor.

Regaining composure as she walked, Angelique inspected her buckets, and with relief, found neither of them broken. The light, flexible birchbark had simply bounced across the ground without smashing. She circled toward a more distant grove of maples and began blending the contents of buckets from several trees. She saw Grandmother re-emerge from the trees just as she refilled both of her containers.

"I'm surprised you're still here," Grandmother said. "I thought your buckets would be full by now."

Tears began to well up in the girl's eyes. "They *were* full," the words bursting through her trembling lips. Recalling the confrontation brought back the feelings of anger and confusion, and she sputtered, "Wind on the Water tripped me! Evil! Why?" Then, looking into Grandmother's eyes, she suddenly felt guilty. "Oh, I'm so sorry! All the sap spilled!"

"It's all right," reassured the old woman. Then, with an arm around Angelique's shoulders, she guided her to rest against the base of a tree. "There's plenty of sap in these old maples. We'll just refill your buckets."

"I hit her," Angelique admitted.

"Did you hurt her?"

"I don't think so. But I wanted to. She tripped me on purpose. Then she laughed at me!"

The Ojibwe matriarch let out a sigh as she pivoted to rest her back against the tree, shoulder-to-shoulder with her granddaughter. "Wind on the Water is jealous of you."

"Jealous? Of me? She is daughter to the chief!" Indeed, Wind on the Water's father was Flat Mouth, leader of the Pillager Band. He gained fame by leading several victorious battles against Dakota war parties. Now he was admired throughout the northern forests as a powerful orator who eloquently represented all Ojibwe people in treaty talks with whites.

"That is true. Wind on the Water is proud of her family's status. But she is envious that the people of our village speak so highly of your mother and father. Jean Baptiste is an honest and successful trader who has delivered many valuable goods and guns to our people. White Loon is an exceptional woman. Perhaps, in her own way, as skillful and wise as her brother Flat Mouth."

"How did my parents come to be married?"

"Because they are worthy of each other," Grandmother answered with a smile. "Your father is a handsome man and very successful. Your mother is a beautiful woman with many abilities. He delivers kindness, and she develops happiness. When White Loon heard your father telling stories and singing songs around our campfires, and Jean Baptiste Reaume saw your mother gracefully dancing, they could not resist each other!"

Grandmother stood and turned her head toward the western sky. A few thin clouds were turning purple where the sun neared the horizon. "Evening is coming. After sunset, colder temperatures will slow the flow of sap flow from the maple trees. Finish with these buckets, and I'll start rounding up the other girls."

Angelique's birchbark containers soon refilled. She gathered them up and continued her journey to the boiling fires. Before long, she could hear young female voices in the distance, and her nose detected the distinct smell of campfire smoke. Approaching a clump of spruces, she could see the fires flickering through needled branches. There White Loon stirred a kettle into which Wind on the Water poured sap. Angelique stopped. Something looked different about both of them.

Her mother had always been just that: her mother. They shared a wonderful loving relationship. But today, after the conversation with Grandmother, she looked at White Loon as others might: an exceptional daughter of the Pillager Band of Ojibwe grown into an admirable woman, the wise sister of Chief Flat Mouth, and the capable partner of a prosperous trader. She imagined how this beautiful woman must have been a pretty girl. Angelique wondered, *Am I like her?*

As the older cousin, taller and stronger, Wind on the Water had seemed superior. However, with both girls now teenagers, their difference in height had diminished. And today's scuffle revealed a similar balance of strength. Wind on the Water's family status may have made the older girl seem a cut above. But Grandmother's counsel revealed that the chief's family was perhaps no more prominent than the family of Jean Baptiste Reaume. Angelique no longer felt anger for Wind on the Water, nor envy. "I'm not an inferior little cousin anymore," she whispered. "I'm an equal."

Eshkibagikoonzhe (1774–1860)

Eshkibagikoonzhe was known as Flat Mouth by white fur traders. Perhaps his nickname came from a tough noncommittal negotiating demeanor when trading, perhaps from his famous neutrality, refusing to involve his people in any fight involving whites. Whatever the origin, his reputation for steadfast leadership was well known.[6]

Born into the Pillager Band of Ojibwe near Leech Lake, Eshkibagikoonzhe earned admiration for his bravery during several victorious battles against Dakota warriors. He was a recognized leader of the band by the age of thirty-two.[7]

Known as a great orator among the Ojibwe, he represented them during major treaty negotiations, including in 1825 at Prairie du Chien, 1837 at Fort Snelling, and 1854 in Washington, DC. Flat Mouth consistently believed that maintaining economic trade was important for his people.[8]

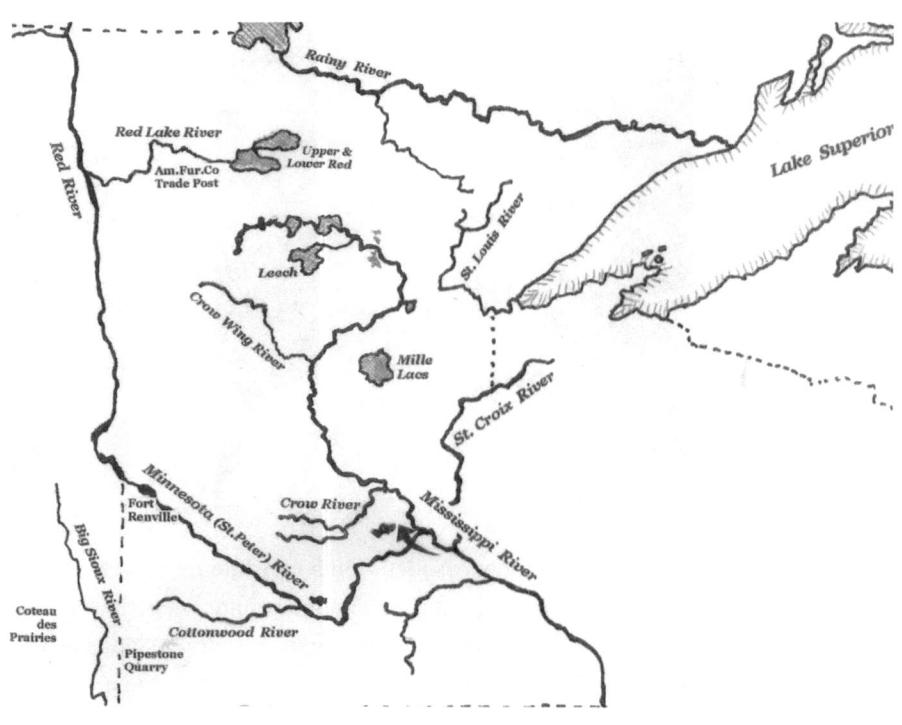

Chapter 3
1831 – St. Anthony Falls

Business and pleasure were the intentions of the expedition to St. Anthony Falls. The team's primary task was to retrieve two wagon loads of lumber from the fort's sawmill, seven miles up the Mississippi River. However, Lieutenant Eastman had scheduled an extra day to hunt game birds around nearby lakes. For him and his new friend Alex, the shooting contest was the start of a three-day vacation from the hum-drum routine inside Fort Snelling.

They sat together on the bench seat of the lead wagon. Eastman handled the reins harnessed to a pair of dapple-gray Percheron draft horses. A pair of black horses pulled the second wagon driven by two carpenters from the fort, Corporal Joe Pratt and Private Pete Jackson. Joe and Pete were working to rebuild the Indian Agency's council house, which had burned the previous summer. They would select lumber needed for this project from the sawmill at St. Anthony Falls.

"You've become a very popular fellow in a very short time," Eastman said to Alex. "The men at the fort really like you."

"I've had a chance to meet almost everybody. During these first several weeks of my deployment, I've been assigned to practically every job at Fort Snelling."

"That's by design. It's a way to find out the work for which a new soldier is best suited. Take Pete back there," Eastman motioned to Private Jackson in the trailing wagon. "He did several jobs at the fort before Joe asked for his permanent assignment to be a carpenter."

"It's beyond that," Alex said. "It's helped me learn how everything fits together here."

"Fort Snelling is at the edge of the frontier. A long way from the nearest supply depot. Colonel Snelling wanted this fort to be totally self-sufficient. The men here feed themselves, doctor themselves, make their own equipment, and clean up after themselves."

Alex chuckled. "Well, I have been cleaning up! In the kitchen and the laundry. I've also dug weeds in the farm fields and tended the livestock, including these horses. But I was probably most helpful in the blacksmith shop. Back home in Detroit, I worked as an assistant to a blacksmith after Father died. I tended the forge and helped to make or repair a few simple iron tools."

"What kinds of tools?" Eastman asked.

"Mother and I both got jobs to supply the fur trade, passing through the Great Lakes. She sewed clothing, mostly warm clothes, for Indian people in the northern forests. I worked on items like animal traps, axe heads and cooking kettles."

"Metal-working skills are valuable in an army fort," the lieutenant stated. "Of course," he added with a grin, "everybody takes their turn on guard duty. You proved today that you're capable of handling a firearm."

"We both did!" The young men shared a hearty laugh.

* * *

The wagons approached St. Anthony Falls about two o'clock that afternoon. In the distance, Alex could see rooflines amidst the trees along the riverbank. "Three buildings?" he asked.

"That larger wooden building on the left is the sawmill. The stone structure beside it is the gristmill. Wheat and corn grown in the fields outside Fort Snelling are brought here where it's ground into flour and cornmeal." Eastman held the reins in his left hand and pointed toward the structures with his right, "That smaller wooden building is the guard shack. A few men are permanently stationed here, on a rotating basis, to protect both mills. They live in the guard shack while they're here."

Twisting Trails

The roar of the waterfall grew stronger as both wagons got closer to the river. "Go take a look at the falls," Eastman said, reining the horses to a stop beside the sawmill.

Alex jumped down from the wagon seat and walked to his left around the buildings where he could see the river. In front of him, water fell in a vertical drop of somewhere between ten and twenty feet. Above and to the left of the falls, the Mississippi flowed quietly, wide and placid, nearly level with its prairie banks, a spectacular contrast to the sudden drop over St. Anthony Falls. Alex could feel the power of the cascade as it crashed into huge jagged boulders at the foot of the falls, creating torrents of whirlpools in the river. He could feel the fine mist from the splashing water against his face. Edging cautiously closer to the falls, Alex craned his neck to the right, where he could see rapids dashing around a pair of small islands and descending into a narrow gorge between steep bluffs on both sides of the river.

"It can really spin that wheel." The lieutenant had walked up beside Alex and was pointing to the water wheel turning alongside the wall of the sawmill. "Let's go inside." Alex followed Eastman into the building and downstairs, where a water wheel spun a huge wooden shaft, in turn, rotating gears that drove the big saw upstairs.

When they climbed back up the stairs, they could see Corporal Pratt and Private Jackson talking with the sawyers who operated the mill. The squeal of gears and whine of the saw obliterated their words, but Joe gestured with his hands, and the sawyers nodded.

Outside, Joe and Pete soon joined Alex and Eastman. "Most of the boards we want are already cut," explained Corporal Pratt, pointing to a shed with a roof but no walls. "The largest timbers we need won't be ready until tomorrow."

"Okay." Eastman clapped his hands together. "Let's get busy." After relocating the wagons next to the shed, Eastman assigned Alex to the horses. He unharnessed the Percherons, provided buckets of grain and water, and then hobbled all four in the shade of tall cottonwood trees where they could graze on lush green grass. By then, one wagon was already half-full of lumber. Joe and Pete had stripped off their shirts, and perspiration soaked through Eastman's.

"Let's load everything we can this afternoon," Pratt said, breathing heavily. "We'll leave enough room on the second wagon to add those big timbers that will be ready tomorrow. Private Jackson and I can handle them with the sawyers." Then, with a sly smile, he added, "You two sharpshooters can spend all day tomorrow hunting."

"It's a deal," Eastman responded. "When you fellows get to Green's Villa tomorrow night, Private Whitney and I will serve you a partridge dinner!"

* * *

"What is Green's Villa?" asked Alex. They were back on the wagon seat, headed southwest after collecting the first day's load of lumber.

"About ten years ago, there was a lieutenant here at Fort Snelling named Platt Green," Eastman explained. "He enjoyed hunting and fishing, and his wife liked getting away from the fort to spend a few days of lakeshore relaxation. So Lieutenant Green built a cabin on the shore of Lake Calhoun, one of a chain of lakes about three miles up this trail. The Indians call it Bde Maka Ska, meaning white banked lake."

"How luxurious is the villa?"

Spontaneous laughter burst out of Eastman. "It's not really a villa. It's actually nothing more than a shack." The lieutenant's tone shifted from silly to serious. "It's a paradise. The water, the trees, the wildlife…and liberty from the stone walls of Fort Snelling."

When they arrived at Green's Villa, it was nearing six o'clock. Alex again watered, fed and hobbled the horses while Eastman prepared their evening meal. Inside, the stew of beef, carrots and potatoes assembled by Eastman simmered in a pot suspended in the fireplace.

Alex sighed when he savored the first spoonful of the stew. "This is a better meal than whatever's being served back at the fort."

Eastman smiled, gently patting his stomach, "I will sleep well tonight. I'm tired. With our shooting contest, the wagon ride, and loading all those boards, we've had a full day."

"I'll wash the dishes," Alex volunteered. "Then I'm going to clean my gun before turning in." By the time the dishtowel was hung up to dry, Eastman was already flat on his bed. Alex carried his shotgun outside and settled on a bench where the gentle horizontal rays of the setting sun would illuminate his work.

As he removed the firearm from its leather sheath, Alex remembered the blacksmith shop back home. The proprietor, Mr. MacIntosh, was a master craftsman who could expertly shoe a horse or edge the blade of a hunting knife. Before Alex's departure from Detroit, he and Mr. MacIntosh had fine-tuned every mechanism of this shotgun. He handled it with a loving touch, just as his father had.

When Alex re-entered Green's Villa, he was greeted by Eastman's gentle snoring. He lay down, closed his eyes and smiled, happy to have friends like Mr. MacIntosh and Seth Eastman.

* * *

Alex awakened slowly, into quiet semi-darkness. He gradually re-alized the dim light was due to shade from sheltering trees around the cabin. When he swung his feet onto the floor and sat upright, he could distinguish a sunlit horizon out the windows. Eastman no longer snored in the opposite bunk. Instead, he was sitting in the morning sun, out by the white shoreline of Lake Bde Maka Ska.

Alex walked to the lakeshore and squatted to splash water against his face. He stood and scanned the panorama across the lake where morning fog reached under branches of surrounding trees and still hovered near the surface. Away from the shoreline, smooth water offered a dappled reflection of the green-leafed canopy and bright clear blue sky above. A gentle breeze sent shimmering ripples across the middle of the lake. Sunlight glinted in the dewdrops clinging to nearby blades of grass. All of the dewdrops and the tendrils of fog quickly disappeared with the rising sun.

He turned away from the lake to face Seth and the cabin. "What are you writing?" Alex asked, pointing to a tablet of paper on the lieutenant's lap.

"Oh, this is for you," Eastman responded. He peeled off the top sheet and extended it up to Private Whitney. Alex looked speechless at the splendid illustration drawn on the paper. It was a lifelike depiction of their shooting contest, detailing himself, shotgun to his shoulder, with the lieutenant and the colonel watching from behind, and the crowd of soldiers in the background and in front and atop the walls of Fort Snelling.

"I like to make sketches of scenes I admire." Eastman held up a simple graphite pencil. "My West Point education was drafting and illustration. I'm trained by the United States Army to draw maps and pictures of potential battle terrain."

Exchanging a look with the lieutenant. Alex had noticed Eastman's eyes before, but now their power of observation became apparent. "You have an artist's vision! This could be displayed in a gallery."

"I've turned a few of my favorites into watercolor paintings. But most of them are just sketches. I have dozens of 'em," Eastman said.

"I will treasure this one." Alex studied the picture with wide eyes and carried it back inside the cabin.

* * *

The two hunters shared a breakfast that did not require cooking—bread, dried meat and apples. Then gathered their shotguns, powder and shells. As they stepped outside, Alex could not help but admire the gorgeous landscape around them. "You're right," he sighed. "This place is beautiful."

"Green's Villa is a popular destination for the married officers to bring their wives. Sort of a romantic getaway, I guess." Eastman repositioned his gun to rest comfortably across his shoulder. "But for men like you and me, this is a hunting lodge. Today we're going to prove it."

From the tree-lined lakeshore, Eastman led the way southeast onto a prairie covered by knee-high grasses and occasional bushes.

"Hopefully, we'll flush some upland game birds from this plateau," he said. "Ruffed grouse or bobwhite quail. If not, we can surely find a flock of ducks on one of these nearby lakes." He pointed, first to the north, "That little one with the islands is called Lake of the Isles. There's a bigger one about a mile to the south named Lake Harriet, after the wife of Colonel Leavenworth, the original commander here." Next, Eastman pulled down the front brim of his slouch hat and squinted toward the morning sun, "A few miles southeast, ahead of us, runs a stream called Minnehaha Creek. It connects several of these small lakes, then drops over a pretty little waterfall just before it empties into the Mississippi River."

As an officer, Eastman preferred to wear his fully brimmed black slouch hat. It shaded his face and neck from sunlight on a hot day and sheltered from raindrops on a wet one. Enlisted men had no choice in the matter of a hat, so Alex wore his army-issued dark blue forage cap.

"Since you're on the left," suggested Eastman, "you shoot first at any bird that flushes your direction. I'll take first crack at one which flies to the right. That way, we won't shoot past each other's heads."

"Nor will we fire a double amount of pellets into the meat of a bird we want to eat," Alex laughed. They separated in order to walk both sides of a copse surrounding a stand of wild plum trees. "What if more than one partridge flies out of this thicket?" he asked.

"Commence firing," the lieutenant commanded, exaggerating his most strict military enunciation. "Fire at will!" Both soldiers burst out laughing and alarmed a rabbit that bolted from the bushes and scampered directly between them. Instinctively, each hunter shouldered his weapon, but neither man pulled the trigger. "We can do better than rabbit stew," Eastman declared, and once more, they both laughed.

Not far beyond the plum trees, a covey of bobwhite quail exploded out of the tall grass, eight to ten birds scattering in every direction. Alex quickly aimed at one quail on the left, and Eastman leveled his shotgun at another on the right. *Boom! Boom!* Two shots.

Two birds. Each man placed into his game bag a contribution for supper.

Before long, Alex noticed an expanse of sparkling water off to the west. "What did you call that lake?"

"That's Lake Harriet. But let's continue walking this direction," Eastman suggested, pointing southeast. "We'll reach Minnehaha Creek inside an hour. Then we can walk the creek upstream for an hour before turning back toward the villa. The entire clockwise circle will get us back to the cabin before mid-afternoon."

"Good. That will give us time to clean our birds and get supper ready for Corporal Pratt and Private Jackson."

As they approached the creek, a larger bird exploded from under the branches of a spruce tree. The thunderous sound of its beating wings prompted Alex to shout, "Partridge!"

It flew in front of Eastman, who took aim, pulled the trigger and the bird tumbled to the ground. Quickly retrieving it, Eastman walked closer to Alex and displayed the tail feathers in the shape of a fan. "Out here on the frontier, people say this is a ruffed grouse. But it's the exact same bird that people call partridge in Michigan and states farther east."

They admired the speckled rusty brown feathers of the grouse and noted the characteristic black bar, which spanned the broad width of the fanned tail. "Whatever you call 'em, I love hunting these birds," declared Alex. "The explosion of beating wings when they take flight. Their acrobatic speed through tree branches. Plus, of course, they make a tasty meal!"

Eastman nodded in agreement and tucked the grouse into the game bag slung behind his left hip. Then pointing along Minnehaha creek, he said, "I'll cross to the other bank of the creek. Then we can walk upstream, westward, with one of us hunting each side."

They had not gone more than fifty yards when a covey of quail sprang out of the creek bed and flushed in front of Alex. He quickly took aim at a bird flying farthest away from the stream and fired. The quail folded to the ground, but seven or eight others veered away from the gunshot and flew across the creek to escape. "Quail!

Coming at you!" A moment later, the lieutenant's shotgun fired, and another bobwhite fell from flight.

"Thanks for the heads up. I got one."

"So did I," said Alex. "Now we have four quail and the one partridge…er grouse."

"We'll need about double that to feed ourselves, plus Corporal Pratt and Private Jackson," Eastman hollered. "Let's keep walking up the creek. We'll likely find more birds in these thickets along your side or mine." He was right. Within the hour, they had flushed three more coveys and put four additional quail into their game bags.

"Hold up," Eastman called. "I'll come back across the stream here." Alex stepped between trees along the creek bank from where he could see the lieutenant cautiously descending the opposite embankment. The stream narrowed here and offered a shorter crossing, but the banks on both sides were steep. As Eastman began wading across, it also proved deeper. "Maybe I should have forded somewhere else." He lifted his shotgun to shoulder height to keep it dry.

Alex edged carefully down the creek bank, holding onto a tree trunk for stability. He reached out over the water to take Eastman's gun and began working his way back up the embankment. With both hands free, the lieutenant grabbed a low-hanging branch and pulled himself up out of the waist-deep stream. The branch broke, and Eastman grasped for another limb, missed, and landed back first into the water. In an instant, he was completely submerged, and his slouch hat bobbed to the surface.

Alex gawked helplessly down at where his superior officer disappeared.

The lieutenant sputtered back above water. Rivulets cascaded from his high forehead and dripped from the bristly goatee on his chin. Wiping a hand across his eyes, Eastman blinked and located the floating hat, which he quickly snatched. To Alex's relief, the lieutenant stood up and burst out laughing.

The commotion flushed a grouse, and Alex turned toward its unmistakable wing beats. The bird descended another forty yards along the stream.

Eastman grinned. "What are you waiting for? Go get him."

Alex walked quietly toward the spot where he saw the grouse land. He stopped about ten paces away, looking and listening intently. Nothing. Five more strides and again, Alex froze in place, but he neither saw nor heard the bird. Finally, he walked to and through the grouse's landing spot, but it did not flush. He wasn't surprised. While hunting these birds back home in Michigan, they had frequently evaded him by scampering along the ground.

Just before turning around, Alex noticed movement in the grass another fifty yards ahead. Something was advancing up and out of the creek bed. He crouched and peered through the waving tips of tall prairie grass. *A wild turkey! Maybe twenty pounds*, he thought. It approached a bush and bent forward. *Perhaps scratching or pecking for seeds.* Alex noted the wind was in his favor, blowing toward him from the turkey. He knew these to be wary birds and was glad the breeze would muffle the sounds of his approach.

I've got to get closer. Dropping to hands and knees, he crawled with painstaking quietness to a spot behind a thick cluster of sumac bushes and cautiously raised his head to peek through the leafy stems. The turkey was still casually scratching at the ground, now only twenty-five yards away. *A young male,* Alex thought, though he could not see a telltale beard protruding from the large, colorfully feathered bird's chest. "Yelp." Alex mimicked a female turkey. Immediately, the tom raised his red featherless head and leaned toward the sound. Now the male's beard and snood were evident, and so was his curiosity. After a pause of several seconds, the hunter called again, "Yelp, yelp." Now the turkey took a few wary steps in his direction. *A little closer and I'll have a clear shot,* Alex thought. He resisted the temptation to call again and depended on the silence to provoke the bird's curiosity. It worked. The turkey advanced into an open space. In one smooth movement, the young soldier stood and leveled his shotgun barrel. *Boom!* The big bird was knocked down, and a few downy feathers floated on the air. Alex bounded forward to make sure it wouldn't run away, but the turkey lay motionless as he approached.

Twisting Trails

He kneeled beside the bird running his fingers over the feathers. Its body was dark, almost black. The wing flashed iridescent colors of copper, green and purple in the sunlight when he lifted it. The hairy beard on its chest, the long fan of tail feathers, and a spur on the back of each long leg confirmed this was a male turkey. Alex encircled his right hand around both legs, just above the four sharp toenails on each shank. He stood and lifted the feathery bulk, estimating the weight. *All of twenty pounds,* he thought and turned back toward Lieutenant Eastman.

As he walked, Alex looked from the wild turkey in his right hand to his father's fowling piece in his left. He remembered a tom turkey feather and beard hanging beside this shotgun on the old gun rack back home in Detroit. Alex wondered how his father's hunt of yesteryear compared to his today. He wished the elder Whitney could see this one today and imagined that his father's smile would match his own expression now.

"A turkey? We'll feast tonight!" Eastman startled Alex from his daydream. Seated on the ground dressed only in his underwear and hat, Eastman grinned. His wet shirt and trousers hung over nearby branches, and sticks poked vertically into the ground suspended each boot upside down. "Let's clean these birds while the breeze and sunshine are drying my wardrobe."

* * *

Upon their mid-afternoon return to Green's Villa, the hunters found Joe and Pete swimming in the lake. "Our workday is done!" Corporal Pratt proclaimed with a happy wave that sprayed drops of water through the air. Private Jackson, however, was quiet, unsure how Lieutenant Eastman would view this lack of military decorum.

"At ease, private," the lieutenant said. Then, with a smile, he gave a relaxed salute.

"But your workday is not totally done. The two of you are in charge of cooking the potatoes for supper tonight. You can bake 'em or mash 'em, whichever you prefer. Private Whitney will take care of the horses. I'll prepare these birds. They are going to be tasty."

That evening the four soldiers enjoyed a delicious meal. They all willingly shared the cleanup before settling down to an evening of relaxation. Each realized they would leave the peaceful beauty of Lake Bde Maka Ska tomorrow and return to the rigid military routine of Fort Snelling.

Seth Eastman (1808–1875)

Seth Eastman was one of thirteen children, born in Brunswick, Massachusetts (later Maine). Eastman went to the West Point military academy at sixteen, where he was an average student who excelled in art. Upon graduation, he was assigned to Fort Snelling, where he served for three years.[9]

He was recalled to West Point in 1833 to teach military map-making and illustration. He taught for seven years, during which time he authored his own textbook, *Treatise on Topography*.[10]

Eastman's marriage to a Dakota girl, Stands Like a Spirit, produced a famous daughter and grandson. But that relationship ended when he returned to West Point and, while there, married Mary Henderson, daughter of a military surgeon.[11]

In 1841, at age thirty-three, he was promoted to Brigadier General and reassigned to Fort Snelling as the post commander. Throughout his military career, Eastman produced hundreds of sketches and paintings, many of which depicted life on the frontier. Most famously, he served as illustrator for H. R. Schoolcraft's six-volume epic *Information Regarding the History, Conditions, and Prospects of the Indian Tribes of the United States*.[12]

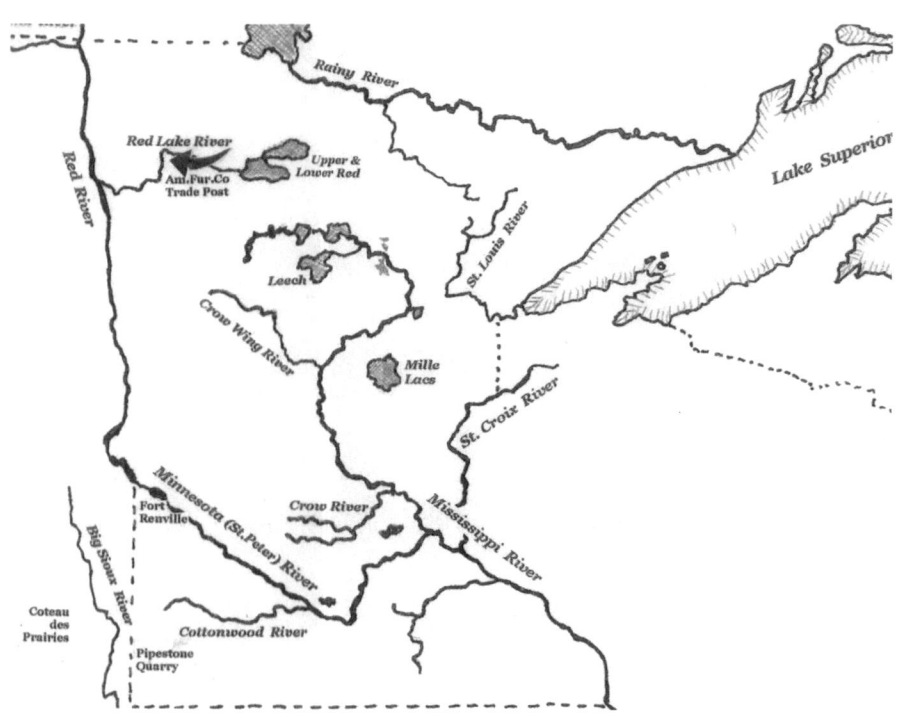

Chapter 4
1832 – Red Lake River

Angelique's slender nimble fingers were tired and sore. She was sewing a fire bag for her brother, but her hands were not familiar with this task. The girl's knuckles were weary, and the sewing needle poked and scratched her tender fingertips. The fire bag would be a gift for Lucien in which he might carry a flint and steel to spark a flame when away from home. Despite her discomfort, Angelique stuck to the project, determined to present her gift during one of these frigid days of winter. She sat on the floor of her family's log home near her mother's feet.

White Loon was also sewing—a new coat for Lucien. With experienced hands, she efficiently laced sinew through the deerskin while she repeatedly glanced at Angelique's handiwork. The mother appreciated her daughter's persistence and grinned as the girl's face contorted from tight-lipped determination to a painful wince. "You are doing well," she encouraged. "It will get easier with practice."

They sat together in the sunlight shining brightly through one of only two windows flanking the front door. Their home faced south, onto the frozen Red Lake River, toward the low mid-winter sun. Across the room, Angelique's little sister Gabrielle fashioned bits of cloth and deerskin around a doll made from birchbark. The younger girl kneeled in the other shaft of sunlight, taking advantage of the warmth and illumination like her mother and sister. Holding up the doll, she said, "I made warm clothes for my baby."

"Your baby *needs* warm clothes on a day like this," responded White Loon. Walking to the window, she scanned the snow-covered landscape and sighed. "I hope your brother and father are staying warm out there."

* * *

Indeed, they were. Jean Baptiste and Lucien were working their trap line along streams feeding into the Red Lake River. Although the temperature was extremely low, the breeze was calm, almost non-existent. The blue sky contained not one single cloud to block the warming glow of the sun. Their exhaled breath floated on the still air as they trudged along the riverbank from one trap to the next. Beneath his fur cap, ten-year-old Lucien could feel beads of perspiration on his forehead. "I'm sweating!" he shouted to his father, who walked several paces ahead.

Without breaking stride, Jean Baptiste answered, "Good! I'll tell your mother she need not hurry with that new coat she's making for you." The boy stopped and smiled. He knew his father was kidding him. Lucien visualized the merry grin that was surely there behind his father's black beard. The boy slid his cap off and wiped the back of a mitten across his glistening brow. When the boy lifted his arm, the coat sleeve exposed his wrist, reminding him of the reason for that new coat. Lucien's arms and legs were growing longer. He might never be as stout and strong as his father, but he was bound to be taller. Both he and Angelique were developing lean bodies that more closely resembled White Loon and her family.

Jean Baptiste moved powerfully and steadily forward on short, muscular legs like pistons. While the snowshoes kept his feet from sinking too deep into the drifts, the fresh, fluffy top layer scattered with each vigorous stride. He pulled the light sled they made together the previous summer. It was built to be a dog sled or, for its current use, to transport traps along this route and the dead bodies of trapped animals back to their home.

Lucien's snowshoes had also been made during the recent summer. Narrow limbs from an ash tree were bent to form the light but sturdy frames. Fur trappers like his father were experts at weaving rawhide leather webbing and straps into the ideal shape for a rugged design enabling them to walk across the snow rather than plow through it.

With his cap off and ears exposed, the boy realized how quiet it was. The new blanket of soft snow muffled every sound. Without a breeze, the towering spruce trees stood still and silent with snow heaped and suspended on their branches. Frost glazed the tall bushes along the riverbank, and their barren limbs sparkled like crystals in the bright morning sunshine. A raven's caw shattered the silence and Lucien's thoughts. His eyes darted toward the gleaming blackbird and then back to where his father continued to advance. He whipped the cap back on his head and over his cold ears and began jogging up the trail just broken by the man and sled. Before long, he had closed the gap, and perspiration beaded his brow.

* * *

"The fire bag will make a wonderful gift for Luc." White Loon smiled. Close friends and family often shortened Lucien's name to Luc, pronounced *Luke*. "It will be a useful piece of gear and make him feel more grown-up."

Angelique modeled the sash across her torso with the bag suspended at her hip, "All of the men wear them."

"When Luc grows old enough to go hunting," White Loon added, "he will carry ammunition in this bag." Her expression shifted into one of slight disapproval. "And, if he begins smoking like your father, his pipe and tobacco may be kept in there."

"Papa's bag is bigger. And much prettier!" Angelique proclaimed.

"I made that one many years ago." White Loon sighed, thoughtfully looking down at her hands and Lucien's new coat. "I sewed brightly colored beads into Jean Baptiste's fire bag and decorated it with dyed porcupine quills. We Métis are sometimes called the *Flower Beadwork People*. Our designs are more than flowers and represent all four parts of plant life—stems, leaves and buds, as well as the blossoms. Métis decorations correspond to the four cardinal directions in nature—north, south, east and west. And every beautiful pattern will contain at least one mistake. Only the Creator is perfect, so we must misplace a bead or stitch to guard against egotistical pride." After a pause, White Loon giggled and admitted, "I committed numerous mistakes while sewing your father's fire bag!" Her smile softened. "But he received my gift as if it were the greatest treasure on earth. He always appreciates me... and I appreciate him."

* * *

For Jean Baptiste and Luc, the next stop along the trap line yielded a beaver, one of the most prized animals for fur trappers. Two days prior, the voyageur chopped a hole through the ice near the riverbank. The hole gave the beavers a temporary avenue in and out from under the ice. Jean Baptiste had also placed a trap immediately beneath that hole and captured this beaver. Sub-zero temperatures refroze the opening; Jean Baptiste chopped the ice away again. After removing the beaver from the submerged trap, he handed it to Lucien. "Here, Luc, this big beaver will make a prime pelt." He began to reset the trap underwater again.

"Its hair is so thick!" Lucien marveled.

"Beaver fur is dense and soft to begin with and especially thick in winter. Furry animals grow longer and warmer hair for protection from cold weather. That's why winter is the best time of year to trap them."

After another hour, father and son completed their circuitous route. Traveling away from their house, they had checked traps along the river's northern bank. Then, after crossing the frozen stream, they worked their way back along the southern shore. Within sight of his family's home, Jean Baptiste paused to study it. Two log buildings stood side-by-side along the waterfront. A thin wisp of smoke curled skyward from a stone chimney poking through the far western roof peak of the house to his left, in which were his wife and daughters. White Loon might be tending the fireplace along that wall where she kept her kitchen supplies. The opposite roof peak extended well beyond the cabin's eastern wall. Within that side were the family sleeping quarters, and outside, a generous supply of firewood was stacked beneath the overhang. "You might split some additional kindling for your mother." He directed Lucien's attention to the woodpile. "But that can wait until tomorrow."

He started across the river towing his fur-laden sled toward the larger building on the right. Perpendicular with the house, its roofline extended over a doorway and open porch that faced the river. This was Jean Baptiste's trading post. For generations, travelers forded the Red Lake River here, and the place was known as the Old Crossing. Within the walls of the well-located post were factory-made goods ready to trade for furs with Native American Indians.

Father and son trudged around to the rear of the trading post, stopping beside a back door. The boy grabbed a few pieces of firewood and entered this back room where his elder was lighting a lamp that burned animal fat. The lard-fueled lamplight illuminated this back room where the Reaume men cared for their furs. Tools to remove the hides, clean them, and keep them soft covered a wooden bench along one wall. Pelts from various animals, in different stages of care, hung from the opposite wall and rafters. Luc kneeled in front of a wood stove and started a fire to warm their workspace.

"You're doing well with your muskrat pelts." Jean Baptiste praised his son. "Here are the additional two we brought in today."

Luc received the two muskrats and watched his father begin to work with the beaver as well as a fisher trapped earlier. First, he removed the fur-covered skin from each animal. Then, the skins were stretched across a wooden beam where fat and flesh were completely scraped from the inside. Before finishing today, the pelts would be stretched flat within stick frames and hung up to air dry.

* * *

The aroma of venison stew encircled Jean Baptiste with his first step through the cabin door. The second step found him encircled by the arms of little Gabrielle. "Papa!" she squealed, tenaciously refusing to let go. With each stride toward the fireplace hearth, she slipped a little lower on her father's body, from waist to thighs to knees. By the time he wrapped a loving hug around White Loon, Gabrielle was clinging onto one foot, and all three of them were giggling.

Looking into the iron kettle suspended within the fireplace, Jean Baptiste inhaled deeply. "M-m-m-m!" He scooped his little girl from the floor and perched her on his hip with one powerful hand, and then extended a finger of his other hand toward the simmering stew.

Whack! White Loon smacked the offending finger with her long wooden spoon and gave him a friendly warning look. "Some of our garden carrots and potatoes are in there." In a clearing just west of the house, her garden lay under two feet of snow today. However, stored in an underground cellar built by the couple were vegetables harvested in autumn, ready to be eaten throughout winter.

Lucien opened the cabin door and stuck his head in. "Someone's coming!" he reported and closed it again. Still in his coat, Jean Baptiste was quickly out the door right behind the boy. Mid-winter sunsets came early in the north woods, and a crescent moon splintered the dark sky just above the horizon. Its light reflecting onto the crystal white snow illuminated the landscape around them.

"Listen," Luc whispered. He pointed eastward up the Red Lake River. A dog's bark broke the silence. Around a bend on the frozen river appeared a team of six dogs pulling a sled and one person. Father and son stood watching while the figure and dogs moved across the snow in expert harmony. As they drew nearer, a deep voice gave quiet but firm commands to the team. Then came a shout. "Jean Baptiste Reaume! Hello the trading post!"

"I know that voice," declared Jean Baptiste. He raised an arm in greeting and strode forward to welcome this visitor, a merry expression spreading across his face.

"Gee!" shouted the visitor, and the dogs turned right, charging up the riverbank. Now the man himself was running behind the sled. He cleared the bluff just before the trading post and called, "Whoa!" The dogs stopped, and the driver commanded, "Line out." They all remained in their places, with some sitting calmly and others prancing.

Lucien wondered if the frisky dogs were still excited to run or if they were nervous in this unfamiliar place. Whichever, they were all beautiful animals filled with powerful energy. Luc marveled at their obedience to the man's simple commands. He thought it best to stay back until given permission to approach the animals.

His father clasped right hands with the visitor, who swept the furry hood off his head to reveal the darkest face Lucien had ever seen. The man stood a full head taller than Jean Baptiste.

"Luc," his father called, "this is George Bonga, a good friend and trader."

"A pleasure to meet you," said the giant man whose massive palm and fingers gently engulfed Lucien's right hand.

"Son, gather meat from the animals we trapped today. George's dogs will be hungry." Turning back toward the cabin, he added, "I must inform your mother that we've a guest for supper!"

When Luc returned with the scraps of beaver, fisher and muskrat meat, Mr. Bonga was arranging his dog team along a picket line. He fastened each separately along a rope stretched between two trees. "Thank you," he said, accepting the pail of morsels. Then he walked along the picket line, speaking kindly to his dogs and tossing a share of food to each.

Lucien opened the cabin door for the man, who needed to duck his head through the entry. Jean Baptiste took Bonga's coat and hung it from a peg on the wall alongside those of the family. "Welcome to our home," smiled White Loon. "I hope you like venison stew." On either side behind their mother, the girls were half-hidden, eyes wide in wonder. North woods visitors were rare on a winter evening, especially one this huge and dark-skinned. "Fill a bowl for our guest," she ordered Angelique and motioned Gabrielle toward the dinner table.

Scanning the young faces around the table, Bonga grinned broadly. "Am I the darkest man you've ever seen?" None of the children spoke but nodded all around. He lifted a spoonful of stew to his mouth, swallowed, and sighed with satisfaction. "My grandfather Jean Bonga was an African slave," he explained, "indentured to a British army officer who commanded the fort on Mackinac Island in the Great Lakes. When granted freedom, he became a fur trader, and so did his son, my father Pierre. Now I am a third generation of fur traders named Bonga."

While Bonga leaned over his bowl for another delicious spoonful, Jean Baptiste picked up the story, "George is a famous voyageur. I lost a bet to him many years ago when I wagered against his strength and stamina."

"Many have," laughed Bonga between mouthfuls of venison stew.

"He claimed he could paddle a canoe north from Lake Superior to Leech Lake in less than a week." George nodded in affirmation. "That's more than 200 miles by water. The route is interrupted by the Savanna Portage, over the continental divide between the St. Louis and Mississippi Rivers."

Bonga continued smiling and offered his bowl to Angelique for a refill.

"Both rivers must be paddled upstream," Jean Baptiste continued. "I knew from experience that trip required more than a week. So, I gambled my share of the trade goods that he would fail."

"I was inspired to reach my mother's people," Bonga explained to the Reaume children. He gestured toward White Loon and continued. "She was a beautiful daughter of the Pillager Band of Ojibwe, just like your mother."

White Loon blushed.

"Yes, George won my coins." Jean Baptiste shook his head, "He quickened every portage by carrying double loads, and his every paddle stroke gained the distance of two ordinary men. His reputation grew at my expense. I will never bet against him again."

"Now it's my turn to tell a gambling story," Bonga said to the children. "Your father has won that amount and more at the voyageurs' summer rendezvous in Grand Portage. His skill at throwing a tomahawk was well known by we *Hivernants* who live year-round in these northern forests."

The children turned curious faces toward their father, but he pretended not to hear. Instead, he blew a cooling breath onto another steaming spoonful of stew.

"But the *Mangeur du Lard,* pork eaters from Montreal, knew him not. None of them could hurl a hatchet with the accuracy of Jean Baptiste. As a result, that lack of knowledge—and skill—left their purses lighter and your father's heavier!"

As laughter subsided around the table, Bonga said to his host, "I am not here to gamble, Jean Baptiste. But in a way, I will ask you to bet on me. I'll explain later when this marvelous meal is complete."

* * *

After supper, both men walked to the neighboring trading post, and Lucien was happy to be invited along. "He is helping with the furs," explained Jean Baptiste, "and I want him to know more about our business."

"In addition to the pleasure of a visit with your family," Bonga said, "my journey is two-fold. First, I would ask if you or the Native people in this area are in need of winter supplies. Second, I am here to promote the interests of my employer, the American Fur Company."

Jean Baptiste unlocked the front door of the trading post. "Go inside and get a lard lamp glowing," he told Lucien, "while George and I light our pipes." Soon there was a warm glow inside the building, although the temperature was cold. When the men entered, smoke curled from their pipes, and the aroma of smoldering tobacco spread about the large room.

"You appear well supplied," said Bonga. Shelves along one wall were neatly stacked with factory-made trade goods—gardening and cooking tools, jewelry such as bracelets and earrings, sewing supplies, cotton and woolen fabric, and ready-to-wear clothing. Against another wall of animal traps and equipment to care for pelts, Jean Baptiste was already accumulating this winter's bundles of finished furs acquired in trade from Native hunters and trappers.

"So much for my first order of business," Bonga said. "Let us discuss the second." He leaned forward, resting both forearms onto the wide trading counter that ran across the back of the room. "The American Fur Company wants your business."

"I like doing business with you," Jean Baptiste answered. "However, many Métis people who live in the Red River Valley enjoy the opportunity to trade with the Northwest Company as well."

"Yes, the Canadian border is near. But it is illegal to sell resources from the United States into Canada. As a British-Canadian company, all of the Northwest trading posts are north of the border."

"Illegal, yes, but not impossible," countered Jean Baptiste. "I can promise that every pelt which comes through this trading post will go to your employer. And most, if not all, of the Ojibwe hunters and trappers in this region will bring their furs to me. But some of the Métis and Dakota people will seek out your competition, hoping to make a better bargain."

"Then I urge you to go to them," George said. "Take some of these trade goods into the Red River Valley. Travel to villages along the Rainy River. Your good reputation extends that far. The Métis especially should be happy to trade with Jean Baptiste Reaume."

"I will consider your advice. Now let us relax and enjoy the remainder of our pipes."

* * *

White Loon dried the last supper dish and returned it to the shelf. "Where is Angelique?" she asked, turning toward Gabrielle. The little girl smiled, pointed outside and squatted down. White Loon could not stifle a giggle at her youngest daughter's pantomime, but she murmured, "Your sister went to the outhouse a long while ago. What could be keeping her?"

The woman stepped out the front door, turned left around the firewood pile, and looked toward the outhouse located approximately thirty paces behind their cabin, away from the river, near a border of spruce trees. There was Angelique, standing still about half that distance away, her gaze fixed above the trees where swirls of purple, green and yellow light flickered through the heavens. White Loon motioned for Gabrielle to join her. She crouched behind the little girl and pointed over her shoulder into the sky. "The Northern Lights!" she excitedly whispered.

The silence broken, Angelique turned to join her mother and sister. "It's beautiful!" she gushed.

"What is happening?" Gabrielle asked.

"Wawatay," answered White Loon. "Our ancestors are dancing into heaven. They are celebrating their lives, thanking the Creator for their blessings here on earth, and making a pathway for other souls to follow into the next world."

The three of them stood motionless, oblivious to the calm, cold air, enchanted by the flaring, whirling flashes and ripples of light. Indeed, they appeared to be lively spirits, frolicking beyond this world.

I met three girls
and all of them were pretty.
Pull on the oars
as we glide along together.

George Bonga's loud and boisterous singing broke the spell. "A fur traders' song to honor three pretty girls!" he shouted from the trading post's front porch.

"Thank you," called White Loon. "You have a wonderful singing voice."

"The name of the song is 'C'est l'aviron.' A favorite of French-Canadian voyageurs who sing it in rhythm with their paddle strokes, and also to remember the pretty girls to be found at the end of their journey."

"We are watching the Northern Lights. They too are especially pretty tonight," White Loon said. The six of them beheld the dazzling display for a long while before retiring into the warm cabin and a restful night's sleep.

* * *

At breakfast, Bonga volunteered to help refill the Reaume family ice cellar. White Loon added a stack of steaming pancakes onto the table already scattered with cups of hot coffee, a platter of bacon, a bowl of blueberry preserves, and a pitcher of homemade maple syrup. "You do not have to do that," she protested.

A gigantic smile filled the trader's face as he spread his hands to encompass the morning feast. "I owe you that and more. Besides," he laughed while delivering a backhanded punch into Jean Baptiste's shoulder, "it's too big a job for one tiny voyageur!"

"We'll all help!" Lucien burst in.

"Yes," Angelique added, "we always help Papa fill the glaciere."

After eating, the men walked onto the frozen Red Lake River. Jean Baptiste led the way to a spot along the near shore where the river widened, and the dangerous under-ice current was slower. He had been clearing snow from these shallows throughout the winter.

"Good ice," Bonga declared. "With the insulating snow removed, it's clear and thick."

They chopped through a foot-and-a-half of thick ice and then cut loose large frozen cubes with a long, heavy saw. Jean Baptiste lifted the first cake of ice out of the river with a large set of iron tongs and slid it to the riverbank, where Lucien waited with the wooden sled they had used to pull traps and furs the day before. Jean Baptiste hoisted the frozen block onto the sled, and Luc strapped it securely with a length of rawhide.

"Away you go," directed Jean Baptiste with a wave and turned to rejoin Bonga. Cutting ice was the most strenuous part of this process, but Bonga pumped the saw with a powerful rhythm, sending sparkling ice chips through the air.

Jean Baptiste shouted over the clatter of the blade's biting teeth, "Let me know when you need a break." He detected a grin on the large black face as Bonga silently continued his muscular strokes of the huge saw.

Turning to watch his son pull the first ice block over the riverbank, Jean Baptiste marveled at Lucien's powerful strides. *I forget he's fourteen and becoming a young man.*

Twisting Trails

* * *

Luc pulled the sled past the western side of their home toward the ice cellar dug into a rising slope about forty feet behind the cabin. A door opened into the cellar's log front before a man-made cave of earth.

White Loon and the girls had been busy, temporarily removing meat and vegetables from storage inside the cellar. When Lucien arrived, his mother laid a wide plank extending through the doorway into the cave. After Luc unlashed the rawhide strap from the cake of ice, he and his mother gave it a mighty shove down the plank onto the cellar floor.

Inside the glaciere, Angelique raked and smoothed a thin layer of sawdust to cover about an eight-foot square of ground. Her mother followed the ice block to the end of the plank and proceeded to roll it into one distant corner. "That's a perfect sawdust layer," she complimented her daughter and motioned toward a heaping pile of leftover sawdust in a front corner. "We'll save that to make an insulating layer on top of the highest level of ice blocks."

Before long, Lucien returned to the cellar door with two cakes of ice nearly identical in size and shape. White Loon and Angelique rolled them up against the first block, creating a neat level row along the back of the cave.

"Father is taking a turn with the saw," Luc announced. "We'll see if his blocks match Mr. Bonga's."

Quietly confident, White Loon whispered, "They will." Angelique looked into her mother's face and saw an expression of tenderness that reflected the trust and fidelity between her loving parents.

"Yes," murmured the girl with unwavering belief, "they will."

They broke for lunch after covering the cellar floor with two layers of ice blocks. White Loon and the girls went into the house to prepare the meal, while the men and boy cut and hauled four additional ice blocks to begin the third layer in the icehouse. Then everyone gathered around the dinner table for a robust feast of venison, carrots and potatoes. They fell into compatible silence when they dug into the well-deserved food. Their muscles felt tired in a satisfying way, and the warm cabin brought a glow of perspiration to their skin. The indoor odor of sweat usually smelled unpleasant. However, on this cold winter day, their shared warmth held a scent of teamwork and accomplishment. They were weary but not worn out.

After the meal, George and Jean Baptiste smoked their pipes. Eleven-year-old Gabrielle was proud to be trusted with dish duty by herself while the others rested. Soon everyone went back to work, and by mid-afternoon, they aligned a fourth and final layer of ice blocks from wall to wall inside the glaciere. Angelique covered the surface with sawdust while Luc and Gabrielle helped their mother replace all of the perishable food back into the cellar.

"You've made an excellent icehouse," Bonga declared. "Inside the earthen walls, those blocks will stay cold and keep your food fresh until next winter."

"And my wife is an excellent gardener," Jean Baptiste proclaimed. "She will fill that cellar with corn, peas, beans, onions, carrots and potatoes." Putting away the pick, saw and tongs, he extended his hand, "Thank you, George. You're a good friend."

Bonga clasped the offered hand and replied, "It is my pleasure to spend an additional day with your wonderful family. Furthermore, this has been a welcome day of rest for my dogs. Their feet were sore last night, but by tomorrow morning, they will be eager to go."

George Bonga (1802–1880)

George Bonga's grandparents were African slaves who served the commander of a British fort on Mackinac Island. They were freed and married upon the commander's death in 1787 when they entered the fur trade. Their son, George's father, was also a successful trader who sent the boy to school in Montreal where he mastered French, English and Ojibwe.[13]

George grew famously large and strong, well more than six feet tall and two hundred pounds. He typically portaged three or four ninety-pound cargo packs, while the average voyageur carried two.[14]

At eighteen, he was hired by Michigan's territorial governor, Lewis Cass, as a guide and interpreter. George's signature is on treaties between the Ojibwe people and the US government, negotiated in 1820 and 1867.[15]

In 1842, George married an Ojibwe woman named Ashwinn, and they had four children. When the fur business declined, he went from employment with the American Fur Company to managing tourist lodges on Leech and Ottertail Lakes. His stories and songs from the fur trade days were especially popular with visitors. Until his death, George continued to advocate for the rights of Native American people.[16]

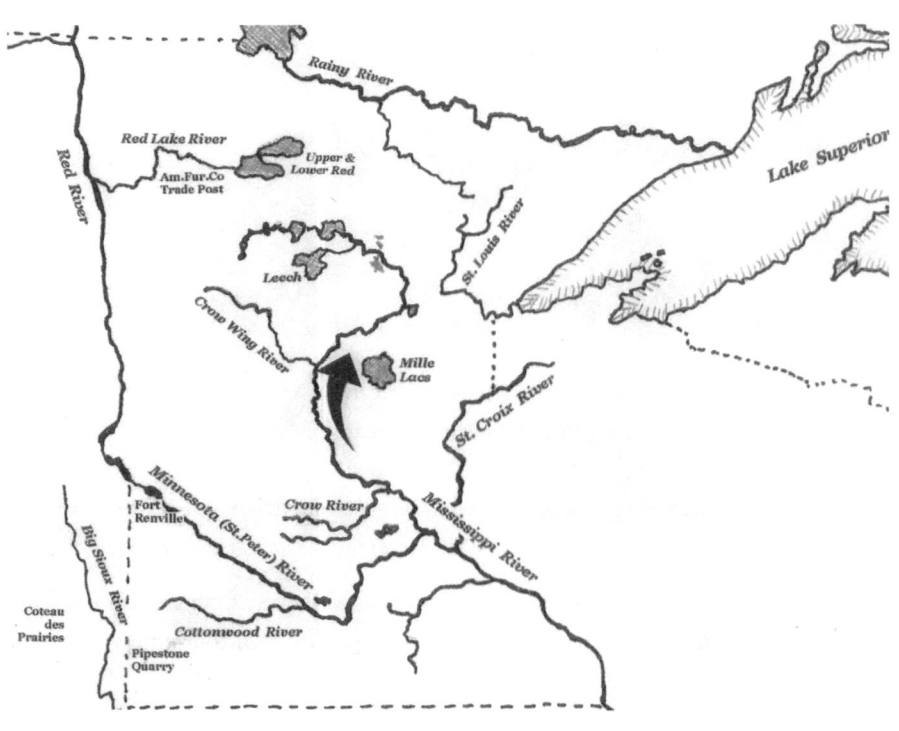

Rainy River

Red Lake River

Upper & Lower Red

Am.Fur.Co Trade Post

Red River

Lake Superior

St. Louis River

Leech

Crow Wing River

Mille Lacs

St. Croix River

Minnesota (St.Peter) River

Fort Renville

Crow River

Mississippi River

Big Sioux River

Coteau des Prairies

Cottonwood River

Pipestone Quarry

Chapter 5
1832 – Mississippi River

"Alex, you've my permission to remove 'dat shirt," said Sergeant William Schmid, Fort Snelling's head blacksmith. Private Whitney's blue shirt was soaked with perspiration as he worked over and around the forge where coals were glowing red and white.

"That's all right, Bill," he answered. "I'll leave it on." He rolled up his sleeves to just below his elbows. Alex straightened his back and wiped beads of sweat from his forehead with one sleeve roll. Both hands were full, a hammer in the right and tongs in the left. Alex and Bill were on a first-name basis inside the blacksmith shop, whereas elsewhere around the fort, military decorum required both men to address each other by rank. This informal arrangement had existed since Alex's first week of apprenticeship under Sergeant Schmid, an immigrant from Germany. At first, his new assistant's skill learned from the metal craftsman in Detroit impressed the sergeant. As the days went by, he gained a greater appreciation for the youngster's character. Schmid soon formally requested Alex's permanent assignment to the blacksmith shop. Now a warm relationship existed between the two men, who were more than two decades apart in age.

On this early summer day, they were making door hardware—hinges, locks and handles for the new Native American council house at the nearby Indian agency. Last year the old council house burned to the ground.

"Whew! I thought it was hot outside." The two men turned to see Eastman stepping through the shop's open doorway. "It must be more than a hundred degrees in here."

"Da' forge is a blessing in wintertime, lieutenant," said Schmid. "But yah, 'tis extra hot in summer."

Eastman leaned against a post, removing his hat to fan his face with the brim. "Sorry to inform you, sergeant, but I'm going to take your apprentice away for a couple of months."

With a quick glance toward Alex, the blacksmith looked worried. "Not to fight dem Injuns!" he blurted.

"No. Colonel Taylor is not sending any troops from our garrison to fight the Sauks," the lieutenant assured him. "Private Whitney is going up the Mississippi River with me to provide a military escort for a territorial Indian agent named Schoolcraft. This is a peace mission."

"Why me?" asked Alex. "Bill and I have a lot of work to do for the new council house."

"That can wait," answered Seth. "We've got to hustle upriver to meet Schoolcraft's party at Big Sandy Lake. I need you to help paddle a canoe, make metal repairs if necessary, and shoot game to provide food for the people in this expedition."

"When will we go?" Alex inquired.

"Pack tonight and leave in the morning." With that, Lieutenant Eastman placed the hat back on his head, gave a brisk salute, and turned on his heel. By the time Bill and Alex returned the salute, he was already out the door.

* * *

June 29th, 1832

Dear Mother,

I will be gone from Fort Snelling for perhaps the next two months, beginning tomorrow. Therefore, I will hurry to complete this letter tonight. You need not worry about the warfare being waged against the Sauk Indians and their war chief Black Hawk. That fighting is occurring far south of here, in and around the new state of Illinois. The soldiers in action there are militia and troops from Fort Crawford at Prairie du Chien. We hear scuttlebutt that our Col. Taylor disapproves of the methods by which that conflict is being fought and he intends to keep us out of it.

In fact, I am going in the opposite direction. Lt. Eastman and I are traveling north, up the Mississippi River to join an expedition led by a territorial Indian agent named Henry Schoolcraft. I'm glad you like the sketch I sent, drawn by Lt. Eastman. He is a very talented artist and has illustrated much of the beautiful scenery in this region. A few weeks ago, I was assigned as apprentice to the fort's blacksmith shop.

My metalworking experience back in Detroit has proven valuable and I enjoy the company of our chief blacksmith. He is a kind-hearted German named Sgt. Schmid. I will miss him while exploring the Upper Mississippi with Lt. Eastman but expect this to be a wonderful adventure!

Your loving son,

Alexander

* * *

Next morning as usual, the soldiers of Fort Snelling assembled on their parade ground for roll call. The color guard raised the flags and played reveille. Eastman hailed Alex. "Private Whitney, after breakfast have one of the cooks assemble a pack of cooking and eating utensils for our trip. I'll have my rifle, but you should bring your shotgun with powder and shells. You'll probably want one change

53

of clothes and bring a rain cape just in case."

"Yes, sir," Alex said. "I'm looking forward to this mission."

"It will be our pleasure!" Eastman declared. "Meet me at the stable. We'll ride to a spot above St. Anthony Falls and launch our canoe from there."

* * *

Two saddled horses were tied to a hitching rail outside the Fort Snelling stable. Eastman was sliding his rifle into a leather scabbard attached to his saddle. An army haversack encircled his torso, slung diagonally from above his left shoulder to just below his right-side rib cage. The haversack was his bedroll, rolled into a flexible cylinder and tied into a circle, with his belongings wrapped inside. Alex was likewise wearing a haversack, toting the pack of cooking and eating utensils in one hand and his shotgun in the other. The two young men climbed aboard the horses and walked them through the fort's main gate. Then, with a nod to each other, they urged their mounts into a canter and began their journey.

Slightly farther than two miles up the trail, they approached Minnehaha Creek, where they allowed the horses a brief midstream stop and drink. Rising out of the creek bed, once again on level ground, the riders allowed their mounts to amble side-by-side. Eastman spoke, "I told Schmid that I need you on this trip for paddling, shooting and metal repair."

"You did," Alex confirmed.

"That's true, but there's more," Eastman continued. "Although we're of different rank, I regard you as a friend. We will be good traveling companions. You're easy-going but smart and capable."

"I value your friendship," said Alex. "Plus, I look to you as an illustration of leadership. I hope to rise to a higher rank in this army, and your style of command is an example I hope to follow."

"You will become your own man," said the lieutenant, "and this mission will provide an excellent experience. We will meet a powerful politician in Mr. Schoolcraft. We will find Indians in their own environment. Every day will present us with problems to solve."

"On the subject of Schoolcraft's expedition," Alex inquired, "you described it as a peace mission."

"We received a message via courier from the office of Michigan's territorial governor Lewis Cass. The message actually specified multiple objectives for Schoolcraft's journey. First, the governor wants to promote trade with Native American tribes who live along the Upper Mississippi River and its tributaries. So part of the mission is to encourage friendly relations between those tribes and the United States. We want the Natives to do business with American traders rather than with British-Canadians. A second part of promoting trade is to discourage hostilities between the Ojibwe and Dakota. It's a lot easier to conduct business with partners at peace rather than war."

"So that's the peace mission part," Alex interrupted.

"Right," Eastman said. "The third goal for Schoolcraft is exploration. He was with a team that tried to find the source of the Mississippi River but failed about a decade ago. He's coming through Lake Superior from Fort Brady. His party will travel up the St. Louis River to Sandy Lake where we are supposed to join them. Hopefully, with help from Native guides, we can paddle to the true source of the Mississippi."

"Exciting!" Alex burst out. "We're explorers!"

"Yes, I suppose we are," Eastman admitted, "but as military escort, our assignment is to protect Schoolcraft's people and help furnish food for them. Additionally, we're expected to provide some guidance on the way home. After finding the Mississippi's source, Schoolcraft wants to come to Fort Snelling by a western route."

"So, we'll see different scenery going north and coming back."

"Yes," Eastman confirmed, "and different Indians. That's Schoolcraft's fourth objective. One member of his party is <u>Dr.</u> Houghton, who is traveling with a large supply of smallpox vaccine. It is his goal to provide medicine for hundreds of Native Americans. I intend to have him vaccinate my wife."

Alex's startled reaction must have alarmed his horse. It stopped.

"Your wife?" He stared at the lieutenant in astonished silence.

The lieutenant turned his horse around to face Private Whitney, "Didn't you know I was married?"

"What?"

"I have a Dakota wife named Wakaninajinwin. It means *Stands Sacred* or *Stands Like a Spirit*, but I call her Lucy."

Alex did not move or speak, so Eastman continued, "She lives with her parents in the village up ahead near Lake Bde Maka Ska. Her father, Cloud Man, is the leader of that village. We'll stop there and pick her up on our way to St. Anthony Falls." With that, the lieutenant pivoted his horse and continued up the trail.

* * *

As they neared the Dakota village, Alex recognized corn and squash plants ripening in a plowed field. People, mostly women, were digging weeds out from between the rows of plants. Some children were running through the field, seeming to chase hungry birds away.

Alex had seen cone-shaped teepees of Dakota people who were traveling to and from the Indian Agency near the fort, but the dwellings in this village were more permanent. Birchbark panels covered sturdy wooden frames. Eastman obviously knew his way, riding directly toward one lodge where a man and girl were standing. When Eastman stopped, the man waved and the girl ran forward. Her face beamed, and she began bouncing happily beside Eastman's horse. He returned the man's wave, then dismounted and gave the girl an enduring affectionate hug.

Could this be his wife? Alex wondered. She was very pretty but also very young, he thought, perhaps in her mid-teens. She wore a buckskin skirt and moccasins like the other females around the village. But her blouse was factory-made, a pretty blue and white calico. When she turned to face Alex, he could see her long black hair was divided into two braids, collected by a decorative shell beneath each ear.

"Private Whitney," the lieutenant said, "meet my wife

Wakaninajinwin."

She remained next to Eastman but offered a shy smile toward Alex as he swung down from his saddle. Holding the reins of his mount in one hand, he whisked off his soldier hat and nodded, "Pleasure to meet you, ma'am."

The lieutenant turned and walked to the man, offering a respectful greeting. Then, turning to Alex, Eastman announced, "Here is Cloud Man, leader of this Dakota village."

"You and my son, Lieutenant Eastman, are welcome," he said.

The girl disappeared into the dwelling while the lieutenant began a conversation with her father. Eastman asked about conditions among the villagers. Cloud Man motioned here and there with his arms, speaking about hunting, farming and the health of his people.

When Wakaninajinwin reappeared, she had changed her calico blouse for a deerskin tunic and a belt around her waist. She also had a satchel, suspended by a shoulder strap, which apparently contained her few personal necessities.

The lieutenant soon finished his conversation with Cloud Man and remounted his horse. When he reached down his left arm, the girl grasped it and swung herself up behind his saddle with the quickness and agility of a bobcat. She gave a wave to her father, and away they went.

Four miles and twenty minutes later, they arrived at St. Anthony Falls. Eastman took the reins of both horses and led them toward the guard shack, where he met one of the soldiers temporarily stationed there. He instructed the man to provide food and care for the animals until they could be returned to Fort Snelling.

Wakaninajinwin trotted down a trail that led to the smooth water above the falls. She located a birchbark canoe among trees along the bank and pulled it close to the shore. Returning to the trees, the girl retrieved three wide-bladed paddles tucked alongside the canoe. After lowering her satchel into the middle of the canoe, she waded into the shallow water and, with cupped hands, lifted a refreshing drink to her lips. Under a bright warm sun, the cool water felt good around her ankles and running down her throat.

The falls attracted Alex, and the roar of cascading water grew louder as he approached. He gazed with fascination as the swift, smooth current above the precipice crashed ferociously onto slabs of rock below. Drops ricocheted in every direction, some scattering high to form a glistening misty rainbow. Turbulent frothy waves swept over and among boulders, rushing into the gorge downstream. Several minutes may have passed while Alex stood mesmerized by this powerful scene.

"Waterfall is gift from creator." Wakaninajinwin had walked to the overlook beside Private Whitney without him noticing. Now he turned, and they exchanged smiles. Gesturing toward a small rocky island in midstream below the falls, the girl said, "Spirit Island."

She closed her eyes and gracefully motioned with her hands while seeming to speak to herself. Alex beheld the young woman; she seemed to stand so delicately on the rocky overhang that she barely touched the ground. *What did Eastman say her name means? Stands Like a Spirit. Yes, she does.*

* * *

Eastman paddled from the stern of the canoe, primarily responsible for steering a straight course while trying to keep the canoe in channels with the slower current. Alex rowed from the bow, the best spot from which to scout for underwater rocks or sunken branches that could tear a hole in the canoe's birchbark hull. Both men were on the lookout for anyone they might meet onshore or on the water. Wakaninajinwin paddled without a break, occasionally switching from side to side when one arm grew especially tired.

Cloud Man's people provided the canoe. Alex guessed it to be about sixteen feet long but amazingly light and swift in the water. In addition to its birchbark skin, cedar wood comprised parts of the craft. The inside bottom was reinforced lengthwise by thin cedar planks. Inside the birchbark, dozens of curved narrow cedar branches formed a rib cage, and cedar thwarts created a sturdy frame for the top of the canoe. Spruce roots lashed each joint along the reinforced gunwales so that everything was held solidly in place from bow to stern.

Late that afternoon, the three travelers rowed ashore. Except for one midday break to snack and relieve themselves, they had paddled steadily since leaving St. Anthony Falls. "We'll stop here for the night," Eastman said. "Lucy, you can set up camp while Alex and I try to shoot something for supper."

A small stream entered the Mississippi here, and they decided to work up the ravine through which it flowed. As they began walking together, Alex commented, "Wakaninajinwin is a good paddler."

"She will prove useful in numerous ways during this journey," Eastman said. "Her paddling power might rank behind you and me, but when it comes to food preparation, she'll put us to shame."

"I recall you did a fine job with our meals at Green's Villa," Alex remembered. "If her cooking is better than yours, I'll be spoiled."

"You will eat better than at the fort. I can guarantee that," Eastman laughed. "Perhaps more significant though, Lucy may help us as a guide and translator. She will be better able to navigate this river and communicate with Native Americans who live in its valley."

"That could be important."

"Also, for me, she's delightful company." Eastman's tone softened. "I love being with her."

Boom! The snowshoe hare had darted out from under a nearby bush and was bounding away before Alex's shotgun knocked it rolling over.

"There will be some meat on him," Eastman said. "But maybe not enough for three. Let's cross this creek and circle back to the river. Maybe we'll find something more."

They did not. Fortunately for them, Wakaninajinwin had been busy during their absence. Laying on the stream bank was a fishing spear she had fashioned from an aspen sapling and beside it a good-sized pike.

"We have fish to fry!" Eastman exclaimed as he leaned down to kiss her. The herbs and roots she had gathered simmered in the campfire pot. He inhaled deeply and laughed with delight. "I will fillet this pike while Private Whitney skins the hare. Then we will enjoy the first delicious meal of our journey."

They did. However, Alex did not enjoy the insects, "These mosquitos are terrible." He tried to swat a tiny bug away from his face.

"I know." Eastman slapped one off the back of his neck. "They are more numerous here in the woods than up on the bluff at Fort Snelling."

Alex nodded in agreement. "And thicker here onshore than when we're paddling up the river where a little breeze will blow."

Sitting downwind from their cooking fire, Wakaninajinwin smiled. "They do not like smoke." The two young men gave each other dumbfounded looks. The Dakota girl continued, "Some people smear themselves with animal grease. Others cover themselves with cloth. But I will endure the smoke." She shrugged. "Mosquitos are worst when the sun sets. They will settle in the grass after dark."

After sundown, the dusk quickly became darker. Tall charcoal-colored clouds began tumbling into the southwestern sky. Occasional rumbles of thunder could be heard before long, and distant lightning flashes soon accompanied them. Abruptly, the leaves began to flutter, and a sudden breeze whooshed up the river. Immediately Alex could feel the hot and humid stillness quickly displaced by cooler air. Wakaninajinwin scooped up her satchel and scurried under the overturned canoe. No sooner had she beckoned the young men to follow than a few raindrops began to fall. Lightning and thunder cracked from almost overhead. Eastman and Alex scrambled for the canoe. Heavy rain instantly gushed from the clouds, and their backs were wet before reaching shelter.

The trio could barely see each other's faces in the dim light under the canoe. The upturned points of the bow and stern were resting on the ground, causing the craft to tilt toward one side. Each of them sat cross-legged with their backs to the grounded side. Alternately, they bowed their heads inside the upraised gunwale or leaned down to peer out toward the river. It was largely invisible except during intermittent lightning flashes when the force and frequency of the deluge generated thousands of tiny geysers across the water surface.

The noise produced by exploding thunder and clattering raindrops against the canoe bottom was deafening. They did not even try to converse with each other. Nor did they attempt to remain completely dry. Some water ran down the riverbank, seeping under the canoe soaking their backsides. The swirling wind blew some mist beneath the tilted canoe, and their shins got wet when heavy drops splattered off the wet ground.

Gradually the storm passed. By midnight, sparkling stars were visible again, and the wind subsided. The travelers tried to get a partial night's sleep, but all were up with the dawn. The rising sun turned their riverside campsite into a glimmering glade, with illuminated rain droplets on every leaf. After eating a small cold breakfast, they were back on the Mississippi, paddling north.

* * *

Twice during the first week of their journey, Eastman, Alex and Wakaninajinwin had to portage the canoe and their gear. They had to pass a series of rapids on the fourth day and around a small waterfall two days later. On those occasions, Eastman and Alex transported the canoe upside-down on their shoulders. Each of them had a knapsack wrapped around his torso and a firearm gripped in one hand while steadying the canoe with their other. Wakaninajinwin walked in front, choosing the best path to carry the canoe. She had slung her satchel across one shoulder and the pack of cooking utensils across the other.

On the ninth day, they arrived at a fork in the river. The width and flow of both branches were nearly equal. Nonetheless, one branch had to be the Mississippi, while the other was a major tributary. "Let's go ashore on that point between the branches," Eastman proposed, "while we try to figure out the proper route." He alternately walked two hundred paces or so up both shorelines, trying to decipher a telltale difference. "Does one become significantly smaller?" he wondered. "Is there a noticeable difference in the current or in the color or temperature of the water?"

Luckily, the lieutenant was rescued from the difficult choice. Two canoes of Native paddlers came downstream on the westernmost branch. They came ashore to meet the white men and communicated through Wakaninajinwin's translation. Their name for the river they just descended was Crow Wing. Now they intended to travel upstream on the Mississippi. In two days of paddling, they expected to arrive at lakes where wild rice could be harvested.

The parties agreed to travel together as far as the wild rice lakes, and they shared a campsite that night. Eastman's well-aimed rifle provided a deer to feed the entire group, which made everybody happy. Following supper, the good fellowship continued with an impromptu sing-along. It started when the Ojibwe women sang a song of thanks to the deer, whose meat had provided a nourishing meal for everyone. Next, Eastman and Alex stood up and agreed to sing the popular soldier song, "The Girl I Left Behind Me." They butchered the lyrics and warbled horribly off-key but sang with such gusto that everyone enjoyed it.

At last, upon urging from the lieutenant, Wakaninajinwin consented to sing a Dakota song. Quietly shy in the beginning, she drew encouragement from the smiles all around, and her sweet voice grew stronger. No one else could understand all of the words, but it did not matter. The beautiful melody sounded like a lullaby in the gathering darkness.—a perfect way to end the day.

* * *

Paddling upstream the following morning, Wakaninajinwin told the lieutenant, "The Ojibwe women are thankful for your gift of the deer hide."

"Maybe we'll get another one tonight," he responded with optimism.

"They recognized my description of the waterfall we passed a few days ago," she said. "Little Falls is their name for it. And the rapids, around which we portaged before that, they call Sauk Rapids."

"Did they say if there are portages ahead of us?" Eastman

asked.

"None as far as the rice lakes. They expect to arrive there tomorrow."

At their evening campsite, Wakaninajinwin asked about the route farther upstream. "The river becomes more winding," they told her. "The trading post at Big Sandy Lake can be reached in three more days."

The hunters found no deer that evening. But they did return to camp with six ducks. In addition, the Ojibwe women had gathered a bounty of wild berries, so once again, everyone was well fed.

* * *

As predicted, they reached the rice lakes the next day. Alex, Eastman and Wakaninajinwin bid a quick but heartfelt goodbye to their new friends, after which they paddled on, hoping to rendezvous with Schoolcraft's party at Sandy Lake.

At the end of two more long days, the lieutenant spied a United States flag fluttering in the distance. Rowing nearer, they saw log buildings on the shore near the mouth of a sizable river flowing into the Mississippi from the east. As they approached the embankment, a man was there to greet them.

"Hello!" he shouted. "Are you from Fort Snelling?"

"Yes, we are," Eastman confirmed as they eased their canoe to the water's edge. "I am Lieutenant Eastman. That's Private Whitney in the stern and my wife, Wakaninajinwin."

The man stepped down into shallow water, where he caught the bow of their canoe before it scraped on the river bottom. "I'm William Aitken, chief trader for the American Fur Company on the Upper Mississippi. Welcome to the Sandy Lake trading post."

"Where is the lake?" wondered the lieutenant.

"Ha," Aitken chuckled. "It's half a mile up this river, as the crow flies. This is the Sandy River."

"We are supposed to meet a large party here led by an Indian agent named Henry Schoolcraft."

"Large is right!" exclaimed the fur trader. "There's more'n

thirty of 'em counting Schoolcraft and his wife's brother, plus a cook, a doctor, the reverend and a bunch of voyageurs. Then there's that Lieutenant Allen and ten soldiers from Fort Brady. You're about a day and a half behind 'em."

"With your permission, we would like to stay here tonight," said Eastman.

"More'n welcome," replied Aitken with enthusiasm. "You settle in, and we'll get a hot supper goin' for you."

After they had eaten, the trader was anxious to talk about the fur business with the lieutenant. He complained about interference by British traders from across the Canadian border. On that subject, he thanked Eastman for coming to the north woods and urged that soldiers from Fort Snelling would patrol the region more frequently in the future.

Eastman promised to relay Aitken's request back to Colonel Taylor. Then he confessed to being a weary traveler who hoped for an early start the next morning.

"We are anxious for a good night's sleep," he said. "However, we should be back on the water by dawn. We hope to catch up with Schoolcraft as soon as possible."

The travelers slumbered in beds beneath a roof that night. They had not slept indoors for two weeks, nor would they do so again for many more.

Wakaninajinwin (Born 1815)

Wakaninajinwin was Cloud Man and Red Cherry Woman's daughter. Her father was the leader of a Dakota village near Fort Snelling during the 1820s and 30s.[17] Translated into English, her name means "Stands Sacred" or "Stands Like a Spirit."[18] Wed in "common law" marriage to Lt. Seth Eastman in 1830, they were fifteen and twenty-three years of age, respectively. She gave birth to a daughter, Winona, later known by the English name Mary Nancy Eastman.[19]

Less than a year after Winona's birth, the army transferred Lt. Eastman away from Ft. Snelling. He declared the marriage to Wakaninajinwin ended at that time.[20]

Nancy Eastman was married to Many Lightnings, a Dakota man with whom she had five children. She died in childbirth with the youngest, Ohiyesa. Later in life, he became known by the English name Charles Alexander Eastman, who became the first Native American licensed medical doctor in the United States.[21]

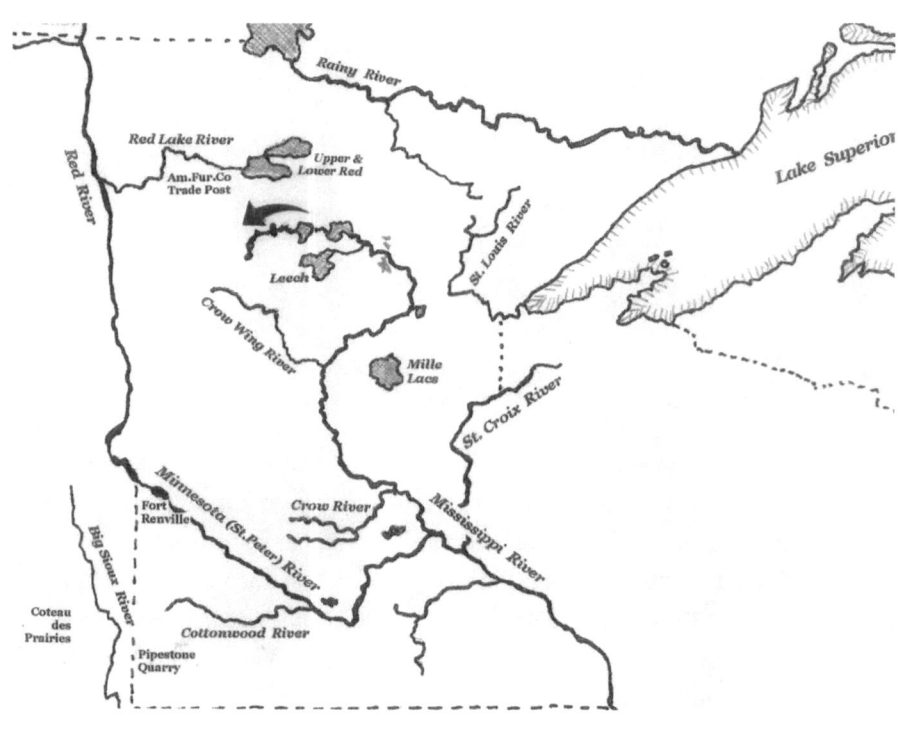

Chapter 6
1832 – Lake Itasca

"Whew!" This was the longest portage of their trip. For more than three miles, Wakaninajinwin led Eastman and Alex as they carried the canoe around boulder-strewn rapids and one prominent waterfall that dropped about ten feet. A narrow path weaved along the river through a forest of red and white pine trees. The existence of the path confirmed that many others, animal and human, had bypassed these rapids before. The earth was cool beneath their feet; only a few slivers of morning sunlight penetrated the long-needled branches of towering pines. Suddenly the girl stopped at the edge of a large clearing. Dozens of people were scattered before them in various groups. This was Schoolcraft's expedition.

This clearing was on the shore of a beautiful lake just above where the long series of rapids began. Lieutenant Eastman quickly identified Henry Schoolcraft sitting in the shade of a large awning. He was in conversation with several other men, both white and Indian. Just as Eastman was approaching, they all stood, and the Native men moved away to join companions. "Mr. Schoolcraft," the lieutenant announced with a salute, "I am Lieutenant Seth Eastman. With compliments from Colonel Zachary Taylor, I welcome you to the Upper Mississippi River."

"Hello!" the Indian agent offered in a friendly voice, extending his arm for a handshake rather than return the military salute. Schoolcraft was a big man with rounded nose, face and torso. A ring of whiskers around his jawline and chin accentuated the shape. The Indian agent's high hairline reminded Alex of the Man in the Moon's face, and he grinned inwardly.

"Let me introduce Private Alexander Whitney," Eastman continued, "and my wife, Wakaninajinwin. We are here to provide some guidance, interpretation and escort to Fort Snelling after your journey to the source of the river."

"Glad for your assistance," Schoolcraft answered. Then, turning to a uniformed soldier near his elbow, "This is Lieutenant James Allen. The lieutenant is in the process of making a fine map of our route."

The two officers exchanged a quick salute, and Allen motioned toward a trio of neat tents along the clearing's edge, "I and my escort of ten men are from Fort Brady at the far eastern end of Lake Superior."

Schoolcraft turned the other direction, "Meet my brother-in-law George Johnston. He and my wife Jane are the children of the well-known fur trader John Johnston and his Ojibwe wife. George speaks the Native language fluently and has traveled in this region as a trader."

They shook hands, and Johnston added, "We also have a local Ojibwe man named Ozawindib traveling with us. He lives near Cass Lake and is familiar with many of the waterways connected to the Mississippi River."

Schoolcraft led the newcomers a few steps out from under the awning and stated that no travel would occur today. "It's Sunday," he said. "The Reverend Boutwell conducted a religious service down by the lake earlier this morning. He is hopeful of fulfilling his mission by converting the Indians to Christianity, but they are skeptical. Some of these Native people accepted his invitation to worship, but I believe they were mostly being polite. Perhaps a little curious."

Gesturing toward a gathering of men further along the shore, Schoolcraft described the voyageurs. "They are French-Canadian and Catholic. Good men with whom to be on the water. They work hard," he paused to chuckle, "and they play hard! Singing, dancing, wrestling—they love rough, rambunctious fun."

Twisting Trails

Turning away from the lake, Schoolcraft directed their attention toward a tent near the middle of the clearing. "That's Dr. Houghton," he pointed. "This afternoon, he intends to vaccinate these Indians against smallpox. The disease has devastated some Native populations, but we hope to save the people we can reach."

"I would like to speak with him about vaccinating my wife," said the lieutenant.

"By all means."

Eastman led Wakaninajinwin to the doctor, while Alex excused himself to meet the soldiers from Fort Brady.

* * *

"Hello, Dr. Houghton. I am Lieutenant Seth Eastman, dispatched from Fort Snelling to assist this expedition."

"Good to have you with us." The doctor looked up from his medical instruments and noticed the Indian girl standing beside the young officer.

"This is my wife, Wakaninajinwin. We would like her to receive the smallpox vaccine."

"It would be my pleasure," answered Dr. Houghton. "If you don't mind, I'll have her wait until the other Native women can see her being injected. I have been vaccinating Ojibwe people along our journey from Lake Superior, and many of them are afraid to have the shot. Usually, if the tribal leaders accept the vaccine, others will follow. In this case, I think it will be very persuasive for them to see the wife of an army officer willingly consent to the injection."

"Thank you," said the lieutenant. "We'll wait."

"I have high hopes for this campaign," declared the doctor. "We are carrying enough vaccine to inoculate 2,000 people."

"I hope you still have some left for my wife's Dakota people when we get back to Fort Snelling," Eastman said. "But I'll be happy for her protection today."

When the Ojibwe villagers came forth, their leaders in front, they saw Wakaninajinwin receive the first inoculation. The people murmured when she smiled and walked into the waiting arms of

69

Lieutenant Eastman. Then, one by one, they followed through Dr. Houghton's line into a healthier future.

* * *

Alex approached a pair of voyageurs who were stirring a strange mixture in a pot heating over an open fire. "That doesn't look like lunch," he joked.

"Oui, you are correct," one of the men responded, mixing his native French with English for the benefit of the American soldier.

"I'm Private Alexander Whitney from Detroit, Michigan."

"Aha! A fellow traveler from the Great Lakes. We are from Montreal. This is Louis, and I am Pierre LaFlamme. I am known as *The Flame.*"

"Is that because of your hot temper?" snickered his partner beside the pot.

"No," Pierre growled dramatically, "it is for the flame of desire, which burns in every girl's heart when she sees my handsome face."

The other voyageur burst out a hoot, and then all three laughed.

"We are going to repair our canoe with this mixture," Louis explained. "The Flame mistakenly believed that he could steer it safely through the Grand Rapids." He pointed sadly toward the bow of their overturned birchbark canoe, where a gash was torn through the hull's underside.

"Oui. My steering was excellent," bragged Pierre. "But Louis's paddling was not good enough." Louis said nothing but wagged his head in disgusted disagreement. "This is a glue made mostly of spruce gum, the sticky sap from pine trees. We are heating the sap to make it softer and mixing it with animal fat and charcoal."

"Any special kind of animal fat?" asked Alex.

"It is tallow from a deer the Indians brought last night," answered Louis. "The charcoal comes out of this fire right here."

"We will place a new layer of birchbark over the tear," Pierre added. "Then seal it inside and out with our black glue. When the mixture cools and hardens, it will be strong and waterproof. It will not crack on a cold morning, nor will it melt during a hot afternoon."

Alex hung around to watch them apply their patch with a stick, one end of which they had whittled into a flat trowel. Then he bid the voyageurs *adieu* and rejoined Lieutenant Eastman and Wakaninajinwin.

* * *

Over the next four days, the river passed through three large lakes that the Native people called Winnibigoshish, Gaamiskwaawaako-kaag and Bemidji. Wakaninajinwin translated the names and their meanings while the trio paddled along.

"Winnibigoshish means brackish water," she explained. "The water is indeed tea-colored, even more so where streams seep through surrounding peat bogs before they enter the lake. Gaamiskwaawaakokaag refers to the many red cedar trees that surround that lake. Bemidji translates into *crossing waters* because the river travels across that lake."

"Schoolcraft is calling that middle one Cass Lake." said Eastman. "He was part of an expedition that tried to find the source of the Mississippi River ten years ago. Lewis Cass, who was the leader of that party, believed the river originated from Gaamiskwaawaakokaag, so those explorers began to call it Cass Lake."

"Lewis Cass was governor of the Michigan Territory for a long time," Alex said. "Now he's the Secretary of War for President Andrew Jackson."

"Perhaps," Wakaninajinwin suggested, "Cass is easier for the white people to pronounce than Gaamiskwaawaakokaag." Eastman and Alex joined her in a hearty laugh.

* * *

Traveling across the lakes should have been fast and easy because the canoes were not fighting a strong upstream current. The trip across Win-nibigoshish began that way in the morning, but before long, a northwest wind began to blow with increasing power. The fleet of canoes was about halfway across the thirteen-mile-wide lake when the wind began whipping the top edges of higher waves into frothy whitecaps.

The surge of each wave quartered into the bow's right side immediately in front of Alex. Each crest lifted and resisted the canoe while splashing a spray over all three paddlers. The tiny wind-blown droplets stung their faces, and they were soon drenched. From the stern, the lieutenant quickly glanced in every direction in search of an island that might provide a windbreak. There were no islands. Winnibigoshish was a broad, uninterrupted expanse of water. In front of them, the voyageurs were changing direction. They had all tacked slightly to the right, angling directly into the northwest wind. A couple of them were waving for other canoes to follow.

"Go straight into the wind," he yelled. Alex and Wakaninajinwin looked over their shoulders at Eastman, but the looks on their faces indicated a lack of understanding. The breeze whipped away the sound of his words. He pointed northwest toward the voyageurs and shouted again, "Go straight into the wind!" This time they nodded and dug their paddles into the lake while the lieutenant tried his best to maintain their new direction.

This was better, Alex noticed. By going perpendicular to each ridge of waves, the bow was no longer being knocked sideways, and the canoe stopped rocking violently from side to side. The lake swells were still big, but the sixteen-foot craft was better able to reach from crest to crest. The canoe remained more level from bow to stern, rather than tipping so drastically forward and backward. So too, he could see the splashing water was now ricocheting off the bow in both directions. The spray was shooting right and left rather than back into the canoe and onto his mates. Looking ahead, he could also detect the western lakeshore was slightly nearer on their new course. *How far to safety?* Alex wondered. *And how long to get there?*

Up ahead, Lieutenant Allen's canoe flipped upside down. The lieutenant was swimming, but the other two soldiers were floundering. The rising and falling waves intermittently obscured the men from Alex's vision. When again he had a clear view, only one of the other soldiers appeared on the surface. Lieutenant Allen was trying to reach the man; his arms were flailing wildly. Suddenly, Pierre and Louis were alongside the desperate castaway. Alex could not tell where the French-Canadians had come from, nor did he know how they had arrived so quickly. Louis extended his paddle to the man while Pierre skillfully kept their canoe pointed into the waves. Another pair of voyageurs deftly lifted the capsized canoe up from the rolling swells and held it upright alongside their own. They held it steady while Louis assisted the awkwardly scrambling soldier back into his own craft.

Lieutenant Allen managed to hold onto his paddle through the entire ordeal. He reached it into the back of his canoe before lifting himself over the gunwale. His vault into the stern showed amazing agility under the circumstances. Eastman saw another paddle floating on the waves, and Wakaninajinwin plucked it from the water when they passed by. They veered near the rescued canoe, and she returned the paddle that the relieved soldier immediately put to use.

Soon they were all earnestly rowing toward the northwest lakeshore once again. *A man has been lost,* Alex realized. He shook the tragedy out of his thoughts because their own desperate situation required his full attention. Again, his mind strayed to the disastrous incident. *The voyageurs were amazing. Without them, all three men may have been drowned.* He looked forward at the skillful paddling of Pierre LaFlamme and whispered with admiration, "The Flame."

* * *

Departing from Lake Bemidji, the river became increasingly narrow and winding. In many places, the canoes could only travel in single file, so the expedition stretched out over nearly a quarter mile. The next day, the river turned into little more than a creek. Their paddles frequently brushed through vegetation and occasionally bumped on the stream bottom. Toward evening, they rowed into a narrow twisting lake that the Natives called Omashkoozo-zaaga'igan, meaning Elk Lake. "This is where the Mississippi River begins," declared the Ojibwe guide Ozawindib.

They found a place to make camp that evening and began to explore the edges of the lake the following morning. A few tiny creeks entered from the south, but Schoolcraft judged them too small to be of significance. Back at the campsite, he gathered the expedition and spoke so all could hear, "I am confident that we have successfully discovered the birthplace of the Mississippi River. Therefore, I will name this lake with the Latin words for truth, *veritas,* and head, *caput.* Lake Itasca, the true source!"

* * *

After their final supper at the Lake Itasca campsite, Schoolcraft gathered his top aides to plan the next leg of their journey. He intended to follow a different path to Fort Snelling rather than retrace their route on the Mississippi. George Johnston recommended they begin with a visit to Leech Lake. "As a fur trader in this region," he stated, "I know that Flat Mouth is an important man, maybe the most respected of all Ojibwe leaders. He commands the large Pillager Band that produces enormous quantities of furs for trade every year. They live on the shores of Leech Lake."

Dr. Houghton spoke, "If the Pillagers are a large population of Natives, I would like very much to go there. We have plenty of smallpox vaccine to administer."

"Yes, and we are near the Canadian border," said Lieutenant Allen. "We should prevail upon Flat Mouth to trade with the American Fur Company rather than British intruders."

"Agreed," Schoolcraft said. "We will start for Leech Lake tomorrow morning. What then?"

"The Crow Wing River is not far beyond," said Ozawindib. "I can guide you there."

"I have seen the Crow Wing," Eastman said. "It is a substantial river, much traveled by the Natives. From where it flows into the Mississippi, we could paddle downstream to Fort Snelling in two long days."

"I will be anxious to reach Fort Snelling," said Schoolcraft. "I look forward to meeting my fellow Indian agent Major Taliaferro and the bands of Dakota people whom he serves." With that, he dismissed the council. "Thank you. We have a good plan."

Henry Schoolcraft (1793–1864)

With a college education in geology, Henry Schoolcraft explored frontier America and wrote about his observations. In 1820, he joined an expedition to find the Mississippi River's source, led by Michigan territorial governor Lewis Cass.[22]

Schoolcraft was appointed Indian Agent for the Michigan Territory, which covered today's states of Michigan, Wisconsin and Minnesota. He held that position for twenty years, during which time he married Jane Johnston, daughter of a prominent fur trader and an Ojibwe woman. He learned to speak the Ojibwe language with his wife, and they had four children together.[23]

In 1832, Schoolcraft led another expedition that found the true source of the Mississippi River, a lake he named Itasca. He also served several terms in the Michigan territorial legislature.[24]

Between 1851 and 1857, he authored the six-volume *Historical and Statistical Information respecting the History, Condition, and Prospects of the Indian Tribes of the United States.* The books were commissioned by the US Congress and illustrated by Seth Eastman.[25]

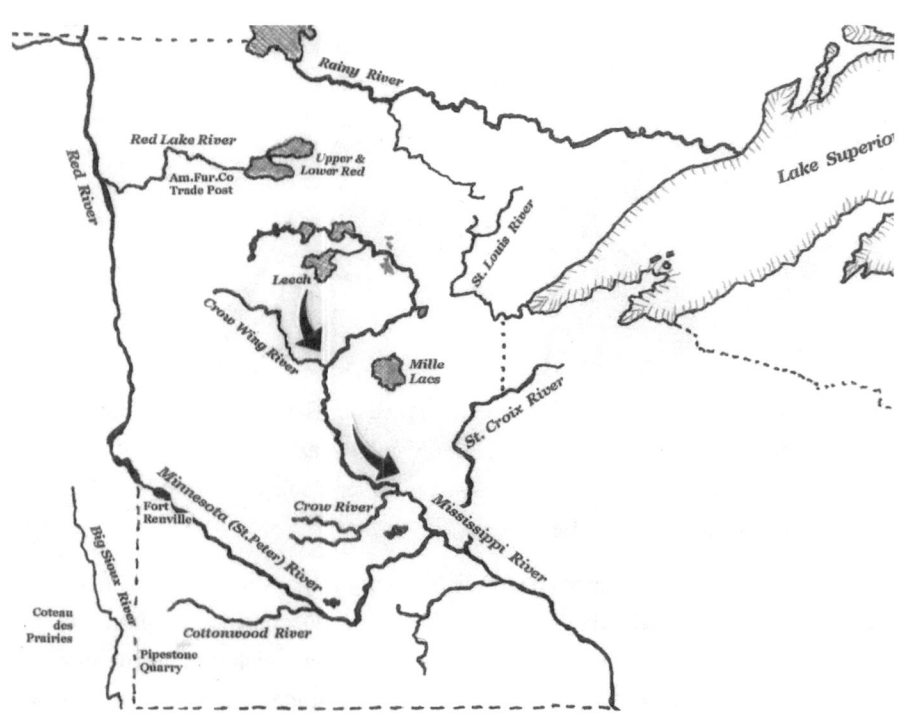

Rainy River

Red Lake River

Red River

Am.Fur.Co
Trade Post

Upper &
Lower Red

Lake Superior

Leech

St. Louis River

Crow Wing River

Mille
Lacs

St. Croix River

Minnesota (St. Peter) River

Fort
Renville

Crow River

Mississippi River

Big Sioux River

Coteau
des
Prairies

Cottonwood River

Pipestone
Quarry

Chapter 7
1832 – Leech Lake

The Ojibwe village was the most impressive Native encampment Schoolcraft had encountered during his entire journey. When the explorers emerged from their portage through pine forest, they beheld the village stretched far along the shore of Leech Lake. The lodges of this Pillager Band were numerous and sturdily built, including a two-story log cabin with glass windows.

The expedition was expected. Four men from this village had met their canoes and guided them along the portage trail. These guides led Schoolcraft's column directly to the log cabin. A tall, powerfully built man who spoke excellent English stood before it. "Welcome to our village, Mr. Schoolcraft. I am Eshkegobecoshe, leader of the Pillager Band. We are honored by your visit."

"We are happy to be here," the Indian agent said. "I am anxious to speak with you about matters of importance to your people and mine."

Eshkegobecoshe invited Schoolcraft and the expedition leaders into his impressive home. During introductions, the Native leader explained that French-Canadian voyageurs called him Gueule Platte. "It means Flat Mouth," he said. "Most whites address me by that name." The hosts then shared cups of Ojibwe tea. The tea had a unique flavor and aroma, with hints of mint and fruit. Some of the Natives mixed a few chunks of maple sugar into their drink.

"We will speak of important matters tonight," Flat Mouth said. "A feast will be served, and then speeches may be heard. But now, you will want to set up your tents and rest."

* * *

Later that afternoon, Alex and Eastman pitched in to help Dr. Houghton erect his medical tent. Also on hand was George Johnston, who shared some of his knowledge about Flat Mouth.

"He is the paramount Ojibwe leader in the Upper Mississippi valley," he said. "During my years of fur trading, his Pillager Band has produced more valuable pelts than any other tribe I know of. And he'll drive a hard bargain. Flat Mouth once imprisoned a trader inside his own house until he negotiated a satisfactory deal."

"Is he prone to violence?" asked Eastman.

"He's known as a great warrior against the Dakota," Johnston said, "but to my knowledge, Flat Mouth has never been hostile to whites. In fact, his people never got involved in the War of 1812, on either side."

"He seems pretty comfortable with the English language," Alex said.

"Oh yes," the trader agreed. "He is considered the most eloquent and persuasive orator among the Ojibwe, and his influence during treaty negotiations is very powerful. I think Flat Mouth's knowledge of the English language gives him an advantage in communicating with whites. That goes for treaty diplomacy as well as fur trade barter."

Dr. Houghton asked, "Do you believe he will approve the inoculation of his people with our smallpox vaccine?"

"I do." Johnston nodded. "You can see by his house that he's receptive to modern ideas."

Just then, eight Native men emerged from the forest, carrying a pair of deer carcasses slung from wooden poles. They quickly had their knives out and began to butcher the meat. One of them turned away and began striding toward the medical tent. "Johnston!" he called and then smiled when the trader recognized him.

Twisting Trails

"My friend, Hole-in-the-Day," Johnston answered. "You are a long distance from your home on Sandy Lake."

"I wish to meet these Americans," said Hole-in-the-Day. "Both they and the British are asking to be our allies. Which whites should we choose, I wonder?" Then with a sly smile, he added, "or neither?"

Johnston shook his hand and smiled himself. "Or both!" The two men laughed.

Eastman turned to Dr. Houghton. "Are they serious?"

"I would suspect they're only half-joking," the doctor guessed. He watched the Natives who were butchering the two deer and marveled, "Look at their skillful slicing of meat from bones and tendons. Many a surgeon would be hard-pressed to match the anatomical dissection those men are performing."

"I'm just looking forward to tonight's venison feast!" interjected Alex. The doctor and the lieutenant nodded in agreement.

* * *

Alex contemplated the amazing circumstance of the panorama before him. Little more than one year ago, he was a city boy, living under his mother's roof. Now he was a soldier of the United States, having explored to the source of his country's greatest river, sitting in council with the foremost chief of the Ojibwe nation. He could scarcely believe his good fortune.

Seated on the ground in the center of a wide semi-circle, Flat Mouth and Schoolcraft faced a large open fire with Leech Lake beyond. Schoolcraft's expedition leaders arced to his right: Johnston, the lieutenants Allen and Eastman, Wakaninajinwin, Alex, Dr. Houghton, and the Reverend Boutwell. Across the semi-circle to Flat Mouth's immediate left sat the Sandy Lake Ojibwe chief Hole-in-the-Day. Beside him were three more tribal leaders, including one of the men who had guided Schoolcraft's approach to this village. At the far end of the arc were members of Flat Mouth's family.

The population of the Pillager Band gathered beyond the open fire all along the lakeshore. The voyageurs and Fort Brady soldiers filled in the remaining portion of a complete circle around the center fire. People swirled to and from other fires, collecting food and eating while they engaged in lively conversations and shared occasional shouts and merry laughter. Children dodged among their elders, with village dogs tagging behind, hoping for dropped morsels.

The sun hung low on the western horizon behind Alex, and towering trees shaded the entire village. Looking east across Leech Lake, the final rays of daylight still bathed the tall pines and clumps of white-barked birches in a golden glow. Gentle ripples across the lake mirrored a shimmering image of trees sparkled with reflected sunlight. He was struck by the contrast between the placid landscape afar and the noisy hubbub surrounding him.

As Alex scanned back around the semi-circle, he hesitated at the sight of a Native girl among Flat Mouth's family. Once seated, she now stood beside an older woman. The girl was very pretty and slender with features not entirely Ojibwe. Alex noticed her demeanor—a serenity that seemed more a part of the lake's landscape than the feast's commotion. He watched her for a while until she turned and moved away with the older woman and another girl.

* * *

"Angelique, you should dance," encouraged Grandmother.

"I don't know how," the girl protested.

However, White Loon reassured her. "You have observed, and I have seen you imitate other dancers. You will do well."

Again, Angelique resisted. "I can't. I have no dancing clothes."

"We can loan you proper garments," suggested Grandmother.

Wind on the Water broke in. "She can just watch," the cousin said impatiently, with hands on hips and a sneer on her face. "After all, she's just a little kid."

The remark shifted Angelique's entire attitude. She had been nervous and bashful about dancing in front of the entire Pillager village and the white visitors. But Wind on the Water's dismissive remark felt like an insult, and now she was angry. "Okay, I'll do it."

Grandmother and the two teenage cousins retreated to the older woman's lodge. Wind on the Water put on a beautiful doeskin dress, and Grandmother helped her attach a full wreath of turkey tail feathers onto the small of her back. For Angelique, the matriarch produced a black vest with brightly colored Métis beadwork on the front and back. For both girls, she provided a pair of bells attached to ankle bracelets.

When they emerged from Grandmother's lodge, Wind on the Water and Angelique joined other girls who were returning to the circle. Flat Mouth stood up and announced that the Pillager girls were ready to perform a dance to honor their white visitors and celebrate the wild rice harvest. Then a ring of drummers started pounding a rhythmic beat, and the girls began to filter out of the crowd into the circle.

Unsure of herself, Angelique moved slowly. She lingered near her family and glanced to them for encouragement. White Loon smiled reassuringly, and Grandmother motioned for her to go ahead. She began to flow with the rhythm of the drum, lifting and replacing one foot before stepping forward. Following with the other foot, up and down, then onward. She circled near to the fire, shying away from the crowd of faces around the perimeter. Soon many onlookers also moved in tempo with the drumbeats, heads nodding and shoulders bobbing.

Wind on the Water was dancing near the outer edge of the circle. It appeared to Angelique that her cousin was paying particular attention to a pair of young soldiers with a Native girl seated between them. *Shameless,* she thought. Wind on the Water was shaking her body in a suggestive manner and twirling around with arms waving above her shoulders. Angelique proceeded around the fire away from her cousin and danced in harmony with the drumbeat. She enjoyed the remainder of the dance, moving gently and carefree.

* * *

When Flat Mouth announced a dance by Pillager girls, young men added sticks to the center fire, and the drumbeat began. A dozen or so young women entered the circle and began stepping around the fire. They all moved in rhythm with the drum, but not in unison.

One girl in particular danced with exceptional fervor. She wore a long deerskin dress cured almost white, and a full wreath of turkey feathers graced the small of her back. Alex noticed her eyes intermittently upon him in between spins of her body.

Then he saw the girl he had been watching earlier. Coming around the fire, she moved with the same calmness he had noticed before. Unlike the previous girl's spirited, agile and energetic movements, she danced with serenity and grace. Alex thought her very pretty. Both young women wore bells on their ankles, and the girl by the fire made hers gently chime in harmony with the drum. In comparison, the more frantic dancer's bells created a non-rhythmic jangling clamor.

The graceful girl circled farther from the fire; the dancing movements of her body in the flickering flames mesmerized Alex. The blaze had its own rhythm, but somehow, she seemed simultaneously in tune with both the fire and the drum. Abruptly, the drum stopped. Alex blinked, and the dancers disappeared, filtering into the crowd on the far side of the circle.

Schoolcraft stood up. He began clapping his hands, and all of the other Americans joined in. When the round of applause subsided, he spoke loudly enough for everyone to hear, "Thank you, Flat Mouth and the Pillager Band of Ojibwe, for the wonderful welcome you have extended to us. This feast has been delicious and bountiful. The dance performed by your maidens was exciting and beautiful." From a hip pocket of his formal coat, the expedition leader withdrew two large bronze medallions, suspended from blue ribbons. Holding them aloft, he proclaimed, "On behalf of the United States, I present these medals to our good friends Flat Mouth and Hole-in-the-Day."

When the two Ojibwe leaders stood, Schoolcraft hung the medallions around their necks. "The image of our President Andrew Jackson is emblazoned on the front of each medal," he announced. "On the back is the symbol of our great nation, the bald eagle. These gifts are intended to demonstrate the respect and gratitude we have for Flat Mouth, for Hole-in-the-Day, and for the Ojibwe people."

Twisting Trails

The three men smiled and shook hands, but Schoolcraft was not done. Reaching into another pocket, he produced two big hunting knives with shining steel blades and extended them handle-first to the Ojibwe leaders. "Let these gifts show our appreciation for the friendship of your people," he declared, "and let them be symbols of friendship to you from our people."

Schoolcraft remained standing when Flat Mouth and Hole-in-the-Day sat down. "The United States hopes to remain friends with you and with all Native people," he said. "Furthermore, we hope that peace and friendship can be maintained between the Ojibwe and your neighbors, including the Dakota. Peace will be good for everyone because men who are not at war can focus on providing for their villages. Men should hunt for furs to trade for necessary supplies and for meat to feed their families."

He finished his speech by introducing Doctor Houghton. "The doctor has brought good medicine," he announced. "The terrible disease of smallpox has killed many Native people. Doctor Houghton's medicine can protect you from that illness. We hope that everyone will come to his tent tomorrow to receive the smallpox vaccine."

Flat Mouth rose when Schoolcraft sat down. Darkness now surrounded the village, but the glowing fire illuminated the Pillager leader. His muscular build made it easy to appreciate the warrior's reputation in battle. Flat Mouth's steadfast eyes seemed to connect with every individual as he panned the circle.

"Thank you for these fine gifts. We are grateful to President Jackson and honored to receive visitors from the United States." He nodded toward members of the expedition. "The Ojibwe also desire peace. We welcome the presence of army soldiers and hope their travels among the Dakota will discourage our old rivals from launching violence against us."

Next, Flat Mouth recalled the Prairie du Chien Treaty of 1825 signed by United States officials and leaders of nine Native tribes, "My friends Schoolcraft and Hole-in-the-Day were at Prairie du Chien six years ago. They signed the paper, which defined hunting boundaries between our neighbors and us. Dakota leaders also signed that paper, yet their hunters continue to trespass onto Ojibwe land. They approach the Crow Wing River in the south and the Red Lake River in the north. The United States promised that its army would help to patrol our borders, but their soldiers are seldom seen." He warned, "If the United States does not help to protect Ojibwe land, we will defend it ourselves."

Pillager voices murmured from the darkness beyond the circle, and Flat Mouth paused until the buzz subsided. "We are pleased to see our old friend Johnston," looking at Schoolcraft's brother-in-law. "He has been a fair and honest trader, but a few who represent the American Fur Company have not been so trustworthy." Again, whispers could be heard among the villagers. "The Pillager Band provides furs of the finest quality. In turn, we expect to exchange them for trade goods of equal value. If the American Fur Company cannot pay fair prices for our pelts, we will deliver them to other traders who can."

After another pause, Flat Mouth extended his arm toward Dr. Houghton. "I am grateful that the doctor has brought good medicine for us. We are aware that other Native people have suffered from terrible diseases. Our people will gladly accept his remedy." With that, he sat back down, and the entire village scattered once again into animated clusters of people. Some gathered around distant fires for the remaining morsels of the feast. Others retreated toward the lodges to begin a restful night's sleep.

Wakaninajinwin rose and headed across the circle toward the women of Flat Mouth's family. Lieutenant Allen leaned in Eastman and Alex's direction and remarked, "The chief doesn't mince words, does he."

"No, he does not," said Alex. "I'm glad he is our ally and not our enemy."

"The US Army would be well-advised," suggested Lieutenant Eastman, "to strive to keep it that way!"

* * *

Twisting Trails

When Flat Mouth finished speaking, the young Dakota woman who had been seated among the army officers approached Angelique. "My name is Wakaninajinwin," she said. Pointing back at the American soldiers, "I am the wife of Lieutenant Eastman from Fort Snelling."

"I am Angelique Reaume," she replied. "This is my mother, White Loon, and my grandmother. Flat Mouth is her son."

"I loved your dance!" said the Dakota woman. "You moved so beautifully."

Angelique blushed while her smiling mother gave her a hug. "I heard Flat Mouth announce that the dance was to celebrate your harvest of wild rice. Is the harvest occurring now?"

"Yes. In fact, that's why we are here," answered White Loon. "My husband is a fur trader, so we live at the trading post on Red Lake River. We come home to my Pillager Band every ricing season for the Leech Lake harvest."

"I do not wish to intrude, but may I go with you?"

Angelique began to explain, "Mother and I will rice together…"

"No, not in your canoe," the Dakota woman interrupted. "I can bring someone to pole my own canoe. Perhaps you can point us to a shallow bay where wild rice may be growing."

"Yes," Grandmother decided. "We will guide you." Pointing a gnarled old finger to the lakeshore, she concluded, "Meet us there at sunrise."

* * *

"I'm sorry," Eastman apologized to his wife. "I cannot go ricing with you. Schoolcraft needs me to join his meeting with Flat Mouth and Hole-in-the-Day.

She was obviously disappointed. "But I cannot do it by myself."

"I'll go," Alex volunteered.

Wakaninajinwin looked into his face, and Alex gave a confirming nod. She took one happy hop and sprinted to the lakeside, where she had pulled their canoe ashore.

"I'm curious about the process," Alex said to the grinning Eastman. "This will be the best way for me to learn about wild rice."

He tugged his cap more tightly on his head and followed after the Dakota girl.

The rising sun illuminated the sky, but the surface of Leech Lake was still in shadow. Here and there, the sliver of a morning sunray sparkled among tall treetops, but dawn was yet to arrive on the lake. Cool night air still hovered beneath the lakeside pines, causing a ring of fog to shroud the shoreline. Out of the fog across the lake, Alex heard the sound of a pulsing *tremolo*. Loons were more common here than at his boyhood home on Lake Huron, but he recognized the call. He knew they had other calls: rising *yodels* to declare territory, haunting *wails* when in search of each other, and quiet *hoots* between mates or to their young. Paddling across Bemidji and Cass Lakes, he had seen several pairs of big, black and white speckled loons.

He had watched them dive and swim under water for a minute or more, emerging perhaps fifty yards away. They appeared to be doting parents. Once he saw a baby chick riding on the back of a swimming adult. Another time, both parents were dropping wounded minnows from their beaks, helping a pair of chicks learn to dive and hunt.

Alex had been gazing across the lake, listening to the loons. Now he was startled to see the pretty and graceful dancer when he arrived at the shore. She stood among the people gathered around two canoes.

"Alex, these are members of Flat Mouth's family," said Wakaninajinwin. "His mother, sister and nieces. They are going to lead us to some beds of wild rice."

"Grandmother will go ashore with my younger daughter Gabrielle," White Loon said. "They will prepare a drying rack for the green rice we harvest. Your canoe will follow Angelique and me to the rice beds."

Angelique, Alex repeated silently to himself. *Her name is Angelique.*

"Take this," instructed Grandmother, handing Alex a long pole about twice as long as he and almost as thick as his wrist, with a forked notch at one end. "Use the pole rather than your paddle when you get into the rice. Paddling would damage the plant stalks, and that notch will grip the soft mucky lake bottom when you push your canoe through the rice bed."

Soon both canoes were speeding gracefully down the shoreline. Wakaninajinwin and Alex pulled hard to stay close behind Angelique and her mother. After about a mile, they rounded a point and turned inward past a small island. Beyond the island opened a wide bay; the shallow end was thick, with green reeds growing three to five feet above the water surface. It appeared to Alex that a small stream might enter the back of this bay, but that was far beyond the expanse of wild rice plants. Angelique and her mother slowed before reaching the rice bed's edge allowing Wakaninajinwin and Alex to pull alongside. White Loon extended her long pole to the lake bottom from the stern of their canoe and stood. Pointing to the summit of a hill beyond the shoreline, she said, "We will harvest to the left of this line. You can work from here to the right."

At first, Alex and White Loon slowly poled both canoes toward the hilltop, staying about fifteen feet parallel with each other. From his spot in the stern, the young soldier could watch each girl, Dakota and Ojibwe, harvesting rice into the cavity of their canoe. They held narrow sticks a little more than two feet long, one in each hand. Alternately, they reached to their right, bending stalks of rice over the gunwale knocking the seeds from the plant heads with their left-hand stick. They repeated the motion on the opposite side of the canoe, back and forth, over and over. Soon kernels of rice covered the floor of each canoe. They would keep going until their boats were half-filled. At that point, they left the rice bed and paddled to an open shoreline where Angelique's grandmother and little sister were waiting near a low scaffold erected for the harvest; it was about twelve feet long and an arm's length wide, supporting a mat of woven reeds. The harvesters began to scoop the rice out of their canoes and spread it upon the mats. The older woman tended hot fires beneath the scaffold that did not burn tall enough to scorch the reed mats.

"This is a drying rack," Wakaninajinwin told Alex. She pointed toward White Loon, who had picked up a wooden paddle. "She will continually turn the rice with the paddle while it dries on the rack. She motioned to include Angelique. "Our job is to pick through the kernels with our hands, removing bits of dirt and weeds or rice worms."

* * *

The teenagers stood along the lakeside of the drying rack with eight-year-old Gabrielle next to Angelique, in the middle, helping to clean debris out of the rice. White Loon and Grandmother tended their paddles and the fires from the opposite side of the rack. Alex sneaked frequent sideways glances at Angelique's pretty profile and admired her quick and graceful hands at work.

She and Wakaninajinwin were comparing this Ojibwe ricing process with that of the Dakota. "We parch the rice on drying racks like this to loosen the outside hull and prevent the inner seed from spoiling," explained Angelique. "Next, the kernels will be hulled by treading feet. We pour them, one basket at a time, onto a clean hide laid over a shallow hole in the ground. Then, with new moccasins, we rub the chaff off the rice by grinding it under our feet."

"Young men in my Dakota village do the hulling," said Wakaninajinwin. "Girls recruit the boys to do the work. The girls gush about how handsome and strong they are, which motivates the boys to tread harder and longer!" They both laughed and thought that was pretty funny. Alex wondered if they were targeting him for that type of motivation.

"Finally," Angelique proceeded, "we winnow the rice by tossing it with birchbark trays. When skillfully flipped into the air, lighter chaff drifts away on the breeze while the heavier seeds fall back upon the tray." Then she concluded, "Rice that is properly parched, hulled and winnowed can be stored all winter long if kept in dry containers. We usually use birchbark, but a bag sewn from animal hide will work just as well."

"Yes," said Wakaninajinwin. "I intend to take my rice home in just such a bag."

Twisting Trails

Later that day, Alex did indeed hull some rice by treading upon the kernels. However, the girls took their turns as well. When the hulling was finished, Angelique's mother suggested that she go berry picking. "We can do the winnowing," proposed White Loon. "Gathering blueberries would be the most valuable use of your time."

"I will winnow my rice," said Wakaninajinwin, "but Private Whitney lacks the experience to perform this task. He should go with Angelique."

"Yes indeed," Alex agreed. He stooped to pick up a pair of birchbark buckets and happily followed the Métis girl inland from the lake.

* * *

Soon the path which Angelique followed led uphill, and Alex had to hustle to stay alongside her. "Your dance last night was wonderful," he offered. She looked quickly at his face and turned away, but her walking pace slowed a little. "I liked it."

"Surely you liked my cousin more," she said. He seemed confused, so Angelique explained. "My cousin was the dancer wearing a white doeskin dress with a fan of turkey feathers on her back. Her dancing is much fancier than mine."

"I remember her," he admitted. "But she seemed kind of frantic. I think your graceful movements were much more beautiful."

Angelique could not stop the smile of delight from spreading across her face, so she quickly turned away, pretending to search for berries. She was pleased this young soldier found her more attractive than Wind on the Water. But it would be inappropriate for her to express those emotions. Improper also to reveal that she considered him handsome, which she truly did. "My father is French," she told him. "A fur trader. We live at the trading post on Red Lake River, almost one hundred miles northwest of here."

"I never knew my father," Alex revealed. "He was killed in battle against the British." The young man spoke about his former home in Detroit and his current assignment at Fort Snelling. Angelique had difficulty visualizing the buildings of stone he described, but she tried to imagine how they looked. Likewise, her description of life among the Métis, with which he had no experience, fascinated him.

Gradually they climbed through a thick aspen grove, emerging onto a rocky hillside more sparsely covered by looming pines and spruces. Angelique stopped and gazed about the sun-dappled slope that was thick with blueberry bushes. She crouched into a spot where clumps of the blue and purple fruit were within arm's reach. Her hands moved quickly but tenderly to close around two or three berries at a time and gently pull them from the foot-tall plants.

Alex watched her for a few moments, then stepped into a likely spot where he began to copy her movements. Many of the berries hung partially hidden and suspended underneath the bush stems. "Don't pick the green ones," Angelique advised. "They're not yet ripe. But a few are over-ripe, too soft with juice oozing out. Don't pick them either." Alex noticed that when he picked ripe but firm berries, they dropped into his birchbark bucket with a delicate pop. He looked around and moved to a nearby area that appeared especially bountiful.

* * *

Before long, Angelique was beside him. Both of her baskets were full. Sheepishly, he gave her his empty one and continued to gather with the half-filled other. They were finished in a short time and stood up, each of them with a bucket in both hands. It felt good to straighten his legs, Alex thought. Suddenly, from this standing view-point, he looked over Angelique's shoulder and saw a black bear emerge from the aspen grove. It was approximately seventy-five feet down the slope, in the direction from where they had come.

Alex pointed, "A bear." It stood upright when she turned to look. "It's a young male," he observed. "Maybe one or two years old."

Angelique was clearly not panicked by the presence of the bear. "He's just hungry for these blueberries," she said. "There will be plenty left for him when we leave."

Twisting Trails

"We should not turn and run," Alex cautioned, "lest we provoke his instinct to chase us. We don't want the bear to think we are afraid. You select a path for us to circle back to the lake. I will retreat with you while facing him. If necessary, I'll raise my hands to appear bigger than him and speak to him in a loud stern voice."

The beast did not follow, and after he was gone from sight, Angelique asked, "How is it you are familiar with bears?"

"I am an experienced hunter," Alex told her. "We have black bears in the forests of Michigan as well. I have seen older males much larger than him."

"We were lucky," she remarked, "that this was not a big female with cubs. Bears are most fierce when defending their babies."

Eventually, they returned to the lakeshore, but because of their route away from the bear, they exited the trees about a quarter mile up the shoreline from Angelique's family. The day had waned into one of those early evenings when the sun was setting onto the western horizon while the moon was rising in the east, full and bright in the clear blue sky. Alex pointed to its vivid reflection on the water surface, "Looks like the Man in the Moon is in the lake!"

"It is the ricing moon," declared Angelique, pausing to face the image. "Last month when the moon became full, it was the berry moon."

"Every full moon gets its own name?" asked Alex.

"My mother's people identify the seasons by connecting each full moon to nature. In the spring, we have the maple sap moon and the flowering moon. When autumn comes, we'll observe the moons for changing leaves and falling leaves. Our winter moons are named for the little spirit and the great spirit."

By the time Alex and Angelique returned, the others were getting ready to bundle their finished rice for transport back to the Pillager village. "Did you find berries?" inquired White Loon.

"Enough to share with a hungry bear!" her daughter exclaimed, and she proceeded to tell the story of their long route back.

White Loon watched Angelique and detected a difference. Unexpectedly, her daughter was not standing, gesturing, talking, or laughing like a little girl. Instead, she was moving and expressing herself as a young woman. White Loon realized that this young soldier also saw Angelique as a blossoming woman. Despite their short time together, a happy ease had bloomed between the two.

As Alex and Angelique laughed and shared their story about the blueberries and the bear, White Loon saw Grandmother from the corner of her eye. The elder woman looked from the young couple to White Loon, and they exchanged a knowing look. Grandmother smiled and slowly nodded her head.

After loading their bundles of wild rice into the canoes, the group launched for return to the village. The lake was calm in the gathering dusk. Little sister Gabrielle had switched into her mother's canoe, and Angelique was now paddling with Grandmother. Alex looked across the water at Angelique and was not surprised to observe that her paddling strokes, like all her other movements, were graceful. *I will remember you*, he thought.

Angelique deftly switched her paddle to the opposite side of the canoe. The change made it easier for her to glance toward the canoe where Private Whitney was rowing from the stern. The gathering darkness obscured the kindness in his face, which she knew was there. She could see the powerful paddle strokes of his long slender arms, and she thought, *I will remember you.*

* * *

The next day, Schoolcraft's expedition left Leech Lake. Ojibwe guides helped them navigate through a series of smaller lakes to the headwaters of the Crow Wing River. Downstream travel was swift, and they reached the Mississippi in two days. At the end of the fourth day, they portaged around St. Anthony Falls and landed at Fort Snelling.

Schoolcraft and his people stayed at the Indian Agency with Major Lawrence Taliaferro. The two Indian agents had much to talk about, and Taliaferro was able to gather hundreds of Dakota people to the agency. The Reverend Boutwell spoke to them about Christianity. Dr. Houghton inoculated them with the smallpox vaccine. They held a feast and Schoolcraft, Taliaferro and Dakota leaders delivered speeches. Members of the expedition, Eastman, Alex, and Wakaninajinwin, were invited to the feast. She was especially thrilled to hear the speech by her father.

Cloud Man acclaimed the ability of his village to become successful farmers. In the process, he retold the well-known story of a perilous hunting trip. Wild game had become scarce near their homes at the confluence of the Mississippi and Minnesota Rivers, so he and other Dakota hunters began traveling farther and farther to find meat for their families. On one such trip, a three-day blizzard trapped his party. Though they survived the ferocious storm, Cloud Man resolved that his people would begin to feed themselves with crops in addition to wild game. He gave thanks to Major Taliaferro, who helped them get started with seeds and equipment. He boasted of their abundant harvest and then had villagers distribute ears of corn among the visiting Dakota bands.

Taliaferro stood. He praised Cloud Man's leadership and the agricultural skill of the Dakota village beside Lake Bde Maka Ska. The Indian agent turned to the other leaders present, including Wabasha from the Mississippi valley to the south and Sleepy Eye from the St. Peter valley to the west. He urged them to follow Cloud Man's example. Furthermore, he pledged support in the form of farming supplies and equipment. Taliaferro also echoed Schoolcraft's plea for peace with the Ojibwe. He promised that providing crops for themselves would promote peace because the rival tribes would have less need for hunting trips into contested territory.

Michael Barnes

Major Lawrence Taliaferro (1794–1871)

Major Lawrence Taliaferro was born into an aristocratic Virginia family of Italian heritage. The family name was pronounced *Tolliver* in America.[26]

He joined the army at eighteen to fight in the War of 1812. He decided to make the military his career and was promoted rapidly through several frontier assignments. Appointed Indian Agent at Fort Snelling in 1819, a post he occupied for almost twenty-one years.[27]

Major Taliaferro forged a reputation for honesty and efficiency. He was trusted by both Dakota and Ojibwe leaders, which helped to maintain the uneasy peace between these traditional rivals. Conversely, he shared mutual animosity with fur traders whom he believed were cheating the Native people, especially those who illegally traded alcohol.[28]

Taliaferro fathered a girl (Mary) with a Dakota woman in 1828, the same year he was married to the former Eliza Dillon in Pennsylvania. He arranged for the daughter to be educated at Samuel Pond's mission school near Fort Snelling, and she eventually married a soldier named Warren Woodbury, who died during the Civil War.[29]

Twisting Trails

Eliza Taliaferro lived at the Indian Agency with her husband, aided by an African American slave girl named Harriet Robinson. As a Justice of the Peace, Major Taliaferro famously married Harriet to Dred Scott (1836). At the time, Scott was enslaved to Dr. John Emerson, an army surgeon stationed at Fort Snelling.[30]

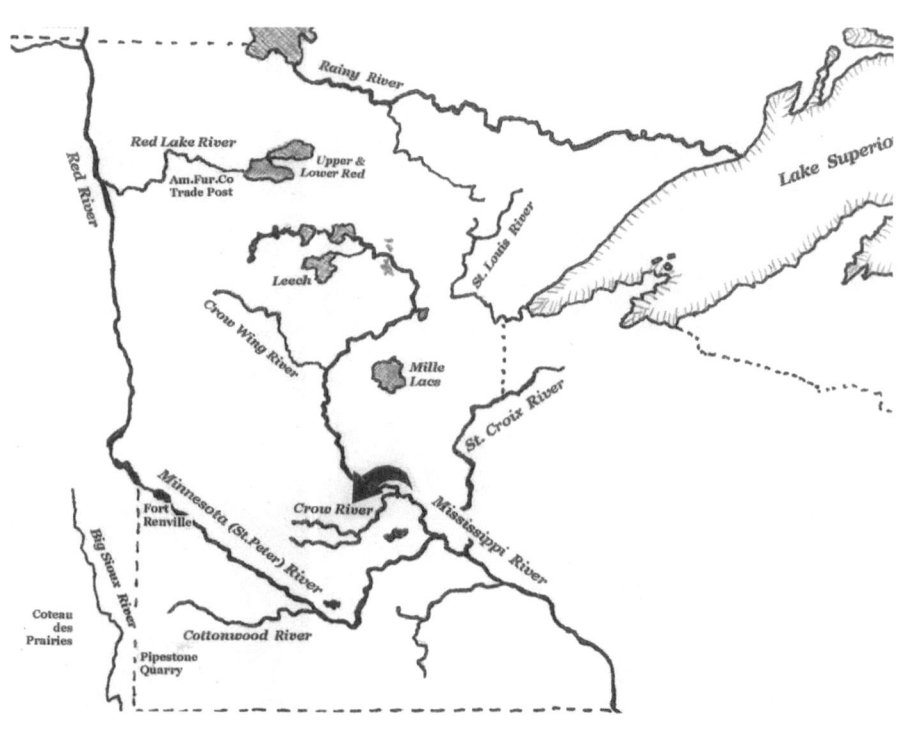

Chapter 8
1834 – Crow River

September 25, 1834

Dear Mother,

Thank you for my birthday presents. The new socks and underwear are better in every way than what I can buy here at the fort sutler's store. They are more comfortable, will last longer, and keep me warmer in the coming winter. At twenty-one years of age, my body has grown more muscular than when I left Detroit. But my height and feet must be the same because the garments fit perfectly. I am proud to report my promotion to the rank of corporal. I believe Lt. Eastman recommended my advancement before he left Fort Snelling. He has been transferred back to West Point where he is teaching art to topographical engineers at the military academy. His young wife gave birth to a daughter before he left, but she remains here with her Dakota family. Apparently their marriage is over.

My promotion carries higher pay and a new assignment. After Sgt. Schmid and I provided all the nails and hardware for the new Council House, I was reassigned to be a liaison between Fort Snelling and the Indian Agency. I report to Maj. Lawrence Taliaferro, the long-time Indian agent for this region. He is much respected and I am told that he requested me because of my service with Native people on the Schoolcraft expedition and at the council house.

Two of my greatest desires are being satisfied with this promotion. First, I am advancing toward a career as an officer in this army. Second, my performance of this position promises to be a splendid adventure!

Your loving son,

Alexander

* * *

Corporal Alex Whitney was familiar with the half-mile ride westward from Fort Snelling to the Indian Agency. He could have galloped the distance in a few minutes but was content to let his horse walk on this warm autumn evening. The silence captivated him. No breeze rustled the tall prairie grasses, so the landscape was quiet. Quiet enough for Alex to focus on the rhythm of each horse hoof clomping along the trail. Farther along, he heard the staccato melody of a lark and paused his mount, scanning the grass tips for a glimpse of the songbird. The musical chirping surrounded him, and Alex wasn't sure which direction to look.

Growing larger and more golden as it settled toward the horizon, the sun shone upon his face. The recently promoted young soldier was enjoying the solitude until the sight of the Indian Agency buildings silhouetted in the sunlight reminded him of his duty. Major Lawrence Taliaferro, Fort Snelling's veteran Indian agent, had invited him to dinner and a meeting. He had never been inside the agent's house. All of his trips with Sergeant Schmid were to work on rebuilding the burned council house, now finished. Taliaferro's residence was a one-and-a-half-story stone house. As

Alex approached, he saw the major step outside the main entrance to welcome his arrival.

As always, Taliaferro's posture was ramrod straight, and he returned the young man's salute, "Hello, Corporal Whitney."

Alex knew, from previous visits, that the major did not always wear military attire, but this evening he was dressed in a formal officer's uniform.

Taliaferro pointed to a hitching rail where Alex could tether his horse and then held open the front door. Upon entry, they turned into a dining room where three people rose to their feet. "Corporal, allow me to introduce my wife. Eliza, this is Corporal Alexander Whitney."

She dipped a quick curtsy and gave Alex a cheerful smile. "We're so happy to have dinner guests," she beamed. "Especially three such talented young men!" Eliza's voice carried none of the southern accent that Alex had detected in the major's speech. She was a pretty woman with beautifully curled dark hair and a stylish dress. Both husband and wife appeared to be about forty years of age with aristocratic demeanor. Elegant furnishings around the dining room also revealed a wealthy family background.

"Have you met the Pond brothers?" asked Major Taliaferro.

Both young men, Samuel and Gideon, stepped forward to identify themselves and offer their hands. "I know who you are," Alex responded, "but we have not been formally introduced." Gideon seemed about his own age. Samuel, the older brother, was probably in his mid-twenties. They stood taller than Alex. Both were more than six feet in height and extraordinarily thin. However, their long slender fingers were strong when they exchanged firm handshakes.

As everyone settled into their seats around the dinner table, the major said, "I am helping Samuel and Gideon to construct a mission near the Dakota village beside Lake Bde Maka Ska."

"We are eager to spread the Christian faith among our Native brothers and sisters," said Samuel. Gideon nodded, and both brothers' narrow faces were bright with enthusiasm.

"Cloud Man's village should be a good place for you to begin," Taliaferro said. "He and his people have successfully implemented our farming methods."

"We both did some farming back home in Connecticut," said Gideon. "I'm an able carpenter too, so I will help build the mission, which will also serve as our home. Additionally, Samuel is a teacher, so he will begin a school for the Dakota children."

"Sounds like you two make a capable combination," exclaimed Eliza.

Major Taliaferro advanced his wife's train of thought. "I am hopeful that the three of you will make an even stronger team. Corporal Whitney, you have demonstrated a unique ability to communicate with Native people. Lieutenant Eastman reported your remarkable service among the Ojibwe while on the Schoolcraft expedition. I myself have seen you interact with Dakota people here while rebuilding the council house."

"Thank you, sir," Alex acknowledged.

"As my liaison from the Indian Agency, I believe you can be valuable to the Pond brothers. Furthermore, their success with the mission, the school and the farm will aid the improvements I am trying to make on behalf of the Native people," Taliaferro proposed. "So, what do you think?"

"To begin with," Alex said, "I know you're not asking about my blacksmith skills, but I could provide a valuable service by repairing metal tools and supplies here at the Indian Agency. Native people are acquiring more metal trade goods every year. When their cookware, or animal traps, or firearms are broken, they have no way to fix them."

"Good idea," said the major, while the Pond brothers both nodded.

"However, with regard to religion and farming," Alex hesitated. "I'll try to help, but I'm not sure the Dakota or the Ojibwe want our help."

Taliaferro's expression reflected understanding, but the Pond brothers looked perplexed. Alex tried to explain, "The Native people have strong faith in their beliefs and their ways of life. On the Schoolcraft expedition, I saw the Reverend Boutwell preach to hundreds of Ojibwe men and women. But I heard none of them vow to become Christian." He continued, "Here at the agency, I saw dozens of Dakota men and women eat the corn from Cloud Man's fields. But I heard none of them vow to become farmers."

"The fur traders are in part to blame for that," the major angrily declared. "They want the Natives to continue hunting and trapping for furs. Rather than become self-sufficient farmers, they want the Native people dependent on the American Fur Company for trade goods."

Samuel interjected, "Christ has guided my brother and me to this beautiful place on earth among these wonderful Dakota people!" His face was radiant with excitement. "We will perform whatever labors are necessary to help the Natives discover the blessings of Christianity, and the good Lord will assure our success." The zeal in Samuel's voice and the optimism in his shared smile with Gideon held the room in silence for a moment.

Eliza raised her glass toward the brothers and broke the lull, "We will pray for our mutual success and better lives for the Native people."

Just then, a Black girl, perhaps twenty years old, stepped in from the kitchen. "Dinner is ready," she said.

"Thank you, Harriet," Mrs. Taliaferro answered. "We may serve it now." Alex was not familiar with slavery, but he perceived immediately that this young woman was a servant. Eliza stood up from her chair, and the two women began carrying platters of food from the kitchen to their dining table. The ham, corn and potatoes looked and smelled delicious. When Mrs. Taliaferro returned to her seat, Harriet filled everyone's water glass from a pitcher and disappeared back into the kitchen.

When their meal was over, Mrs. Taliaferro summoned the girl to clear the dishes. Alex had no doubt that she was also expected to wash them. Taliaferro escorted Alex and the Pond brothers into the main room of the house, where Eliza seated herself at their piano.

She played and sang a beautiful song. Then invited all of the men to sing along while she played the old English folk song "What Can the Matter Be? Johnny's So Long at the Fair." Samuel and Gideon joined her with full-throated enthusiasm. Alex and the major also knew the tune but timidly held their off-key voices to a much lower volume.

* * *

The following week, Taliaferro sent Alex to Bde Maka Ska to check on conditions at the Dakota village and the Pond Brothers' mission. Stopping first at the village, he found Wakaninajinwin grinding corn with a stone outside her father's lodge. The young woman waved happily to Alex and scooped a nearby toddler into her arms at his approach. This was surely her daughter with Eastman, but he thought it more polite to ask. "Who is this pretty little girl?"

The girl clung tightly to her mother but gave the blue-uniformed stranger a shy smile. "This is my Winona," said Wakaninajinwin. "It is the typical name for first-born Dakota daughters."

"I miss her father," Alex disclosed. "He was a good friend."

"I miss him too," she answered, "but we are not lonely."

Her seeming lack of emotion surprised Alex. Her face betrayed no more sorrow for the departure of her husband than if he were a worn-out pair of favorite moccasins, fondly remembered but no longer of any use. He decided not to pursue the subject. "Is your father here so that I might speak with him?"

When Wakaninajinwin answered, yes. Alex asked that she remain to help translate the conversation. They entered the lodge where Cloud Man immediately recognized and greeted the young soldier, "Welcome, Private Whitney."

Alex grinned and quickly informed the Dakota leader about his promotion to the rank of corporal. "I am now under the supervision of Major Taliaferro," he explained.

"My son is a good man."

Thinking that Taliaferro was similar in age to Cloud Man, Alex asked, "Why do you refer to him as your son?"

Twisting Trails

Wakaninajinwin responded instead, "He has a daughter with my oldest sister. They were married before the major took his white wife."

Alex's mouth fell open with astonishment. Before he could digest this revelation about Taliaferro, the Dakota leader continued, "The major is fair and honest. He tries to serve the Ojibwe and Dakota evenly. His efforts to keep peace between our tribes has been mostly successful. He does not lie to us. Sometimes we are unhappy with his words, but he does not hide the truth."

Alex regained his composure enough to provide more information. "I will also be providing a blacksmith service. From now on, Dakota people may bring broken metal items such as tools and traps to the Indian Agency. I will repair them."

Father and daughter exchanged a nod.

Alex continued, "Major Taliaferro wants me to travel to Native villages along the Mississippi and Minnesota rivers to inquire about conditions among the Ojibwe and Dakota. We seek your advice. What can the Indian Agency do to help your people?"

"It has been a good year," Cloud Man answered. "We are at peace, and the harvest has been bountiful. But I warn you, the scarcity of wild game makes life harder for other bands of the Dakota you will find. Down the Minnesota River, the Wahpeton and Sisseton bands of our people reject the idea of farming. Even the leaders of our own Mdewakanton band refuse to plant crops in the Mississippi valley, as do the Wahpekuta to our south."

"Why do they resist?"

"The men consider farming to be women's work," answered the Dakota leader. "Traditionally, our young men have gained prestige by hunting or in battle. They rise to manhood by defending our people against enemies or by providing their families with meat for food and animal hides for clothing. They believe their skill with weapons, not farm tools, will bring them greater honor."

"Major Taliaferro blames the fur traders," said Alex.

Cloud Man agreed. "Indeed, the people desire trade goods. Woolen blankets, iron kettles, and steel knives make life easier, and the only barter to exchange for those items are furs."

Alex nodded in understanding, and after a moment's pause, he stood. "When I leave here, I will visit the Pond brothers at their mission house. What do you think of them?"

"They are hard workers," said the Dakota leader. "They helped here with our harvest of corn and potatoes. At the same time, they were building a log home for themselves."

"They intend for that log structure also to be a meeting house. The brothers wish to share their Christian beliefs with the Dakota," Alex said.

Wakaninajinwin said, "They have made it known that we are welcome. Perhaps some of the people will listen to them."

"The older brother Samuel has asked to accompany our winter deer hunt," Cloud Man said. "I believe we will let him come."

* * *

The discovery that Major Taliaferro, like Lieutenant Eastman, had been married to a daughter of Cloud Man preoccupied Alex after he remounted and headed to the Pond brothers' mission house. Both of them had fathered a child by their Dakota wife and then dissolved the marriage before taking a white wife. Alex had grown up with the understanding that marriage was a permanent bond. But here on the frontier, wedlock seemed to be a temporary convenience. The casual attitude with which husbands and wives, fathers and mothers regarded the breakup of their families amazed the young soldier.

When a maple leaf fluttered within inches of its nose, his horse tossed its head and danced sideways. Alex looked up to see from where the leaf had fallen and noticed the spectacular multi-colored autumn vista into which he was riding. Many of the trees surrounding Bde Maka Ska held onto their dark green canopy beneath the clear blue sky, but aspens and birch were glowing with golden yellow leaves. Mother Nature had splashed the maples with bright splotches of orange. On the edges of prairie, blazing red sumac bushes seemed ready to burst into flame. Then, in a clearing near the lake, the Pond brothers' wooden log mission came into view.

Twisting Trails

Samuel came forward to greet Corporal Whitney with a wave and a shout. Behind him, a great blue heron rose with a squawk from the shallow shoreline of Bde Maka Ska. The tall bird's gangly neck and legs on land transformed into a magnificent spear when its six-foot wingspan launched above the lake. Alex thought Samuel looked much like the bird. The missionary's beak-like nose bobbed above his narrow neck as each long-legged stride lifted above the waving grass. Even Samuel's arm, raised in greeting, resembled the heron's long slender wing.

"Gideon will be sorry he missed your visit." Pointing southward, the older brother explained, "He has taken a plow and our pair of oxen to the Dakota village of Kaposia. He will help them till a plot of soil to make it ready for planting in the spring."

"Your log building looks solid," Alex said, nodding toward the mission.

"Come in." Samuel opened the door and praised his absent younger brother, "Yes, it shows Gideon's skill as a carpenter."

Somehow, the structure seemed more spacious on the inside than Alex expected, perhaps because the main room was intended to be open, a place for worship and school. "May I offer you some coffee and fresh bread?" Samuel asked. He motioned toward a kitchen stove that occupied one corner.

When they settled, Alex explained that he had come by way of the Dakota village. "You and your brother have made a good impression. Cloud Man says you are kind, capable, and hard-working."

Samuel smiled. "I am also impressed with them. These are wonderful people, cheerful and generous. I have asked to go with them this winter to their deer hunting camp in the north."

"Cloud Man told me that. I believe you will be welcome."

"I am so excited to live within their winter village. I have already begun to create a dictionary for the Dakota language. By asking the people to pronounce their words, I am spelling those words phonetically, using the English alphabet." Samuel's face came alive. "Dakota people will have a written language to record their own history. We will be able to translate hymns and Bible verses into that language."

* * *

Three months later, the elder Pond brother was every bit as enthusiastic when Alex found him at Cloud Man's winter hunting camp in the Crow River Valley. He made the journey on horseback, leading a packhorse loaded with a tent and camp supplies twenty-five miles up the Mississippi River to the mouth of the Crow, and then following that tributary fifteen miles to the southwest where it divided into north and south forks. The Mississippi waters were frigid but flowing, while the surface of the Crow was mostly frozen. Alex found evidence of Cloud Man's encampment at the forks, but the village had moved on. Following their trail another ten miles up the North Fork, he arrived at the Dakota camp.

"We stayed only a few weeks where the forks divide," Samuel confirmed. "Game was scarce. Thankfully the hunters have fared much better here, and we are surrounded by many small lakes where the muskrats are plentiful."

"I have brought my shotgun along," Alex said. "Hopefully, I can make a contribution."

"The hunters gather in Cloud Man's lodge every night. That's when everybody gets their hunting territory assignment for the next day," Samuel said. With a chuckle, he added, "That's also when the men report whatever hunting success they've had each day. Sometimes the storytelling gets pretty hilarious. Those who bring in the meat can be fantastic braggarts, while others who are unsuccessful might be targets of sarcastic teasing. Both can lead to uproarious laughter."

Later that night, at the hunters' council, there was talk about moving the camp again. Day by day, the skilled Dakota hunters were harvesting most of the meat-bearing animals within a few miles of the village.

Alex and Samuel were designated to hunt an area several miles upstream. They would be on horses and able to travel farther to the west. They mounted up the next morning, the soldier with his shotgun and the missionary carrying a rifle.

"My shotgun shells will be good for small game such as rabbits or grouse," said Alex, "but your rifle bullets are the better ammunition for a longer shot or at a larger animal."

"Cloud Man said we are chosen to go a greater distance because of these horses," said Samuel. "That is true. But he is trying to protect us by asking that we hunt near the river." With a sly grin, he continued, "He's afraid we'll get lost without the waterway to guide us home."

Alex produced a compass and held it up with a look of confidence.

"The Dakota hunters do not have compasses," said the missionary. "Yet they navigate this wilderness as if they were following lines on a map. They are natural woodsmen, and their abilities of observation are amazingly keen."

For several miles, the young men rode in conversation until they reached their designated hunting area. "How is your Dakota language dictionary coming along?" asked Alex.

"This opportunity to live among the people has been a godsend. Yes, I have accumulated dozens of words into the dictionary, but my appreciation for their values and traditions and way-of-life has grown even more."

"Do you think the camp will be moved again?" asked Alex.

"I don't know. But it will be a consensus decision. Dakota leaders like Cloud Man have influence because they have earned respect. But they aren't dictators." Samuel paused and then concluded, "If the council decides to move our encampment, the women will pack our entire village and have it relocated by the time the men come in from one day's hunt.

"Each teepee is constructed of hides," Samuel described the process. "It's wrapped around a framework of twelve-foot poles. Those are converted into travois, laden with all their belongings, and dragged to the next encampment by horses, dogs and people. It's amazing."

"When I traveled with Schoolcraft," said Alex, "I saw that work roles between Ojibwe men and women are also clearly defined. I notice here that winter clothing for men and women are pretty similar."

"Yes, everyone wears sturdier moccasins with leggings and a coat. Some people prefer woolen coats acquired from the traders, while others wear buckskin. Males and females have knives sheathed at their waist, but women wear skirts over their leggings whereas the men wear breechcloths."

The corporal's mind wandered to the abbreviated marriages between Cloud Man's daughters and the white men from Fort Snelling, Lieutenant Eastman and Major Taliaferro. "What have you learned about family relationships?" he asked.

"I know that a man must provide payment to a girl's father in order to gain her hand in marriage," said the missionary. "Then it is customary for the man to live among his wife's family and become a provider for them."

A vision of the Métis girl Angelique Reaume came into Alex's mind. *What would it cost to marry a girl like her? And what would it be like to live with her family?* He shook his head. *Where did that idea come from?*

"Up ahead, on the left." Alex blinked, and the vision of Angelique disappeared. Samuel was pointing to a high knoll with stalks of tall prairie grass poking up through the snow. "That must be the hill we're supposed to be looking for."

"Let's ride to the top," Alex suggested. "We should get a good view of this area from there."

Riding up from the river bottom, they gained a view of a small ice-covered lake that had been out of their sight. Beyond the hilltop, among the prairie grass tips on the far downslope, Alex glimpsed several deer. He dismounted and signaled Samuel to do likewise. Peering over his horse's neck, he spied the deer, which appeared to be pawing through the snow to graze on the grass beneath. Two of them lifted their heads to stare up the hill, but the men remained hidden behind their mounts. One of the deer flicked its white tail but seemed more curious than fearful and returned its attention to the grass.

"Balance your rifle over the horse's back," Alex instructed. Samuel nodded while Alex held short rein on both horses. The tall missionary's smooth, confident handling of his long-barreled firearm demonstrated that he was an experienced marksman. He held a breath, squeezed the trigger, and stood motionless when the rifle boomed against his shoulder.

Alex turned to see all the deer jump and run toward the river valley. Then the largest one stumbled and pitched forward before reaching the tree line. It did not move.

Together the two men field dressed the deer and strapped it across the withers of Samuel's horse. Briefly, they returned to the hilltop from where they scouted the terrain in every direction. Surely, they would be expected to report on this area at Cloud Man's council back in camp. Covering a wide circle, they rode farther west and dropped back into the river valley.

"I'll cross over," Alex said. "We can return to camp on opposite sides of the river. It's narrow enough for us to see and hear each other all the way back." Not far along the far bank, he spotted a snowshoe hare. Depending on its winter coat of white fur, the rabbit sat motionless in the snow. Still, the corporal saw its outline against a thicket of willows and dispatched the hare with a quick shot from the saddle.

Surprised, his mount reared up and bolted forward, thrusting Alex's backside into mid-air nearly a foot above the horse's rump. By the time of the rider's descent, neither rump connected with the other. The corporal's backside descended all the way into a snowbank. Although the deep snow softened his landing, it engulfed him from his armpits in back to his knees in front.

After a great deal of wiggling and squirming, Alex got himself upright so he could retrieve the rabbit. The horse was not far, and soon he was back in the saddle.

"I cannot wait to tell this story at council tonight!" cackled Samuel from the opposite riverbank. Alex could not help but grin while using his fur cap to whip snow from his legs.

Not much farther along the river, Alex spotted another snowshoe hare. This time he dismounted before taking aim. This hare also tried to hide in plain sight and suffered the same fate. When the hunters neared the Dakota camp, Alex saw a good place to cross the river and drew alongside the missionary.

"How is your religious work going?" Alex asked.

"I cannot say there are very many converts yet. I believe these people have accepted me. Some have shown curiosity and respect for my Christian beliefs. But they are not ready to put their faith in the universal power of God. Instead, they hold to their belief that all things and places are possessed by spirits or ghosts. This river, those trees, the deer and rabbits, even the winter weather—all have their own mystical power."

Samuel's deer turned out to be the only large game brought in this day, though other hunters brought in muskrats and fish caught through the ice. As usual, the villagers shared the meat equally. The hide of the deer, per custom, belonged to the hunter who killed the animal. At council that night, Cloud Man displayed the hide and declared that his daughters would make it into a garment for Samuel. The missionary was proud and thankful for the generosity of his Dakota friends. However, it seemed he took far more delight in telling his story about Alex's seat-first flight from horseback to snowbank.

SAMUEL POND (1808–1891) and GIDEON POND (1810–1878)

The Pond brothers, Samuel and Gideon, traveled from their native Connecticut to the Minnesota Territory, arriving at Fort Snelling via steamboat in 1834.[31]

Presbyterian missionaries who aimed to bring Christianity to Dakota people who lived in the Minnesota River valley were welcomed and assisted by Major Lawrence Taliaferro, the long-time Indian agent for the Minnesota Territory. Taliaferro granted the Ponds permission to build a mission near a Dakota village, with the understanding that they would promote agriculture among the Natives. The small log mission, built near Lake Bde Maka Ska, served as their home, church and schoolhouse.[32]

The Ponds became fluent speakers of the Dakota language and are best known for developing a written Dakota language. They adapted the English alphabet to include oral Dakota sounds, which led to a dictionary and grammar book, as well as translations of the Bible and Dakota stories.[33]

Michael Barnes

The brothers published a thorough description of Dakota culture as it existed in the 1830s and worked to promote positive relations between whites and Native people. To that end, they published a newspaper, *The Dakota Friend*, and Gideon joined the Minnesota Territorial Legislature.[34]

They were less successful in spreading Christianity among the Dakota people. By the 1850s, they were ministering primarily to a rapidly increasing population of white settlers. Gideon's church was in the present-day community of Bloomington, while Samuel settled in Shakopee.[35]

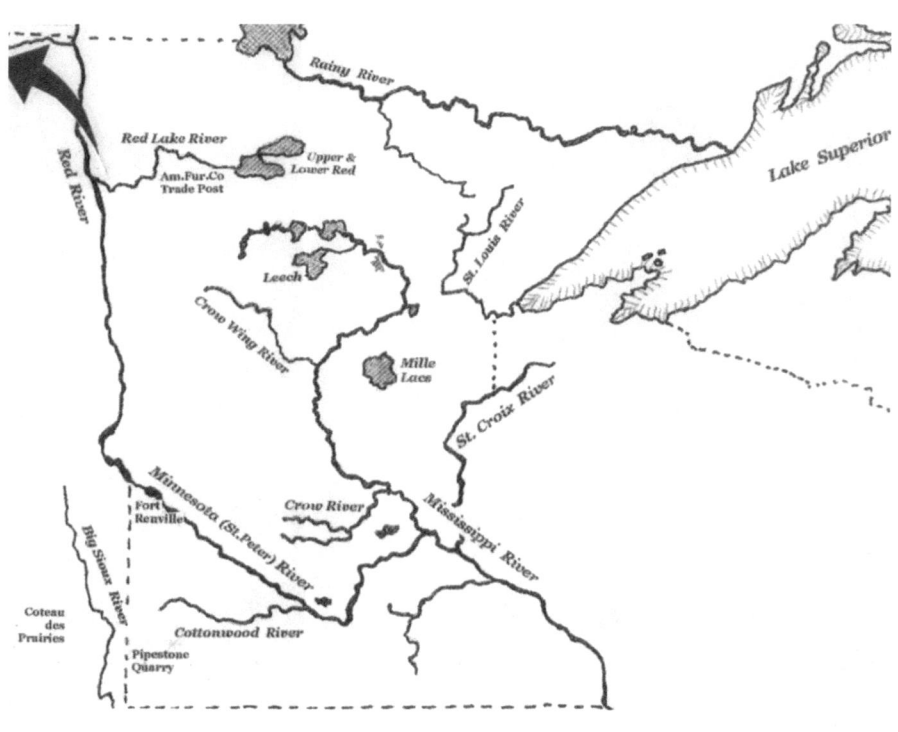

Chapter 9
1835 – Red River

The Red Lake River had broken free of ice. Water ran high between its banks, boosted by melting snow and a few early spring rains. White Loon and the girls had returned from maple sugar camp to find that much of the snow around their home had disappeared. Not only did things look different, but the scents and sounds had changed. New grass was not yet growing, but she could smell the fertile odor of earth as the ground began to thaw. A few migrating birds were returning, and their songs blended into a welcome concert with the hardy winter flock.

Lying beside Jean Baptiste in their darkened cabin, White Loon occasionally heard the passage of floating ice or branches scraping along the shoreline. "It will soon be time to plant our garden," she whispered to her husband so as not to disturb their sleeping children.

"Yes," he murmured. He was on his back, eyes open toward the rafters with both hands clasped behind his head. "And then I would propose an adventure for us."

She rolled onto her elbow to look down upon his face. "An adventure?" She quizzically cocked one eyebrow, which drew a smile from Jean Baptiste.

"I think we should join the Pembina Métis on this year's summer buffalo hunt."

"What about the children?" she worried.

"The buffalo hunts have been Métis family endeavors for years," he said. "Lucien and Angelique can work as well as any adults. And Gabrielle is eleven—not a baby anymore."

White Loon sighed. "Why do we need to do this?"

"Fur-bearing animals grow scarcer in our forests as the years go by," he admitted. "Furthermore, demand for those furs is beginning to decline on the European fashion market."

"Aren't buffalo just another fur-bearing animal?" she asked.

"In part. But bison hides can also be used for leather. And these animals are a food source. Each buffalo yields more than one hundred pounds of pemmican and dried meat."

"All right." White Loon dropped onto her back. "I can tell you have been thinking about this for some time. We should discuss it with the children tomorrow morning."

"At breakfast," he agreed.

* * *

The children were excited. All three peppered their father with anxious questions. However, there was work to be done before they embarked on the hunt in early June. "First, Lucien and I must load our winter pelts into the canoes. We will paddle to George Bonga's trading post and return with trade goods for next winter."

Luc nodded with anticipation. He could hardly wait to see the giant voyageur again.

"Next, you girls must help your mother prepare and plant our garden. Then remove every weed, so her young vegetables can thrive until we return in late July." Angelique and Gabrielle gladly accepted this responsibility. They knew White Loon was proud of her garden, and they loved to help her make it bountiful.

"Finally, we will catch as many fish as possible during the spring run. I'll smoke the fillets, and we can store them with our other meat in the ice cellar."

With their tasks completed just several weeks later, they launched both canoes and headed downstream. Angelique was in the bow of Jean Baptiste's canoe, and Gabrielle paddled between her brother in front and her mother in the stern. It was a swift and easy journey, traveling with the current of both rivers; a short one-day voyage westward on the Red Lake River followed by a longer dawn-til-dusk trip north on the mighty Red River to Pembina.

* * *

Angelique heard voices coming from a path leading to the house where her family slept. Peering out a small window, she saw her father and brother talking with a small circle of men. The tallest of these men fascinated her, partly because he appeared to be leading the discussion and also because he looked younger than all the others except Lucien. The young man wore buckskin and moccasins with a brightly colored Métis sash tied around his waist. His dark hair was cut straight across so that it barely touched his square shoulders. His darkly tanned complexion, no doubt from constant exposure to wind and sunlight, enhanced a youthful face.

"Pierre is my youngest." The voice came from behind Angelique's shoulder and belonged to Marguerite Bottineau. She was the Ojibwe wife, Clear Sky among her people, married to a well-known Hudson Bay Company trader named Charles Joseph Bottineau. Charles had died, leaving his widow to raise the Bottineau children. With them now grown and out of this house, Marguerite had room to host the Reaume family.

Angelique smiled at her hostess, then turned back to watch the front-yard conference. "He's eighteen," Marguerite said, "but he's always behaved like a grown man, especially since his father died."

"When did that happen?"

"Eleven years ago." After a pause, she continued. "He can speak French and English and all of the regional Native languages. By his early teens, he was guiding settlers between here and Fort Snelling. Last year, he brought a herd of cattle to the Selkirk settlement, all the way from Prairie du Chien."

"Will he be the leader of this buffalo hunt?"

Marguerite smiled. "Older men will claim the title of governor, but none of them will make a decision without listening to Pierre's opinion. Everyone knows he is the best hunter in Pembina."

The door jerked open, and Pierre strode in, roughly hugged his mother, and gave her a loving kiss. He seemed even taller inside the house, and Angelique felt uncomfortable while his gaze lingered upon her. He abruptly smiled and motioned for Jean Baptiste and Lucien to join him at the dining table.

"Come, Angelique," called Marguerite. "Let's bring some tea and bannock." In the kitchen, the woman fed some kindling into the big iron stove and repositioned a tea kettle above the flame. She handed a knife to Angelique and asked her to slice the round cake of bannock into pie-shaped pieces. The knife spread open a bounty of wild berries baked into the heavy, unsweetened bread, and the girl's mouth watered with anticipation. She lifted the plate to smell the aroma and breathed a pleasurable sigh. "Here," smiled Marguerite, "we'll warm it a little on the edge of the stove." When they returned to the table, White Loon and Gabrielle were there as well, so Angelique fetched a seventh chair from the kitchen. They passed around the tea and bannock and began to discuss plans for the coming hunt.

"These large, organized Métis hunts began several years ago," said Pierre, "led by Mr. Grant from White Horse Plains."

"His given name is Cuthbert," Marguerite interjected, "but no one calls him anything but Mr. Grant."

"Well, some have taken to calling him Warden of the Plains," Pierre added. "He's an educated Métis man who, by a combination of diplomacy and violence, has become the unquestioned leader of his people in Canada. Grant began leading a caravan of Métis hunters onto the Dakota plains to systematically harvest bison."

"Is it dangerous to travel onto hunting land which the Dakota believe is their own?" asked Jean Baptiste.

"They don't like it," Pierre admitted, "and there has been conflict. But Mr. Grant has developed a military structure for the Métis hunts."

"Military?" asked White Loon.

"We will be a small army when we leave Pembina," Pierre said. "A large one when the Turtle Mountain Band joins us. Scouts will constantly patrol our perimeter in all four directions. If suspected enemies are spotted, the scouts will report, and our two-wheeled carts will interlock together to form an unbreakable circle with our people and livestock on the inside. Except for our soldiers, who will be mounted and ready for battle around the outside."

"And all of us will be armed," asserted Marguerite, looking purposefully at White Loon and Angelique, "including women and children."

"The Dakota may try to scare us," conceded Pierre, "but they will not dare to attack our caravan. It would be suicide for them to try."

Pierre changed the subject, "I am confident that our two families will merge into a successful buffalo hunting team." Then, turning to Jean Baptiste, he smiled, "I have acquired a good horse who will be a dependable buffalo runner for you."

"Buffalo runner?"

"Yes, these are horses with the speed, strength and confidence to carry a rider alongside a running bison. Your runner, Falcon, has experienced several hunts, and he will serve you well."

Jean Baptiste smiled nervously, glancing toward White Loon, who cocked an eyebrow in return. They both knew he had done little riding...very little.

Noticing the exchange, Pierre reassured them, "There will be time to practice between here and the Turtle Mountains. You and Falcon will become able partners!"

"And I will help your family become efficient buffalo butchers," Marguerite said.

"We will load our carts with dried meat, bags of pemmican and prime hides."

"We will have three Red River carts between us," Pierre explained. "When it's time to run a herd of bison, White Loon will follow with Lucien to process your kills. Mother and Angelique will bring another cart, tending to my carcasses." Again, Angelique felt the young man's eyes dwell on her. His gaze made her shy and want to look away, but then he flashed that easy smile again.

"What about me?" Gabrielle's protest broke the silence.

"Oh, you will have a job," Marguerite assured the girl. "Some of the young people remain at camp with the elders during buffalo runs. Boys tend the livestock herd, and girls take care of the youngest children. How old are you, child?"

"I'm eleven!" Gabrielle sat tall.

"Well, you and your mother can decide. You are old enough to join her with the butchering if that is your choice."

Noticing that teacups were empty and only crumbs of the bannock remained, Angelique stood up. "More tea for anyone?"

"There is much to do before departure tomorrow," said Pierre. He stood, leaned to kiss his mother's head, then started toward the door. "Come along, Jean Baptiste. Time for you to meet Falcon."

* * *

With fifty horse-drawn Red River carts, around one hundred people gathered to leave Pembina the following morning. Thirty men were the actual hunters, and their valuable buffalo runners were herded along behind the caravan, inside a crew of outriders.

Jean Baptiste Wilkie, a well-respected man in his mid-thirties, was elected governor of the hunt. As such, he would choose the route to travel, judge any camp disputes and take command, if the expedition were attacked. Final decisions rested with Wilkie, but it was understood that he would consider the counsel of the other leaders. He appointed Pierre and two additional men as captains, and they, in turn, divided their soldiers into groups of seven or eight men.

On the first day, Wilkie's carts led the procession. The governor's lead cart flew a Métis flag, flapping from a pole that extended up several feet. It displayed a white infinity symbol embroidered onto bright blue fabric. One of Wilkie's captains directed scouts far in front and on both flanks of the caravan. Another captain took charge of the remuda, the horse herd, making sure to keep their valuable buffalo runners in close proximity. Pierre and his soldiers, including Jean Baptiste, occupied carts at the rear of the convoy. They would be expected to serve alternate shifts on night patrol for the first encampment. Thus, among Wilkie and the captains, a four-day rotation was established.

"Yeow!" Angelique's hands shot up to cover her ears. She was not prepared for the shrieking squeal of turning wheels on fifty Red River carts.

"Relax," said Marguerite. "You'll get used to it." She lightly tapped the horse that drew her two-wheeled cart and threw back her head. "To me, it's a welcome sound. When you love the buffalo hunt as I do, this is considered the music of northwest fiddles."

"More like *broken* fiddles." The girl grimaced. "Can't they make them quieter?"

"If we greased the wheels, dust would collect on the hubs and turn into glue," the older woman explained. "This way, any Métis family can repair their own cart on the plains because they are made entirely with wood and shaganappi."

"Shag a what?"

Marguerite laughed. "Shaganappi is a strip of bison hide, sometimes braided into a strap. The joints of these carts are wrapped with wet shaganappi that shrinks and tightens as it dries to form a tough and durable bond. With no metal parts, our Red River carts are light."

Angelique examined the cart as they walked alongside it. The horse was harnessed to wooden shafts that extended back, parallel and four feet apart to form the base of the cargo bed. Wooden fences, about six feet long, surrounded the bed. A buffalo hide tarp covered some of the carts, including Marguerite's.

"They're tall." The wheels on either side of the cart extended higher than Angelique's head.

"That gives them good clearance," said Marguerite, pointing underneath the cargo bed. "These carts can roll above rocks and through shallow streams without the contents getting wet or damaged."

The girl noticed the twelve wooden spokes on each wheel angled outward from hub to rim. She pointed, "Why are the spokes dished out like that?"

The older woman grinned, placed her feet far apart and swayed her walk. "Makes 'em harder to tip over," she giggled.

Marguerite was effectively steering both of the carts belonging to her and Pierre. While walking, she carried a long stick with a tassel of leather strips attached to the tip. She could guide the lead horse forward, left or right with gentle taps upon his rump or withers. The mare pulling their second cart was connected to the first by a tether, keeping both animals in single file.

Angelique noticed behind them that her mother, brother and sister had paused to jump down from their cart in which they had been riding. Gabrielle frowned and rubbed her bottom.

"Uh-oh," Marguerite remarked. "That's one shortcoming for a Red River cart—a rough ride." The widow Bottineau stopped beside the trail and waited for Gabrielle to come alongside. "It will be more comfortable to walk," she consoled the little girl. "When your feet get tired, you'll find a softer ride on the back of your cart horse."

* * *

Late that afternoon, the caravan forded a shallow stream and made camp on the far side. The remuda drank before grazing on lush grass in a slight hollow along the stream. People waded upstream to gather buckets of water not muddied by the horses for drinking, cooking and washing.

Mr. Wilkie supervised the formation of carts into the interlocking circle that Pierre had described. Angelique judged it slightly more than one hundred feet across. Soon families were assembling tents and extending awnings inside the circle from their carts. Cook fires appeared next, and before long, an aroma of burning wood was mixing with the smells of first night feasts.

After supper, the cart circle was briefly opened, and the horse herd was gathered within. The first shift of night guards, including Jean Baptiste and Lucien, went out. Halfway through the night, they would come back in to sleep, and the second shift of Pierre Bottineau's soldiers would patrol until dawn.

Twisting Trails

On the second day, Jean Baptiste and Luc took their turns riding with the remuda. That evening after supper, Pierre sat down with a tightly wrapped bundle on his lap. "We are scouting tomorrow," he told Jean Baptiste. "It will be a good day for you to become familiar with Falcon."

Unrolling the bundle, Pierre revealed four flintlock muskets with shortened barrels. He handed one to the voyageur, saying, "This one belonged to my father. It served him well, and I will teach you to use it tomorrow."

"I brought my own gun," said Jean Baptiste. "A .36 caliber rifle."

"Yes, and you are free to use it," said the young captain. "But these short-barreled muskets are ideal for the buffalo hunt. Easier to load and aim from the back of a running horse."

* * *

They began day three with a hearty breakfast. The scouts would be out all day. Lucien went north with Sharlo, another Bottineau brother, two years older than Pierre. Two more scouts patrolled to the south, and one rode back east behind the caravan. "You can't be too careful," cautioned Pierre. "We could be followed as easily as we could be intercepted." After cantering about a mile away from the convoy, Sharlo slowed his horse to a walk and signaled for Luc to do likewise. "We'll stay on this right flank, keeping pace with the cart train, or slightly ahead of it."

"Are we looking for Dakota?"

"Yes, but we're pretty far north of their territory," said Sharlo. "Up here, we'd be more likely to find our friends the Turtle Mountain Ojibwe. Even so, they're not likely to be this far away from their lakes and tree-covered hills."

"How far are the Turtle Mountains?"

"Several more days. They're a little more than one hundred miles from Pembina. We're also looking for any sign of buffalo or prairie fires. Plus, we should be ready to describe the terrain we've seen." He reached forward to pat the stock of his hunting rifle, which rested in its saddle scabbard. "If we could bag a deer or prairie elk, that would be an extra bonus for the menu back at camp."

"It's beautiful out here," said Lucien, "but I can still hear those squeaking cart wheels."

"Yeah," Sharlo chuckled, "you will, unless we get upwind from 'em."

Pierre and Jean Baptiste were upwind from the caravan. They had ridden west and were a full two miles in front of the cart train, beyond earshot. Much of the land was flat, but where low slopes angled in front of them, Pierre carefully rode just below the ridgeline so they would not be silhouetted against the sky. He approached those crests cautiously, peering carefully beyond, before exposing the two of them to the far horizon.

Through a wide shallow gully, the young captain spurred his horse into a full gallop, dodging right and left around scrubby bushes, then waved for Jean Baptiste to follow. As promised by Pierre, Falcon was fast and sure-footed. The buckskin gelding showed his buffalo running talents by weaving swiftly around or through every thicket.

"Good!" Pierre cheered when they were back together. "You stayed with him."

"Barely," Jean Baptiste admitted, breathing heavily. "I almost zigged each time he zagged."

"In a few more days, the two of you will be a reliable team." Moving forward to a small mesa, Pierre dismounted. "Time for shooting practice."

He pulled one of the short muskets from his saddle scabbard. Jean Baptiste produced old Charles Bottineau's gun, given to him by Pierre the previous night.

"We're going to fire these muskets a few times," Pierre announced, "so you should hobble Falcon. He's probably heard enough gunshots to stay calm, but let's make sure he doesn't run off."

Jean Baptiste tied a short length of rawhide rope into a circle. Twisting it into a figure-eight, he placed each of Falcon's front hooves through the loops on each end. The horse would be able to take small steps, but it couldn't run. When Jean Baptiste came next to Pierre, the young man's left hand was holding both his horse's reins and the barrel of his musket. With his free right hand, he reached into a pocket of his leather hunting jacket to withdraw three musket balls of lead which he popped into his mouth. Next, Pierre used his right hand to take the cap off his powder horn slung over one shoulder on a leather cord. He tapped a measure of gunpowder straight down the barrel and dropped the powder horn back to his hip. Grabbing the gunstock in his right hand, just behind the trigger, Pierre spat a saliva-covered lead ball straight down the barrel. He punched the butt of the musket down against his thigh, assuring the powder and ball were seated in the bottom of the barrel. Then he leveled the gun and fired a one-hand shot into a nearby bush. *Boom!*

The horse's head jerked back in surprise, but Pierre was still holding its reins in his left hand. The entire process took less than ten seconds.

Jean Baptiste started to ask a question, "How…" But the young captain was loading again: powder, ball, punch, boom.

He produced the second shot even faster.

"That takes practice," admitted Pierre. "We will do it here on the ground at first. But eventually, you should learn to reload and fire from horseback."

Jean Baptiste smiled but shrugged his shoulders with doubt.

"Yes!" Pierre raised his voice, and his expression turned stern. "The buffalo hunt is serious business. You are a capable man. You have a good horse and good guns. When the time comes to run a bison herd, you will be prepared, and our families will harvest many hides and bags of pemmican."

Jean Baptiste nodded. Despite being short of years, this young man was long on wisdom. His confidence was reassuring, and the older man was ready to learn. They practiced loading and firing the musket several times.

"That is enough for today," said Pierre. "Now you know what to do. Each day while riding, you can handle this weapon and go through the motions of using it." They nodded to each other and remounted.

A few hours later, Pierre identified a place where the caravan could camp that night. There was no water, but it offered good grass for the horses, and the young captain judged it a defensible position. "I'll scout the perimeter of this location," he told Jean Baptiste. "You ride back to the cart train. Tell Wilkie we have found a place to camp and lead them here. Everyone should have brought a supply of water from last night's camp in their barrels and canteens."

The caravan arrived just before sundown, and there was Pierre, butchering the carcass of an elk he had shot. There would be fresh meat to share around the campfires.

* * *

On day four, the Bottineau carts rotated into the front position. Pierre and Mr. Wilkie fixed on a far western butte as their aiming point, and Marguerite steered her lead horse steadily toward that target. Pierre began the day walking and talking with his mother and Sharlo. He spent many of the remaining hours communicating with almost every member of the caravan. He discussed plans with the other captains, shared jokes with fellow young men, spread compliments among the women, and teased the youngsters. After checking on the remuda, he allowed Gabrielle to ride his horse while he led it by the reins, strolling in conversation with Jean Baptiste and White Loon.

"The Pembina River is off to our north," he said and motioned with his right hand, "It swoops down out of Canada and meanders back east to our home town. Today will be a long day, but we want to camp beside that bend in the river. Our route between there and the Turtle Mountains might cover two or three days of dry ground."

"As long as it takes," Jean Baptiste agreed. "We'll go until we get there."

For Angelique, two new points of view came with their families' turn in front of the caravan. First, she noticed the lack of dust. During the first few days, a fine powder stirred from the trail by plodding hooves and turning wheels that covered her clothes. At day's end, she whacked off the dust with her hands. But where it touched the perspiration on her skin, the powder formed a slick brown grime that needed a wet cloth to be removed. Most bothersome were the tiny particles that floated into her eyes causing red irritation and flowing tears. Thankfully, today the air was clear and clean.

Second, when she looked forward, the panorama seemed bigger. Her entire field of vision was unobstructed by anyone or anything. The outstretched rolling prairie extended from side to side and as far as her eye could see. No wagon ruts cut through the gently waving prairie grasses of green and brown. Here and there, tiny splotches of colorful wildflowers peeked through, white or yellow or purple. Above it all, the limitless dome of blue sky reached from beyond one horizon past the other. She relished the endless vista.

They did indeed travel farther this day to reach the Pembina River bend. When Angelique finally saw the curving belt of trees lining the river channel, the sun was beginning to sink into the western skyline. As the blazing yellow sphere slowly disappeared, it cast a bright orange glow above the distant hills. Dazzling pink illuminated the bottom edges of a few far-flung clouds. The tops of those clouds flushed with shades of purple and lavender as the fading sunlight struggled to pierce through. Gradually the clouds began to tumble into an ever-scrambling kaleidoscope of colors.

"Beautiful, isn't it?" Pierre walked beside her.

"Y-y-yes-s," she stammered, not knowing what else to say.

The young captain simply smiled at her, at the sky, and continued walking at her side.

* * *

Late in the morning of day seven, the Bottineau soldiers were scouting again. Sharlo and Lucien were patrolling the caravan's northern flank, but Luc was allowed the responsibility of riding separately today. He rode about a quarter mile behind the older Bottineau brother, giving them two perspectives on the landscape. They were close enough to occasionally see each other and would certainly hear a gunshot, but sufficiently far apart so no enemy could capture them both.

Luc glimpsed the dust of riders charging toward Sharlo. The boy headed into a shallow depression and laid low along his horse's neck to avoid being seen. Faraway shouts reached his ears, but Luc's partner remained strangely still. From that distance, the three riders and their ponies appeared to be Native. They came upon Bottineau at full speed and rode circles around him, shouting and lifting weapons into the air. Sharlo dismounted and stood erect, whereupon the riders jumped to the ground and began hugging him in a wild backslapping embrace.

The scout broke apart from the small group and waved for Lucien to join them. When the boy pulled abreast of them, Bottineau announced, "Meet our Turtle Mountain Ojibwe brothers."

Luc dismounted to exchange greetings, and Sharlo continued, "These boys are on a hunting trip," he laughed. "They found us, but no game!" At that remark, the Ojibwe lifted Bottineau off the ground and pretended to drape him across his horse's back as if he were a deer carcass. They all howled in laughter and stumbled to the ground when Sharlo struggled to get free.

When the merry group was back on their feet, dusting themselves off, Bottineau turned to Lucien, "I'm going to leave with these fellows. Perhaps I can help them find some food as we reenter the Turtle Mountains." He cast a sly glance at the hunters. "You ride back to the cart train and tell Wilkie that we have made contact with our Ojibwe brethren."

Luc remounted but sat on his horse for a few minutes watching the others gallop away. Then he pivoted to the south and carried the good news back to the caravan.

By the time Lucien reported their close proximity to the Turtle Mountains, Angelique had begun to notice changes in the landscape. The flatlands had already given way to low, rolling hills. Some craggy rock bluffs began to jut up out of the hills, eventually giving way to tree-covered slopes and ridges containing dozens of small lakes. She turned to White Loon and observed, "It looks like home."

"That's what this band of Ojibwe people thought when they first came out here," responded her mother. "Their ancestors lived in the northern forests as we do. A few generations ago, their hunters migrated westward in search of more abundant game. They found the buffalo herds near these mountains and decided to stay."

"With their families," Angelique surmised.

"Yes," Marguerite said, "And they have been joined by many Métis families. You will find these Ojibwe have different customs than your mother's people back in the pine forests. They have adapted to the plains, and their lives revolve around the bison. These Ojibwe are horsemen, every bit as skilled as the Dakota."

That horsemanship was soon evident when dozens of Ojibwe and Métis riders came out to meet their caravan, shouting happy greetings. Men and boys galloped alongside the cart train, as well as a few girls younger than Angelique. She envied the unrestrained freedom these girls displayed on horseback and yearned to join them.

Upon arrival at the Turtle Mountain settlement, Angelique observed a scattered oval of small log homes, perhaps thirty in number. The Pembina cart train gathered on the outskirts of this village but did not need the customary interlocking circle. A crew of night scouts would be on guard, but they felt safe within the perimeter of the settlement.

After the evening meal, a faint scent of tobacco smoke began to float through the air. Angelique noticed that even Marguerite puffed on a pipe. Soon the cheerful sound of a fiddle arose from among the houses. When a second fiddle joined in, the music became more spirited and soon people were gathering toward the center of the village.

One man picked up the rhythm with a hand drum, and soon others were keeping time with sticks and clapping hands. When the song ended in a lively crescendo, everyone was smiling and laughing with delight.

Sharlo stepped out of the crowd with his own fiddle and shouted, "How about a Red River jig!" He began stomping his foot, tucked the instrument under his chin and began bouncing the bow across its strings. Angelique noticed he was wearing a vest and moccasins decorated with Métis quill and beadwork. Before she could think twice, Pierre whisked her out of her place and into the haphazard circle surrounded by the assembly.

With his left arm behind her waist, Pierre bounced enthusiastically. This was a drastically faster cadence than any dance Angelique had ever seen, let alone performed. She felt awkwardly out of sync with Pierre and the music, and she struggled to follow the uncoordinated timing of all three fiddlers. She tried to watch Pierre's feet which alternated between taps of his heels and toes along with a scuffing forward of each foot or a quick backward lift of one moccasin then another.

Nervously, Angelique glanced at the faces of people around the circle, fearful of finding scornful expressions. However, everyone was smiling broadly and clapping energetically. Just when she looked toward White Loon for a helpful signal, her father twirled her mother onto the earthen dance floor. All at once, dozens of couples from the Pembina contingent joined in the joyous free-for-all. Their movements were as uncoordinated as Angelique's, but now it didn't matter. She relaxed and kicked up her heels with everyone else.

Sharlo's bow made one last dynamic stroke across his fiddle strings, and the music stopped. Cheers burst forth, and Pierre lifted Angelique off her toes in a powerful embrace that brought their torsos together. He kissed her squarely on the lips. Though the kiss lasted more than a moment, she didn't know how to react or respond. Luckily, she didn't have to. When he set her down, a pair of friends clapped him on the back and led him away with a jug to quench his thirst.

Angelique's mind whirled around these two first-of-her-lifetime events. The Red River jig was fun. She had no idea if her dance steps had been halfway correct, but she was anxious to try again. The kiss was even more confusing. Here too, Angelique was unsure about her performance. She didn't know if she had done it correctly, or how she might do it the next time, or with whom she might like to try it again.

Pierre Bottineau (1817–1895)

Pierre Bottineau was born in the Red River valley to a French-Canadian fur trader, Charles Joseph Bottineau, who died when Pierre was seven years old. His mother, Marguerite Ahdik Songab, "Clear Sky," was the sister to a leader of the Ojibwe Lake of the Woods band.[36]

At the age of thirteen, Pierre made his first long journey as a fur company courier, from the Selkirk settlement in present-day Manitoba to the southwestern Wisconsin fort at Prairie du Chien. While still in his teens, he brought a herd of cattle 400 miles to Selkirk and guided several Canadian families to Fort Snelling.[37]

Growing to more than six feet tall and 200 pounds, Bottineau was eventually known by the nicknames "Kit Carson of the Northwest" or "Daniel Boone of North Dakota." He gained fame as a hunter and guide for future Minnesota governor Henry Sibley and to survey a route for the Northern Pacific Railroad. Others called him "the walking peace pipe" for his multi-lingual skill and repeated ability to settle disputes without bloodshed. He was highly respected among whites and Natives as well as his own people of mixed ancestry.[38]

Pierre was twice married and fathered more than twenty children. During his middle years, the Bottineau families lived at three different locations in present-day St. Paul and Minneapolis, along the Mississippi River. But at the age of fifty-nine, he moved back to northwest Minnesota where he founded and fostered the town of Red Lake Falls.[39]

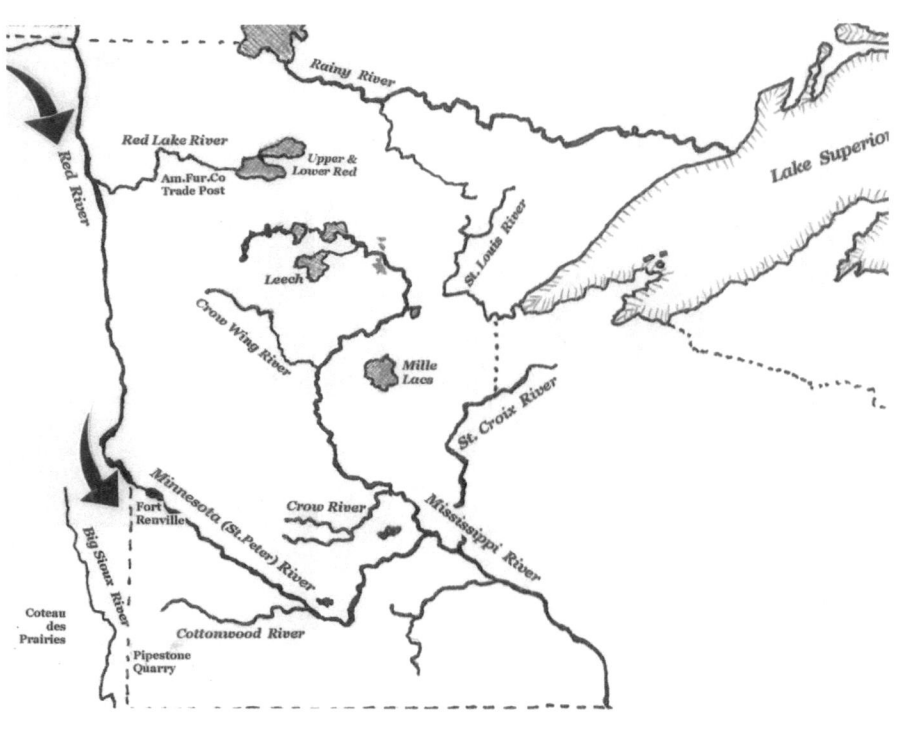

Chapter 10
1835 – Dakota Prairie

When the caravan left the Turtle Mountains, its number of Red River carts was nearly doubled. The combined Métis and Ojibwe hunting groups angled southwest into a wide basin through which the Souris River and its tributaries drained northward. They hoped to find a bison herd before mounting the continental divide with the Missouri River Valley and the heart of Dakota Territory on the other side.

Late that afternoon, when the cart train stopped to make camp beside a stream, Pierre approached the Reaume family leading a pair of horses. Addressing Jean Baptiste, he said, "I have noticed Angelique admiring the horsemanship of the Turtle Mountain girls. I'm willing to give her a riding lesson if she would like." He paused to look at her, then back to Jean Baptiste, "With your permission, of course."

Her father turned to face her and inquired, "Angelique?" She did not speak but nodded to affirm her interest, glancing back and forth between the two men. Jean Baptiste pivoted back to young Bottineau, "Thank you. Angelique will surely benefit from your expertise."

"We will be back before supper," Pierre promised.

As the two teenagers walked away leading the horses onto open prairie, White Loon stepped alongside her husband. "He is courting her," she said.

"Yes," Jean Baptiste answered slowly. "He is." Mother and father stood shoulder to shoulder, watching their daughter from a new perspective. "You will need to speak with her."

White Loon laughed aloud. "Why not you?" she giggled and playfully punched him in the ribs. He winced and gave her a quizzical look, but she eased his worry, "We have already had some conversations about romance. Now we will have a particular boy to discuss." When she could see her husband's relief, White Loon warned, "Your time will come," she smiled, "with Lucien."

When they were clear of the cart circle, Pierre remarked, "I enjoyed our dance last night."

"I'm afraid I wasn't very good," Angelique apologized.

"The Red River jig is not about proper or improper," he reassured her. "It's about fun. Did you like it?"

"It was delightful!" she exclaimed, which brought a smile to Bottineau's face. Looking squarely into his eyes, she thought about the kiss and hoped he would not ask her about that. She would have no idea what to say.

Pierre handed the reins of a bay mare to Angelique, "This is Breeze. She will be a good gentle girl to learn on. Stop here and let her get to know you. You should touch her in a friendly way and talk to her with a calm, relaxed voice."

While Angelique stroked the curve of Breeze's neck, Pierre commented, "She can tell you're not afraid. That is good. A horse will be made skittish by a nervous rider." He looped the far rein around to the saddle horn and held the stirrup steady for Angelique to mount up.

Holding Breeze's bridle with his left hand, Pierre put his right hand on Angelique's thigh. "Use your legs to communicate with a horse," he advised. "Your hands should hold the reins lightly while you apply pressure with your thighs and knees to direct her action. You want to be centered and balanced in the saddle." Then tracing a vertical line with his right arm, "Think of a line pointing straight down from your ears, through your shoulders and hips, to your heels." He slightly flexed his legs to model a wide-stance squat, "If the horse disappeared, you'd want to land on the ground in perfect balance." Then he backed away and grinned, "You look very pretty up there."

Twisting Trails

Angelique could not suppress a bashful smile, "Thank you."

Pierre directed her to begin walking Breeze ahead. Then he mounted the black stallion he called Stone and drew alongside her. For several minutes, they simply walked and talked. They stopped and restarted their horses, turning them this way and that. Unexpectedly, Pierre declared, "My mother likes you."

"I like her," Angelique responded. "Marguerite reminds me of my grandmother in the Pillager Band of Ojibwe. The young man gave her a look of understanding, then twisted in his saddle and looked back toward camp. "We should be returning to our families," he declared. "First, let's have you break Breeze into a canter." He pointed a direction across the prairie, "Urge her forward with your knees." The mare responded eagerly and surged forward with longer, more powerful strides, causing the girl to bounce uncomfortably upon the saddle. Stone instinctively kept pace with Breeze, and Pierre yelled across, "Let your hips flow with her movement."

Angelique squeezed her knees to stay firmly mounted and began to feel the reach and rhythm of the mare's pace. Soon she adjusted to the cadence of each hoof beat and the action of Breeze's body. Pierre was right. She stopped bouncing on top of the horse. Rather, she began to move with the running animal. It was thrilling. When they finally slowed back down to a walk, she was excited, "That was amazing!"

He grinned.

"It felt like we became one running creature," she gushed, "rather than two separate things."

"You are becoming a rider."

* * *

The next morning, Angelique noticed the caravan cart circle was larger. It was now almost two hundred feet across and contained a remuda of nearly one-hundred-fifty cart horses and buffalo runners. She scanned the herd, trying to spy Breeze from among the animals released to graze outside of the circle.

With the horses gone, she turned her attention to the cone-shaped tipis that some Turtle Mountain families had erected near their carts. One group had already removed the outer covering of their tent. The stitched-together bison hides were lowered by the shaganappi rope used as a pulley to hoist them up and around the lodge poles the previous evening. The pole framework was more than double the height of the people disassembling it, and the circular base provided enough room to sleep eight or ten if necessary. Another shaganappi rope was unwound to release all the lodge poles except three, still bound together near the top. These three formed the initial tripod upon which the entire structure was based. This family had their tipi totally apart and rolled up onto their cart in a matter of minutes.

"How was your horse ride last night?" Angelique turned to find her mother close behind.

"It was wonderful."

"What about your riding instructor? How do you feel about him?"

"He was very helpful."

"And?" By the tone of White Loon's voice and the expression on her face, the girl could tell that her mother had a deeper interest in Pierre than his ability as a riding instructor. "How do *you* feel about *him*?"

"Pierre is a much-admired man among these people, both Métis and Ojibwe. He is an able horseman and scout and hunter. Everyone respects him."

White Loon stepped closer to her daughter, "I'm sure that you respect him." She paused, "I'm asking if you have deeper feelings of affection for him—romantic feelings."

Angelique looked down, "I don't know. He kissed me after the Red River jig in the Turtle Mountains."

"Yes, I saw."

"I think he likes me." She examined her mother's face for a reaction.

White Loon giggled and reached to hold her daughter's hands, "It is plainly evident that he likes you."

Twisting Trails

"But," Angelique's brow wrinkled, "maybe he likes himself more than he could ever like anyone else."

White Loon folded her arms around her daughter and appreciated the young woman's wisdom. "Time will tell," she said. "This buffalo hunt will last a few more weeks."

* * *

Over the course of several days, the caravan crisscrossed the Souris River as it flowed southward out of Canada and then curled northward again to join the Assiniboine. Hours of daylight remained when they climbed up the western bank of the Souris, but Mr. Wilkie decided to make camp there. It was a good place to dry out from the river crossing, graze the horses and replenish the fresh water supply before leaving the next morning.

Wilkie called a meeting of the captains to address three issues—food, buffalo and the Dakota. One group of Turtle Mountain soldiers divided into two hunting parties. Half of them went upstream along the Souris valley, the other half downstream searching for meat to fill the caravan's stew pots. They expected to pursue wild game until dark, stay out overnight and resume the hunt from dawn back to camp.

Two Métis captains, including Pierre Bottineau, would deploy their soldiers overnight in search of bison. So far, the scouts had seen no buffalo nor sign of a passing herd. Pierre's soldiers explored from a line to the setting sun at intervals to the south. The Métis captain from Turtle Mountain spread his soldiers to the northwest, beginning from that line toward the setting sun.

Wilkie's soldiers and another group of Turtle Mountain Ojibwe would double the night patrol. They were deeper into Dakota Territory than at any time during this hunt. Like the buffalo, they did not find any sign of them. But that did not prove their rivals were not nearby.

Jean Baptiste and Pierre rode their horses southwest at a gentle lope across the empty prairie. After an hour or so, a long grassy ridge began to rise on the horizon, stretching from their right to left as far as they could see. This was the Missouri Escarpment, a continental divide separating the Missouri River Valley from the Red River Valley. All of the streams on their side of this height of land flowed east and north into Canada until they emptied into Hudson Bay. However, just over this ridge before them ran the mighty Missouri River. Out of the Rocky Mountains it came, eventually to join the Mississippi and south to the Gulf of Mexico.

The sun was settling lower to the horizon as the scouts rode nearer to the escarpment. The sky was turning an unusual color, darker than a normal prairie sunset. Not bright and pink but a deeper red, almost brown. Jean Baptiste pointed at the ominous view. "Is that a coming storm?"

"I don't think so," answered Pierre, slowing his horse to a walk. "Smell the air."

Perhaps the scent had changed so gradually that the voyageur had not noticed, but now he detected a faint odor, "Is that smoke?"

"I believe so," confirmed the young captain. "I think our friends the Dakota have set the prairie afire to drive a buffalo herd into the range of their hunters." He lifted his chin toward the ridge, "Let's proceed, but with caution."

They trotted Stone and Falcon up the ever-steepening slope until they came near the top. Now the smell of smoke was unmistakable, and the horses snorted as if to clear their nostrils. Bottineau came to a stop and dismounted. Quickly hobbling his horse, he told Jean Baptiste to do likewise and walked until he could see beyond the rim. Then the two men descended to their hands and knees, moving forward without exposing themselves to the horizon. When a wide vista of rolling hills came into view, they dropped to their stomachs and elbows.

Now the billowing smoke was evident though still a few miles away. Black and gray clouds churned upward from distant valleys. Then as the fluttering soot lifted above the hilltops, it began to tumble and disperse, chased by a northwest breeze. The smoke moved almost parallel to the escarpment upon which the two scouts lay.

Twisting Trails

Once more, Jean Baptiste suspected a coming storm when he began to hear a faraway rumble, "Is that thunder?"

Pierre shook his head. "No." He eyed the landscape, and an eager smile spread across his face. The rumble became more distinct, and Jean Baptiste began to feel the ground vibrate. In the next instant, their horses began to whinny and stamp their hooves. The young captain jumped to his feet just as the leading wave of bison crested the nearest hill. They were running fast, with more and more of the big hairy beasts galloping behind them.

Jean Baptiste chased his fellow scout back to their horses. Falcon was jittery and difficult to mount, but the older man was able to climb into the saddle. He circled near Pierre, who had regained the ridge top aboard Stone to view the stampeding herd. The buffalo were still a quarter mile away, but their size and speed combined with the sheer number of animals made their arrival seem imminent. Bottineau displayed more excitement than fright, but he decided to flee and motioned for Jean Baptiste to follow. Down the escarpment they rode, back onto the flat prairie from where they had come.

After gaining a safe gap, they reined up and turned around just in time to see the herd come over the ridge and spill down the slope. The leaders were still running, but not as fast. Those coming behind were slower still and were walking by the time they reached the bottom, where the two scouts watched from afar. The animals just kept on coming! In a few minutes, the slope and prairie floor were covered less by the green of grass than by the brown of buffalo hides. Many of the larger bison were darker, even black across the head and shoulders. The younger calves, some now braying in search of their mothers, were a much lighter tan color.

Thirty minutes later, when the remainder of the herd trickled over the escarpment, dusk was beginning to settle. While the scouts continued to watch in silence, another pair of riders appeared from the north. Though a half-mile distant, Pierre recognized his brother Sharlo at once. He was riding with Lucien. Upon meeting, the Bottineaus quickly shared their common understanding of the situation. "We saw the prairie fire," Sharlo reported.

"So, Dakota hunters are not far away," Pierre said.

"Yes," said Sharlo. "But it will take them tomorrow to harvest the carcasses they have killed today."

"Perhaps we are lucky the Dakota transport their buffalo meat and hides on travois rather than Red River carts," Pierre said. "They may head back to their Missouri River village when they are done."

"If they are done," Sharlo wondered.

"That is the concern," Pierre said. "If they pursue this herd, they will find us."

The brothers turned to face father and son. "Ride back to the caravan tonight," instructed Pierre. "Jean Baptiste, use the stars to guide your way to the Souris. You and Luc can split up if you miss the camp, up or downstream at the river."

"Tell Wilkie we have found buffalo," Sharlo added. "The carts should be headed this way at first light."

"We will be busy here," Pierre said. "My brother and I will spy on the Dakota hunters and try to determine their next move. We will also attempt to find our fellow Pembina and Turtle Mountain scouts and gather them here. Then, by daylight, we will relocate the buffalo and be ready to guide the first charge on this herd."

The small group separated to ride in opposite directions. The Reaumes were lucky. Father and son encountered a pair of Pembina soldiers on night patrol who took them directly to Mr. Wilkie before reaching the Souris River. The governor wasted no time. Though dawn was still a couple of hours away, he roused the entire camp. Before long, all ninety carts were rolling under starlight, and everyone consumed uncooked breakfasts on the move.

Wilkie left a few men beside the river to greet returning Turtle Mountain hunters who trickled in after sunrise. Several of them had been successful and were leading packhorses that carried field-dressed game. Everyone hurried to catch the caravan as soon as they arrived.

Despite the early start, it was midday when Pierre Bottineau galloped up to meet Mr. Wilkie at the head of the cart train. "The buffalo have moved southeast," he pointed, "but they are not far.

Our scouts are watching the herd, but they will not attack until you are ready to command the entire caravan of hunters."

"Jean Baptiste Reaume informed us that Dakota burned the prairie yesterday," Wilkie reported. "Where are they?"

"They are camped several miles beyond that ridge," Pierre gestured toward the escarpment with a sweep of his arm. "They killed many buffalo yesterday. Sharlo and I saw them celebrating with a feast. Their women tended fires to dry the meat late into the night."

"What will they do today?"

"I don't know, but my brother is still watching them."

"Well," Wilkie declared, "we have come to hunt buffalo. Let's get busy."

The hunters did not need to be told. Most had already retrieved their buffalo runners from the trailing remuda. Now they were collecting their weapons, inspecting powder horns and checking ammunition. Marguerite stepped beside Pierre, giving him a handful of short Métis sashes, brightly decorated with red, white and yellow stripes, each tied through by a short segment of bison bone. Pierre gave his mother a quick hug and tucked the sashes into a pocket of his leather jacket.

Holding the reins for his black stallion, Angelique noticed a fancy blanket beneath Stone's saddle decorated with Métis embroidery in the same red, white and yellow colors. The young captain produced two short muskets, shoving one under his belt and holstering the other into the saddle scabbard. "Good luck," she said, handing him the reins.

He gave her a smile as he launched into the saddle just when Jean Baptiste rode up aboard Falcon. Away they galloped, kicking up dust to join the combined group of Pembina and Turtle Mountain hunters. White Loon, Lucien and Gabrielle came running alongside Marguerite and Angelique to watch them go. Everyone could feel the excitement, but the widow Bottineau was all business. "We need to follow them as quickly as possible," she said. "White Loon, I'll get you started with butchering when we find one of our kills. Then Angelique and I will continue on to the next one."

White Loon wondered, "How will we know which bison have been shot by our men?"

"They will identify their kills by throwing a Métis sash near the body," Marguerite answered. She directed Angelique to mount their lead cart horse while she climbed into the cart and began wielding her long, tasseled whip.

Luc pointed behind the caravan, "I'm supposed to help the other boys wrangle the remaining remuda," he called to his mother and took off running to the rear.

Up ahead, the hunters were trotting their buffalo runners abreast of one another, more than fifty in number. When the bison herd came into view, Wilkie, roughly in the middle, brought his horse to a stop. The squeal of Red River cart wheels was faint behind them, and the faraway buffalo seemed to be peacefully grazing. "Maintain this line," the governor shouted, waving his arms straight out to each side. "We will move forward at a walk, with no one in front of me. When I see the herd is about to break, I will thrust my hand forward," he demonstrated the motion of throwing a spear, "and the attack may begin."

Pierre and Jean Baptiste were on Wilkie's far-right flank. During their approach toward the bison, Sharlo had appeared coming down from the escarpment, and now he was the last man on the line. Everyone kept glancing back and forth between the buffalo and the governor. Falcon was moving calmly, but Pierre had to keep a tight rein on Stone, who kept prancing sideways. Within smelling distance of the bison, he was obviously anxious to begin the pursuit. A large bull lifted his head with a snort. His tail flipped, and he whirled to face the oncoming hunters directly. Wilkie's arm flashed forward, and the charge burst ahead.

Jean Baptiste immediately recognized the effectiveness of this Métis hunting strategy. Every buffalo runner was quickly on the heels of a bison, and the animals were running in a uniform direction before the wide sweep of hunters. Ahead and to his right, Pierre was almost immediately beside a buffalo. His musket boomed, and the beast faltered. Then after a few more strides, it stumbled, fell, and slid, raising a cloud of dust. The young captain threw one of the Métis sashes near the body and hastened his black stallion forward again.

Falcon was gaining on a running bison, and Jean Baptiste got ready to shoot. But as the buckskin gelding edged closer to the buffalo's flank, it continuously veered away. Then Jean Baptiste noticed Pierre and Stone shadowing the animal from the opposite side, forcing it to hold a straight line. Falcon carried the voyageur within point-blank range. He extended his musket muzzle within an arm's length of the buffalo's rib cage and fired at a spot just behind its front shoulder. The force of the blast knocked the bison sideways and down. It tumbled and landed awkwardly on its back, then lay still.

Pierre quickly circled around and tossed a striped sash beside the beast. "Reload!" he shouted to Jean Baptiste, then brandished his musket in the air and charged after the fleeing herd again.

Not so adept at reloading on the run, Jean Baptiste allowed Falcon to walk forward while he tamped a bit of gun powder down the musket barrel and spit a lead ball into the muzzle. Thumping the stock down onto his thigh, he urged the horse ahead with a lurch of his knees and barked, "Giddyup!" Despite weighing more than a thousand pounds, the bison ran with amazing speed and stamina. Most of the herd was pulling farther away from Jean Baptiste. However, off to his left, one of the Turtle Mountain buffalo runners had collided with a buffalo bull, and both animals had fallen. The rider was thrown clear and quickly got to his feet, but the horse was struggling on the ground, apparently unable to stand. Now the bull was trying to follow the stampeding herd, but he was limping badly on an injured leg.

Jean Baptiste steered Falcon toward the wounded bison, and the long-legged buckskin drew near in a hurry. This time the buffalo was to the voyageur's left, so he aimed the musket across his body and above his horse's neck. *Boom!* He was sure his shot had hit its mark, but the massive beast barely flinched. Gradually the bull slowed to a walk. He then stopped and turned to face his pursuer with bold defiance. Jean Baptiste dared not move Falcon within striking distance of the buffalo's menacing horns. He most certainly was not going to dismount. Carefully, he withdrew his own .36 caliber long rifle from the saddle scabbard and put the short musket away. The rifle was already loaded. "Whoa," he eased out the soothing command to hold his mount motionless. He leveled his gunsight just under the bull's bearded chin, aiming directly into his chest. He squeezed the trigger, and though Falcon jumped at the rifle blast, the bullet found its mark. The big bull sank to his knees and toppled over.

By now, the remainder of the herd was too far gone for Jean Baptiste to pursue. Instead, he rode back a couple hundred yards to find the Turtle Mountain hunter who had been thrown from his horse. He seemed physically unhurt but emotionally wounded. His buffalo runner had been fatally injured, requiring a gunshot to relieve the animal of its misery.

"My name is Francois Lacombe," he said, extending his hand. "Thank you for coming back to me." He sadly removed the saddle and bridle from his horse. Then the two of them walked forward to where the big bison bull lay dead.

"I was just about to shoot this buffalo," Francois explained, "when he swerved into my horse and hooked a horn just behind his front shoulder. They got tangled, and both fell down with the bull on top. I was lucky to jump clear, but my runner's left foreleg broke clean in two."

"The buffalo got hurt too," Jean Baptiste told him. "Otherwise, I could never have caught and killed him."

"Lucky for you."

"Lucky for both of us," the voyageur countered. He sympathized with the Métis hunter, whose valuable buffalo runner lay dead. The fatal accident would also deprive the Lacombe family of food on the table from this buffalo hunt. "Were it not for your deadly collision, this bull would still be running with the herd. I will take the hide, but his meat belongs to you."

Francois looked from Jean Baptiste down at the massive bison that would yield six or seven hundred pounds of food. He withdrew a butchering knife from his belt and lifted his grateful eyes to the voyageur's face again, "Thank you."

Twisting Trails

Half an hour later, Jean Baptiste could hear and see the cart train rolling up to where the buffalo charge had begun. He shook hands with Francois Lacombe. Then rolled up the bison hide and draped it across Falcon's rump before riding to rejoin his family.

White Loon was watching Marguerite skillfully butcher the first buffalo that Pierre had shot. Angelique had spread the hide, shaggy side down, across the floor of the Bottineau's Red River cart. Now, as Marguerite continued slicing apart the carcass, the girl carried cuts of meat and piled those upon the hide.

After harvesting every usable part of the beast, White Loon thanked the widow for her lesson, "I will try to follow your example," she pledged, "and now my husband is here to help." Jean Baptiste could lead the Reaume cart directly to his first kill. For Marguerite and Angelique, he could only point the direction he had last seen Pierre riding.

Reunited with his wife, Jean Baptiste excitedly described both of his thrilling bison encounters. He admitted how Pierre had steered the first animal his way. Then explained the circumstances of Francois Lacombe and the giant buffalo bull. She felt sympathy for the other man and readily agreed with Jean Baptiste's decision to share the animal with his family.

Together, husband and wife butchered Jean Baptiste's first kill, aided by Marguerite's carving lesson and the voyageur's experience with carcasses of other wild mammals. It took a long while because of the animal's size and their meticulous work, but they did a remarkably good job.

Eventually, they caught up with the Bottineau cart, where Marguerite was busy dissecting Pierre's third and final kill of the day. The young captain was erecting a drying rack out of wooden poles where Angelique was hanging some of the long strips of bison meat. She was the first to notice their visitors. "Who are they?" She pointed toward two riders on the crest of the escarpment, a quarter mile to the west.

"Dakotas," answered Pierre, his voice level and serious. "I'll get Wilkie, and we'll try to find out what they want." While the

Pembina and Turtle Mountain captains gathered with their governor, four more Dakota warriors appeared beside the original two scouts. When Wilkie rode toward them, with the captains abreast of him, the Dakotas began walking their ponies down the long slope.

"Pierre," the governor said, "you do the talking. Your ability to speak their language is better than the rest of us."

The Dakota were not painted for battle, but their spokesman was loud and fierce. "You trespass on our land and kill our buffalo!"

In a much quieter but unyielding voice, Pierre said, "The land belongs to no one, and the buffalo belong to themselves. Our presence here is as natural as this ground and these animals as well as the Dakota people."

"You will leave half of these dead buffalo for us," demanded the Dakota leader. "Take your half and go away today. Otherwise, we will destroy you and take them all!"

Pierre quickly translated for Wilkie. Then turning back to face the Dakotas, he emphatically declared, "No, you will not." He paused before proceeding, "I watched your hunting camp last night after you burned the prairie. We are greater in number than you. You would need two or three days to bring reinforcements from your Missouri River villages. Our soldiers have guns while many of your warriors are armed with bows. You know our carts can be locked into an invincible circle."

The Dakotas began to murmur among themselves, and their confident expressions turned anxious. The spokesman was silent.

"We will leave when we are ready," Pierre announced, "with all of our meat and hides." Then the Métis and Ojibwe turned their horses and deliberately walked away toward their families. The half-dozen Dakotas briefly watched them go before whipping their ponies over the ridge and out of sight.

"Will they be back?" Wilkie wondered.

"I don't know," Pierre admitted, "but we better be ready."

"We will assemble the circle now," the governor ordered. "Pull the entire remuda inside. Every man will take a turn on guard duty tonight, and every cart will be ready to roll by dawn tomorrow."

Twisting Trails

After making those safety preparations, the Reaume and Bottineau families treated themselves to a supper of delicious bison steaks. "Wow, this tastes good!" Lucien proclaimed between mouthfuls.

"Enjoy it tonight," Sharlo advised. "The next few days will be long on travel and short on sleep."

"Yes," added Marguerite. "Fires must be tended tonight and during the coming nights to dry our meat as we travel back through the Souris River valley. We can wait to make pemmican when we have safely returned to the Turtle Mountains."

The Dakota never came.

* * *

It was a successful hunt. Pierre and Jean Baptiste had collected five valuable hides between them. Each cart was laden with a thousand pounds of food. Other parts of the bison, including bones and sinew, would be used to make many useful supplies.

Upon their arrival back into the Turtle Mountains, Marguerite directed the pemmican-making process. In large kettles provided by Marguerite, White Loon heated buffalo fat to form a thick liquid. Angelique received a wooden mallet to pound some of the dried meat into tiny flakes. Gabrielle's job was to separate flavorful saskatoons and cranberries into portions, which would be added to the mixture.

"I'm fussy about my pemmican," Marguerite declared. "Angelique, make sure no small particles of bone are left in the meat. Gabrielle, don't be stingy with the abundance of berries." When all were ready, the widow held open bags made from buffalo hide. White Loon poured in the hot fat, to which her daughters added plentiful helpings of meat flakes and fruit. Mother briefly stirred the mixture, and Marguerite sewed each bag shut with stitches of strong sinew.

"Those are big bags!" marveled Gabrielle.

"The Hudson Bay Company will expect each one to weigh ninety pounds," the older woman explained. "Canadian voyageurs will paddle far into the wilderness with these bags in their canoes.

They will eat this pemmican along the trails as a snack, or fried, or boiled into rubaboo stew. It will provide nutritious and filling meals without spoiling for at least a year."

Later, Marguerite showed the Reaume girls how to use some of the buffalo fat to create soap. She also demonstrated the cleaning and softening of hides in preparation to make new bags, moccasins or clothing.

The men were also busy. Sharlo taught Jean Baptiste and Lucien how to make shaganappi straps and ropes. Pierre set to work with bison bones and horns, carving them into useful tools. Then on the last evening before they left the Turtle Mountains, he approached Angelique apart from the others, "I have a present for you." Pierre reached into a pocket of his vest, decorated with Métis embroidery, and produced a necklace. A turtle-shaped amulet carved from bright white bone hung from a thin leather strand. The Métis infinity symbol was engraved on the shell of the beautifully lifelike chiseled figurine.

"Thank you," she said and hung the necklace around her neck.

Pierre took Angelique into his arms and kissed her. It was longer and more passionate than the one that ended their Red River jig. This time she kissed him back. When their lips parted, her ribs were still contained in his powerful embrace. "You have earned this gift with your help for my mother and me. We are very grateful."

From within his hands, Angelique asked, "Is that the only reason for my present?"

"I know that the turtle plays a sacred role in the creation story for your mother's people," Pierre began. "The interlocking circles of the infinity emblem are symbolic for the joining together of our White and Native ancestors, and it is a sign that the spirit of our Métis society will live forever."

"I will remember you forever," she said.

He hugged her tightly and then guided her back toward their families' campfire with his arm around her waist. Upon their return, Pierre and Angelique witnessed another gift exchange. Francois Lacombe was there with his family. "This is a horn from the big buffalo bull you killed. It is decorated and filled with gunpowder to honor you and your generous gift of food to our family. Thank you." He extended the powder horn to Jean Baptiste and then shook his hand.

"It is a treasure," said the voyageur. "I will wear it proudly and fill it with powder once again when I return to hunt with you next year."

Everyone smiled and clapped both hunters on the back in happy laughter.

* * *

When they departed the next morning, the Reaume and Bottineau carts showed evidence of Jean Baptiste's trading activity. He had acquired fifteen bison hides and more than a dozen bags of pemmican in exchange for manufactured trade goods. "These Turtle Mountains are far from the nearest trading post," he told Lucien. "People were happy to trade for the merchandise I brought from home, especially the clothing, kitchen utensils and tobacco."

"What will we do with all of the hides and pemmican?" asked Luc, gazing at the loaded carts.

"Trade for even more in Pembina!" his father laughed. "The Hudson Bay Company will buy all of the pemmican we can supply. They provide it to their voyageurs, who consume the portable food while scattering north and west across Canada to gather furs."

"I thought we were trading for the American Fur Company."

"We are," granted Jean Baptiste. "Pierre and Sharlo have agreed to take our pemmican north across the border to Fort Garry, the Hudson Bay trading post at the confluence of the Red and Assiniboine Rivers. Meanwhile, you and I will take all of the hides south, down the Red River Trail to the American Fur Company post at Fort Renville."

"Another adventure!" Luc beamed.

"Yes, a profitable one. Eventually, Pierre and I will meet to share the earnings between his family and ours."

Indeed, when the caravan returned to Pembina, many of the hunting families were eager to trade their hides and pemmican to

Jean Baptiste for factory-made trade goods. The Bottineau brothers needed two carts to haul all of the pemmican bags one hundred miles north to Fort Garry. The Reaume family required a third canoe for their upstream trip on the Red River. One each for father and son to paddle the 250 miles to Fort Renville, packing twenty hides apiece. The third canoe to carry mother and daughters back to their cabin on the Red Lake River.

For the first few days, the family traveled together. Then the girls turned east toward home while the boys continued south. A week later, Jean Baptiste and Lucien paddled into a long narrow lake, Lac Traverse, the source of the Red River. The height of land was actually a marsh-filled valley, through which father and son slogged on foot for four miles, pulling their canoes behind.

Mosquitos tortured them, buzzing around their heads and biting any exposed skin. They made Lucien wish that he was back on the dry and breezy Dakota prairie where the tiny insects were less of a nuisance. Eventually, he and Jean Baptiste arrived at another slender lake, Big Stone, headwaters of the Minnesota River. They camped overnight at the south end of this lake, hoping to reach Fort Renville the next day.

Indeed, near the following evening, they pulled their canoes ashore in front of a stockade at the confluence of the Minnesota and Lac qui Parle Rivers. Log posts, at least ten feet tall, formed exterior walls of the fort. Through a large gate, facing the riverbank, came striding two Native men, and one of them shouted, "Welcome!"

"I am Jean Baptiste Reaume, and this is my son Lucien." He motioned toward the canoes. "We have come down the Red River with some buffalo hides to trade."

The men retrieved a handcart onto which they tossed hides before leading father and son through the gate. Once inside, they glanced around the stockade, which appeared to measure approximately one hundred feet along the riverfront and fifty feet deep. The most conspicuous structure was a watchtower, standing more than a dozen feet tall, in the center of the fort. A single sentry stood atop its platform, holding a rifle in his hands. Inside the back wall stood a row of simple log structures. One of the Native men gave a quick wave to the sentry and wheeled the cart of hides toward the right, "We'll stow your hides in the fur post." Pointing to a door on the opposite side, he said, "You can go on into Joe's reception room."

Just as they ducked through the doorway, a man appeared from what seemed to be living quarters in the back. He was beyond middle age and neatly dressed. Short but powerfully built. Thick black hair was trimmed at his collar. The Native features of his dark-skinned face immediately broke into a smile, "Visitors!" his voice boomed, "You have arrived in time for supper. I am your host, Joseph Renville."

Mealtime was busy. Many of the fort's residents came and went from their supper plates while Renville entertained the Reaumes at the head of the table. The man was clearly a generous benefactor for these people. He put off any talk of business, telling Jean Baptiste that trading could wait until morning. Instead, he politely but enthusiastically queried the voyageur about news from the north. Renville had spent many of his younger years along the Red River, and his face lit up at the mention of Pierre Bottineau. He listened intently to the account of their buffalo hunt and shared delightful stories from his own memory of Pierre's father.

The next morning, they talked trade. Jean Baptiste was satisfied with the price received for the buffalo hides. As part of the exchange, he bartered for vegetables to take home. "My wife planted a garden before we left on the buffalo hunt," he told Renville, "but she dared only to sow plants which would ripen underground like potatoes, carrots and onions. We feared that critters would eat anything growing above the soil."

"I'll show you our fields, and you can pick what you like," allowed their host. "Corn, beans, peas…our crops grow well in this valley." Later, during a walk outside the fort, he showed them a pasture where herds of horses, cattle and sheep were grazing.

"You employ a lot of people here," Jean Baptiste said.

"My mother's people are Dakota," he answered. "This valley has been a traditional campsite of theirs for generations, so they would be here without me. But yes, approximately fifty of these Dakotas work for the fort. They are farmers, herdsmen and voyageurs. They cook, clean and haul cargo. Plus, they are all soldiers. So we are perfectly safe here, as are visitors to this outpost like yourselves."

"Fort Renville is known as a welcoming haven by all travelers of the Red River Trail," said Jean Baptiste. "Sadly, my son and I must be going soon. However, I would like to buy some presents for my wife and daughters. Do you have any suitable items?"

By noon of that day, the Reaume men were on their way home. Tucked in the firebag, which Luc had received from his older sister, was a new comb for Gabrielle's growing hair and a handheld mirror for Angelique. Wrapped neatly beneath Jean Baptiste's seat in the stern of his canoe was a pretty blouse for White Loon, made of beautiful blue cotton fabric with fashionable European tailoring.

Joseph Renville, Jr. (1779–1846)

Joseph Renville, Jr. was born at Kaposia near the confluence of the Mississippi and Minnesota Rivers. The marriage between his Dakota mother and Joseph Renville, Sr. did not last, so the boy was taken by his French voyageur father to be raised and schooled by a Catholic priest in the Red River Valley of Canada.[40]

By his early teens, young Joseph had lived enough with those three adults to achieve a working knowledge of English, French and Dakota languages. That multi-lingual ability served him well in later years as a guide, trader and translator.[41]

Working for the Hudson Bay Company, Renville, Jr. actually fought on behalf of the British during the War of 1812. When the United States prevailed, he helped start the Columbia Fur Company by establishing a trading post at Lac qui Parle near the headwaters of the Minnesota River. He built the post inside a stockade, which became known as Fort Renville. Eventually, the American Fur Company bought out Renville's syndicate, but he continued to operate the trading post at Lac qui Parle.[42]

He was married to a Dakota woman and maintained friendly relationships throughout his life with Dakota and Ojibwe people as well as whites, not an easy accomplishment during the early-to-mid-1800's. Fort Renville was considered an oasis of peaceful hospitality on the Red River Trail under his twenty-four-year proprietorship from 1822 until his death.[43]

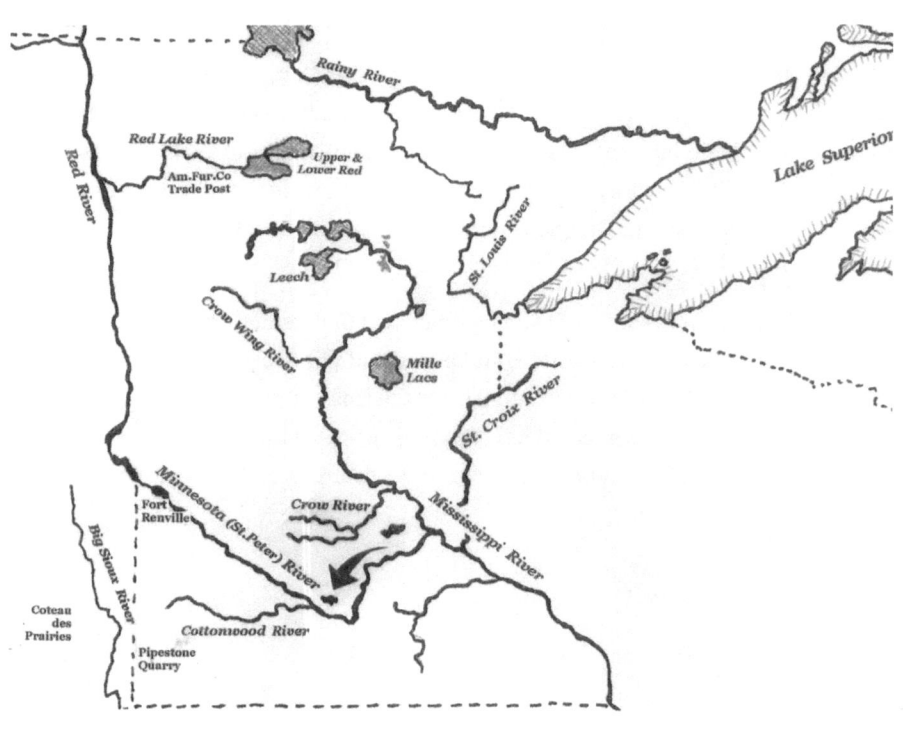

Chapter 11
1836 – Minnesota River

Alex Whitney stepped to the front door of the American Fur Company's trading post at Mendota and knocked. He turned to look over his left shoulder, knowing that Fort Snelling was just a half-mile away across the Minnesota River, high on the bluff above Pike Island. The door opened, and Henry Sibley smiled, "Good morning. Have you had breakfast?"

Stepping inside, Alex could smell fresh coffee and biscuits, "That sounds great." He sat down beside a table where a coffee pot and two cups were already waiting. "Hopefully, the fish will wait for us."

The two young men had arranged to go fishing this morning. Alex was now twenty-three years old. Sibley, at twenty-five, was the proprietor of this trading post and already a partner in the American Fur Company.

The young trader's confident face had a prematurely receding hairline above sharp-edged eyebrows. He wore a neatly trimmed Van Dyke style mustache with a jaunty tuft beneath his lower lip. Sibley's posture seemed relaxed but alert at the same time. He had quickly gained a reputation for competent leadership of the trading network that extended upriver from this Mendota post.

"I've been spending time with a Mdewakanton girl named Red Blanket Woman. Her brothers tell me there are a lot of fish off the eastern point of Pike Island where the Minnesota River joins the Mississippi."

Alex snickered, "You can practically see that spot from here!"

"Yes, we'll meet the brothers there. We are going to fish together."

"That's good," said Alex. "They know where the fish are."

"Yes, but I'm supplying the equipment," Henry remarked. "They do most of their fishing with nets or spears. I promised to show them some of my techniques with hook, line and pole."

Taking a bite of warm biscuit, Alex looked around the room. "Your new buildings look great." Both the warehouse next door and this structure, which doubled as the trader's house and store, were constructed of stone.

"Thanks," Sibley responded. "I decided to replace the old log buildings with limestone blocks like Snelling did at the fort. It forms a visible connection that is impressive to visitors. Plus, the walls are stronger and warmer."

Alex tried to remember, "How long have you been here?"

"I've been so busy, the two years have gone by quickly. Before that, I worked five years at the American Fur Company post on Mackinac Island. I was just eighteen when I left Detroit."

"Detroit? I'm from Detroit!"

"What a coincidence," declared Henry. "My mother and father still live there. He's a supreme court justice for the Michigan Territory."

"My mother is living there too," Alex revealed. "I'll tell her about your family in my next letter home."

Sibley dabbed wild raspberry jam onto a biscuit and popped it in his mouth. Then, with a final swallow of coffee, he slid the pot onto a cool portion of the stovetop. "Let's go," he said while striding toward the door. Once outside, he wiped both hands down the front of his shirt and trousers, scattering biscuit crumbs onto the stoop.

As Alex emerged, Sibley grabbed four fishing poles that he had leaned near the door. "I'll carry these," offered the trader, "if you will take the bait and tackle?"

Alex bent to collect a box of Sibley's fishing equipment next to a small bucket of dirt and worms. Then down to the river they proceeded, where Alex had pulled his canoe ashore.

In a matter of minutes, they paddled to the eastern point of Pike Island, where a pair of Dakota boys crouched on opposite sides of a small fire. "Those are Red Blanket Woman's brothers," Sibley confirmed. Then he guided their canoe into the gently sloping sandy shoreline, alongside the boys' canoe. "Let's wait here until they're ready."

"What are they doing?" Alex asked.

"Natives call this place Bdote." Henry pronounced the word *buh-DOH-tay.* "The Dakota believe their people first came to earth on this place where the two great rivers converge. This land and water are sacred to them."

Alex watched as one of the brothers lifted his arm to the north, south, east and west—up and down the Mississippi, up the Minnesota, and opposite to the far shore. Then he tossed some twigs onto the small fire, causing sparks to erupt. In a few moments, the flame receded, and wisps of smoke curled upward, filtering through the cottonwood leaves above.

"That's red willow bark," Sibley continued speaking softly. "Those shavings hold spiritual significance for the Dakota. The boys are giving thanks for this place and all living things that exist here."

Soon the brothers stood up and approached the beached canoes. Henry introduced Alex and produced a napkin that contained biscuits for both. After exchanging greetings, Sibley handed each boy a fishing pole and provided a brief demonstration of its use.

With both canoes launched off the point, Alex noticed a strong current down the middle of both rivers. The water was still high because of spring runoff. However, the brothers held their canoe in the relatively placid space between the two channels, protected by Pike Island.

"The river bottom is sandy here," the boys explained, "because silt is deposited by both streams. Fish like to gather in this spot where they don't need to swim so hard against the strong current."

Sibley attached a squirming earthworm to his hook and gave the line a flip into the water with his fishing pole. A minute later, the end of his pole throbbed downward, and the trader had a fish on the hook. The handle of his fishing pole was thick and sturdy, but it became slender and more flexible nearer the tip. If a fish fought harder, the pole could bend farther to allow a constant strain on the line. The line itself was not merely tied to the end of Henry's pole; rather, it was strung through several small rings permitting the angler to pull line in or let line out from the handle. Soon a frisky perch was thrashing alongside the canoe. Holding the pole in one hand, Sibley grasped the fish with his other and fetched it over the gunwale.

Alex watched the entire process with interest, as did the brothers. Within a few more minutes, one of them hooked a fish, and the fight was on. He had hooked a bass that jumped above the water a couple times, leading the other brother to whoop in laughter. This battle lasted quite a bit longer, in part because of the angler's inexperience with his equipment but also because the big bass had strength and stamina.

During this time, their canoes drifted out into the faster current and were swept downstream. Henry picked up a paddle and steered them back into the shallower, calmer water near the point. No sooner had they slowed down than Corporal Whitney hooked a small perch and pulled it in.

"These perch will make a tasty meal," declared Sibley. "Their meat will turn white and delicious in my fry pan, along with an onion and carrots. *M-m-m-m!*"

"We're not done, are we?" asked Alex.

"Oh no, of course not," Henry replied. "Let's catch a bunch of 'em and send some home to Red Blanket Woman."

They had done just that by midday and paddled back to the trading post for lunch. Sibley told the brothers to keep their new fishing tackle, and as promised, he gave them most of the fish. He knew they would share with other Mdewakanton families and was glad of that.

When Alex and Henry were finishing their fried perch feast, the trader disclosed, "We will be dining together again tomorrow night."

Twisting Trails

"We will?"

"Yes, at Major Taliaferro's house," Sibley explained. "I'm invited to join your dinner with Joseph Nicollet."

* * *

Dinner at the Indian Agency turned out to be quite a festive affair, with ten people in attendance. The hosts, Major and Mrs. Taliaferro, had invited the fort commander Major John Bliss and his wife. Half of the guests were men about to embark on an expedition deep into Dakota Territory, southwest of the Minnesota River.

Taliaferro began the occasion by inviting everyone to be seated in the parlor. "Several of you have already befriended our guest of honor, Mr. Joseph Nicollet. Though he is the oldest man in this room, you know him to be jovial and energetic. I would like to begin by making sure that everyone is aware of his professional accomplishments."

"I am a very young fifty-one!" Nicollet laughed, flexing his wiry arms as if to display vigorous muscles.

Taliaferro continued the introduction. "Before emigrating from his native France, Joe was a noted scientist at the Paris Observatory where he taught math and astronomy. Political upheaval brought him to our continent."

"I was also broke," Nicollet admitted. "Tried to play the stock market using my own theory of probability and lost everything." Then he laughed again at his own expense.

"Over the last two summers, Joe has mapped much of the US territory north of here, beginning with the Upper Mississippi River. He has traveled east, up the St. Croix, all the way to Lake Superior and down the Rainy River, along the Canadian border. Then west to the Red River Trail and back to Fort Snelling via the Minnesota River."

"I am indebted to the American Fur Company for financing those explorations," said the Frenchman, pointing to the Mendota trader Henry Sibley. The company partner returned Nicollet's tribute with a nod.

"That was also good fortune for the fur company," Taliaferro said. "I have seen the beautiful maps you drew for them. The detail and the accuracy make them tremendously useful."

"I agree," declared Sibley. "Our voyageurs have better maps of this territory than the US government."

"Well, that is about to change," Taliaferro announced. "Which brings me to the purpose of our gathering tonight. Let me introduce Lieutenant John Charles Fremont." He extended his arm toward the twenty-four-year-old officer sitting next to the scientist. "He is a member of the newly formed US Army Corps of Topographical Engineers. A commissioned aide from the War Department to escort Mr. Nicollet on a mapping expedition of territory south and west of the Minnesota River."

"It will be my pleasure," expressed the handsome, able-bodied Fremont. He had a full head of wavy brown hair and a neatly trimmed beard.

"Your team will travel onto the Coteau des Prairies plateau, which rises between the Minnesota and Missouri rivers. This trip will travel over land occupied by outlying Dakota bands, including their pipestone quarry. I have arranged to have three men who are familiar with Native leaders in those areas accompany the expedition—my Indian Agency liaison from Fort Snelling, Corporal Alexander Whitney; Mr. Sibley's dependable voyageur, Joseph LaFramboise; and proprietor of the American Fur Company trading post at Lac qui Parle, Joseph Renville."

The three acknowledged their identity in turn, but no one spoke. However, Mrs. Taliaferro jumped to her feet, clapping her hands. "How exciting," she cheered, inspiring everyone to applaud in a spirit of fellowship. Then, motioning toward the dining room, she proclaimed, "Let's eat."

The guests savored Eliza Taliaferro's delicious dinner. Then everyone returned to the parlor where she provided piano music, and Mr. Nicollet played his violin. Both musicians were skillful and performed a number of old favorites, with which everyone could sing along until late into the night.

Twisting Trails

* * *

The mapping expedition did not get started until after breakfast the next morning. Joseph LaFramboise led their column of equestrians. Alex's hand-picked mount was a chestnut Morgan named Justice. Compact but strong, the gelding had the stamina and disposition for long-distance travel. Food supplies and Nicollet's cartography equipment were secured to the backs of additional packhorses. Segments of their journey would be along rivers, but most of the intended route was over prairie terrain where canoes would be useless.

LaFramboise was a voyageur for the American Fur Company, whose trading activities made him extremely familiar with the lower Minnesota River and the Native people who lived there. He led the procession above the northern rim of the Minnesota Valley, riding a trail that was drier than the river bottom and less congested with trees. Near the end of the second day, the guide reported they would turn away from the river altogether, "Tomorrow morning, we will strike due west."

"Traverse des Sioux," agreed Joseph Renville. The Métis trader was also familiar with this shortcut across higher ground, which avoided the southernmost bend of the Minnesota.

Then LaFramboise chuckled, "But tonight, we stop to see our old friend Louis Provençalle."

"LeBlanc!" Renville roared. "My Dakota family still call him The White Man because he was about the only one when he came here."

"You should see Louis' trading post ledger," LaFramboise remarked. "He does not read or write, so his record books are filled with pictographs—little hieroglyphics he draws to represent different pelts and trade goods. They are difficult for me to decipher, but the Natives he trades with understand them perfectly."

Upon arrival at the Traverse des Sioux trading post, LaFramboise and Renville enjoyed a boisterous reunion with Provençalle. The fifty-six-year-old trader exchanged rough hugs and laughter with his friends. Half a dozen children appeared from the trees, and

Provençalle instructed the two oldest boys to help the travelers with their mounts. They skillfully removed saddles and led the horses to the river where they could drink and graze.

When his wife appeared at their cabin doorway, the trader announced that additional food would be required for supper. The Dakota woman surveyed the five hungry men, and her eyes grew wide. Lieutenant Fremont took a step forward, "We are prepared to pay for our meal," he told her. Then turning to Provençalle, "and for the care of our horses. This is an official expedition of the US government."

The trader turned an inquiring look to LaFramboise, who explained, "These men are making a map of territory south and west of the river." He pointed to Nicollet and Fremont.

"Well, come on in." Provençalle led the way inside his long, low log cabin. Once inside, the men could see the structure was divided in half—trading post on one side and living quarters on the other. There were no spare beds, but their host pointed to the store area and offered, "You can sleep with a roof over your head tonight if you choose."

Over supper, Renville provided some of the details for their journey, "We intend to follow the Cottonwood River valley to the pipestone quarry. Then west onto the Coteau des Prairies, before turning north to the Height of Land. My role will be finished when I get home to Lac qui Parle."

With a wary expression, the trader glanced back and forth between his friends, "Does Sleepy Eyes know you are coming?"

"No," admitted LaFramboise, "But I have an edge with him. My wife is his daughter."

"The quarry is sacred to the Dakota. They won't like the idea of white men setting foot on that ground."

Nicollet spoke up, "A painter by the name of George Catlin was allowed to travel there last summer. I hope to make it a very important feature on my map."

After supper, the old friends stayed awake a long while sharing memorable stories and a jug of whiskey, but in the middle of the night, just when they decided to lay down, Nicollet and Fremont got up. Responding to a quizzical look from the fur traders, the lieutenant said, "It's time for Papa Joe to read the stars."

Fremont had taken a liking to the scientist and started to address him by that nickname. Nicollet was more than twice his aide's age and a full head shorter. These midnight measurements to determine latitude, longitude and elevation were a regular routine whenever clear skies allowed observation of the stars. The lieutenant hoisted a satchel of instruments onto his shoulder—sextant, barometer, thermometer and chronometer. Nicollet checked for the compass in his pocket and hung a spyglass around his neck. Together they walked outside and sought a clearing that would give them an unobstructed view of the heavens. An hour later, Papa Joe had conducted his tests, his aide had recorded the readings, and they were back inside the cabin hoping to sleep again.

* * *

They traveled the Traverse des Sioux shortcut the next day but split into two groups. LaFramboise led Nicollet by the shortest route past the southern shore of Swan Lake. Renville became a hunting guide, taking the two soldiers through an area of small prairie lakes where they hoped to supplement the team's meat supply. By nightfall, everyone was to gather at the mouth of the Cottonwood River.

The three hunters galloped ahead, leading a packhorse that they hoped might carry a deer carcass by day's end. Reaching the crown of a low mound, Renville stopped. Miles of gently undulating grassland bordered the south end of a larger lake in front of them. However, the northern end of the lake disappeared into a series of tree-covered hills and ravines.

The Lac qui Parle trader turned to Alex and waved to the left, "Take your shotgun and work across this prairie. You may find quail or partridge in the meadows. There might also be ducks or geese along the lakeshore."

Alex pulled his trusty fowling piece from the saddle scabbard and checked to see that it was ready to fire.

Renville pivoted to the right and pointed into the deciduous forest. "Lieutenant Fremont and I will carry our rifles through those trees looking for deer. Eventually, we'll meet on the opposite side of this lake." He pointed to a spot where the hardwood trees dwindled in number to meet the prairie shoreline.

"Good luck," Alex waved and watched his partners lead the packhorse away. Moving across the grassland, he walked Justice in a zigzag pattern, weaving a hundred yards away from the lake and back to its banks. The corporal's eyes and ears were alert while his horse thoroughly covered the ground, working back and forth around the water. Alex held his firearm diagonally in front of his torso with his right hand low, near the trigger. His left hand cradled the gun barrel and loosely held the reins, allowing the Morgan gelding to walk at its own leisurely pace.

Halfway around the lake, he had seen nothing but prairie songbirds. They kept up a welcome chorus, some pecking at the seeds of wildflowers, others swooping to snatch insects in flight. *Crack!* A rifle shot from the woods shattered the gentle meadow melody. Alex snapped his gaze north across the lake, but he could detect no movement. "If they have successfully killed a deer," he wondered aloud, "it will take a while to field dress." Realizing that only Justice could hear those words, the corporal snickered to himself but continued, "We may have additional time to hunt for upland birds."

Alex began riding wider loops, casting an occasional glance toward Renville's proposed meeting place. If the other men reappeared, he should be able to join them quickly. He was riding down a gentle slope approaching the lake's southwest corner when a covey of quail burst out of the grass. At least a dozen of the birds exploded off the ground almost beneath his mount's feet. Justice spun away from this unexpected cloud of buffeting wings, so Alex could barely hang onto his gun, let alone aim and fire at one of the quail!

Frustrated, Alex dismounted and hobbled his horse. Fortunately, he had noticed that none of the birds flew toward the water. Rather, they scattered up and over the slope he just descended. "Now they're spread apart," Alex said to Justice. "That's lucky. Maybe I can find 'em and flush 'em one at a time instead of the entire covey taking off at once."

Leaving the horse hobbled near the lakeshore, he trudged a large circle beyond the crest of the slope. Sure enough, the birds took flight at his approach one and two at a time. He was able to flush six of them and shot four.

Striding back over the ridge, he saw that Renville and Fremont had gathered beside Justice. As he neared the men, Alex realized that a large black bulk, not a deer, was heaped across the back of the packhorse.

"I love bear meat!" he shouted.

"Me too," Fremont beamed. "I didn't even have to chase this one. He stood up on his hind legs and growled at me!"

Bear stew was on the menu when these hunters reunited with LaFramboise and Nicollet at the confluence of Minnesota and Cottonwood Rivers. Arriving first, the scientist had gathered a bundle of edible roots and plants that were added to the recipe. Everyone happily ate their fill and then reclined upon their bedrolls, but their voyageur guide voiced a caution, "We're in Sleepy Eyes' territory," he warned. "I will stay awake for first watch, but I will need relief."

"I'll stand guard when Papa Joe and I get up for stargazing," the lieutenant offered.

Then Alex volunteered, "I'll take the last shift until morning."

* * *

Alex actually awakened before his turn on guard duty was scheduled to begin. He wiped the sleep from his eyes and decided to go find Nicollet and Fremont. He was curious to see how the mapmakers used their instruments. Alex found the scientist gazing at constellations of stars using a telescope and a sextant. Nicollet quoted his measurements to Lieutenant Fremont, who recorded the numbers into a journal.

"Papa Joe will use these recordings to draw his map when the expedition is finished," the lieutenant told Alex. He gestured across the star-lit landscape, "The shapes and locations of these hills, valleys and waterways will complete his map of the entire Upper Mississippi River basin."

For a long while, after the cartographers returned to their bedrolls, Alex continued to observe the night sky. The crescent moon was only a thin sliver, leaving the earth around him in near-total darkness. That made the thousands of twinkling stars appear even more brilliant. He could find the North Star and identify particular constellations after Fremont pointed them out, but the clusters of light were a shining mystery to him. *Pop!* He was startled by the sound of a crackling ember in their dying campfire. Shaking his head, the corporal scolded himself. *Fine sentry I am. Any enemy could have walked right into our camp while I was hypnotized by the heavens.* He moved to a more concealed position and double-checked the readiness of his firearm.

As the next pair of hours passed, a grayness crept up from the eastern horizon. While Alex's teammates continued to doze in pre-dawn shadow, a few wild creatures began to stir. From the nearby prairie, he could hear the coo of mourning doves. Songbirds started to twitter and flit in the treetops. Then came a skittering sound among the branches above. A squirrel scampered headfirst down the trunk of an ash tree to within a few feet of Alex. Suddenly realizing a person was there, the animal froze in place. The sentry lifted his gun and quietly said, "Bang." The squirrel darted around the tree to perch on a branch and flip its bushy tail. When the corporal softly chuckled and lowered his gun, the varmint burst into a noisy chatter as if to scold the young soldier.

That clamor resulted in groans and movement from the bedrolls. Renville sat up and turned toward the amber glow that was beginning to fill the eastern sky. When he moved to pull on his boots, Alex decided to gather fresh water from the river to splash on their faces and fill the coffee pot. Soon everyone was awake and preparing for the new day.

Henry Hastings Sibley (1811–1891)

Henry Hastings Sibley was born in Detroit, son of a successful businesswoman and father who would become chief justice of the Michigan Territorial Supreme Court.[44]

He was drawn to the pursuits of hunting and fishing as a boy. These interests lured him away from law school at the age of eighteen to clerk for the American Fur Company at Mackinac Island. He rose quickly, becoming a partner in the company five years later.[45]

Twenty-three-year-old Sibley arrived at Mendota in 1834, where he operated the American Fur Company trading post until the company's demise in 1847.[46]

Sibley fathered a baby girl named Helen *(Bird)* in 1841. He did not maintain a permanent marriage with the girl's Dakota mother, Red Blanket Woman. However, his father-daughter relationship with Helen was supportive and life-long. At the age of thirty-two, Sibley married twenty-year-old Sarah Jane Steele, whose brother, Franklin, rose from Fort Snelling sutler to wealthy local land speculator and businessman. Henry and Sarah had nine children, but only four survived to adulthood.[47]

By the time of his marriage, Sibley had become active in politics. He was elected Minnesota territorial representative to the US Congress beginning in 1849 and narrowly defeated Alexander Ramsey to become Minnesota's first state governor in 1858.[48]

Sibley served one term as governor, during which time the Civil War began. He was appointed colonel in command of the Minnesota state militia. However, the troops he led into battle became engaged in the Dakota Conflict of 1862 rather than the Civil War.[49]

Twisting Trails

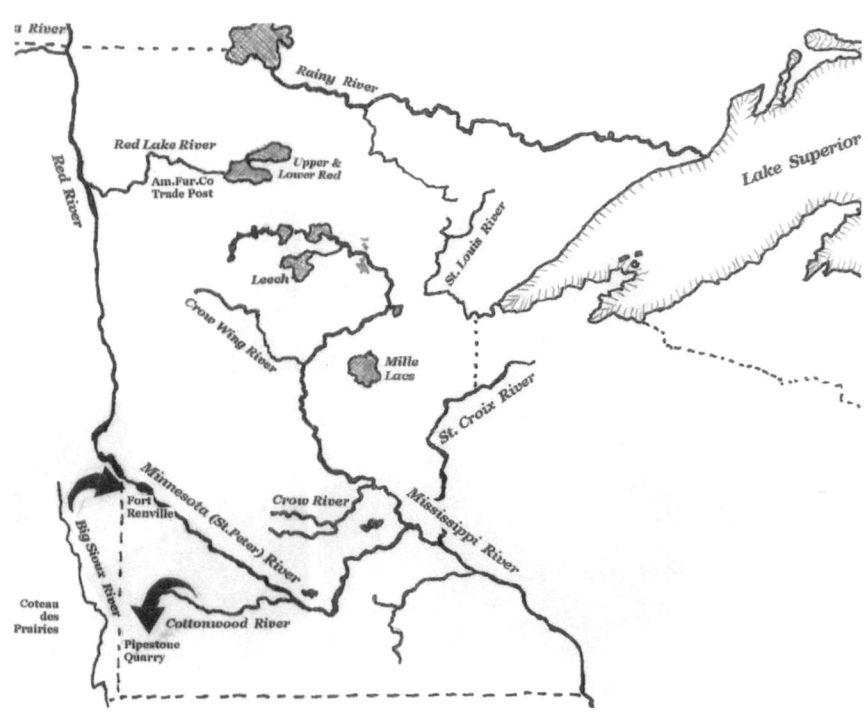

Chapter 12
1836 – Coteau des Prairies

The expedition proceeded westward from the confluence of the Minnesota and Cottonwood Rivers. They moved upstream, staying above the southern banks of the Cottonwood.

"I thought this was Dakota Territory," challenged Fremont. "I haven't seen a sign of a single Native."

Joseph Renville responded, "You can bet they have seen you." His comment silenced the lieutenant and caused him to peer suspiciously all around. Come midday, the Métis trader's words proved true. Three Dakota warriors popped up in front of Joseph LaFramboise at the head of their column. All three were riding ponies that suddenly bounded up from a deep ravine where a stream entered the Cottonwood from their left. An instant after the middle rider shouted a command, several more Natives appeared to surround the column. They were all on foot with weapons ready. Two with bows had come off the ground on their left, and two more with muskets jumped out of the river gulch on their right.

LaFramboise showed empty hands to the warrior who had spoken and delivered a greeting in his friendly tone of voice. At that, the Dakota seemed to relax. He walked his pony forward and engaged the guide in conversation. Presently, he motioned for the surrounding Native men to lower their guns and bows.

Both fur traders were capable with the Dakota language. While LaFramboise spoke with their visitors, Renville quietly translated,

"The speaker belongs to the Swan Lake Band led by Sleepy Eyes. He recognizes our guide as an American Fur Company trader. They are having a friendly conversation, but he insists that we come to their village. Lucky for us, they are camped upstream on the Cottonwood, right where we are headed." An eighth Dakota warrior appeared, this one leading ponies for the men on foot. They all mounted and proceeded to escort the expedition forward, some in front and some behind.

They reached the Dakota encampment late that afternoon. The Dakota leader received LaFramboise with special enthusiasm, "Husband of my daughter! Welcome!"

Corporal Whitney looked around and realized, upon seeing their tipis, that this was no permanent village. These people were actually on the move. Sleepy Eyes confirmed the fact. "We are on our yearly summer journey to the buffalo grounds," he explained. "These men who escorted you here are scouts and hunters."

The visitors were invited to share the evening meal and gather afterward for conversation. Alex was puzzled how their tall, handsome host came by the name Sleepy Eyes because he appeared the opposite. He expressed enthusiastic curiosity about Nicollet's map, and his eyes keenly examined the astronomical instruments displayed by the French scientist.

A ceremonial pipe was lit and passed around the circle of Natives and whites, its bowl carved from unmistakable, red-colored pipestone. Nicollet prompted LaFramboise to inquire about the quarry, "Our scientist is most anxious to visit the pipestone quarry."

"That is sacred ground. Only the feet of Dakotas are welcome to walk there."

Nicollet started a panicked objection, but LaFramboise silenced him with an extended hand. "Father, the quarry is supreme among all of the places our mapmaker wishes to locate. We seek to honor the place of precious stone. I promise that nothing will be damaged."

Sleepy Eyes turned and whispered briefly with the warrior who had led their escort before turning back to LaFramboise, "My son, you and Renville," he nodded to the Lac Qui Parle trader whose mother was Dakota, "you know our red stone is holy. You must caution these others to show respect." Motioning to a pair of warriors, "Broken to Pieces and Tip of the Horn will guide you. If the place of sacred stone is violated, our relationship will not lessen your punishment."

The next morning when they broke camp, the expedition veered away from the Swan Lake Band of Dakota. Sleepy Eyes led his buffalo hunters northwest, continuing upstream toward the source of the Cottonwood. The explorers followed their Dakota guides slightly southwest on a direct path to the pipestone quarry. A full day's travel brought them to the shores of Lake Shetek, where an arrow from Tip of the Horn's bow provided a venison supper. "One more day will bring us to the red stone," predicted Broken to Pieces.

However, the next day proved difficult. They woke to the approach of low gray clouds scudding above their heads. By late morning, the cool dawn breeze grew into a whipping wind that blew directly into their faces. Alex was subconsciously aware that the horses were gradually climbing. Each rolling hill they topped seemed to give way to another taller one. As the terrain got higher, the wind blew stronger. Finally, a long high ridge stretched from south to north in front of them. The corporal twisted in his saddle to face Tip of the Horn, who rode nearest behind him. He gave the warrior an inquiring look and pointed along the rise.

The Dakota yelled into the gale, "Buffalo Ridge! Wind here is always fierce!"

The combination of clouds and wind created an unusually cold July day, but it got worse. The afternoon brought squalls of rain that swept across the prairie like random waterfalls. Each squall could be seen for miles, the falling moisture resembling lavender curtains that waved down to the ground. Some passed by in the distance. Others merely unleashed a stinging wind-driven mist. Twice the riders were drenched by heavy rain that soaked through their coats and made their wet bodies shiver.

Alex had just begun to feel dry when the second downpour came. Justice did not seem bothered by the cool rain, but even the horse lowered his muzzle against these pelting droplets. The corporal hunched forward behind his Morgan's neck, but then chilly drips trickled down his neck, underneath his jacket and shirt. Wetness saturated the pants around his hips and down his legs. Wet skin, buffeted by the cold wind, chilled him to the core. Every frigid muscle tightened into a shivering clench. Thankfully, Lieutenant Fremont insisted they stop after fording the Rock River.

"We can reach the red stone before nightfall," shouted Broken to Pieces.

Fremont pointed to Papa Joe, whose lips had turned purple, "We need to stop here where there is cover and warm him up." The men dismounted and began to build a sizable lean-to using the plentiful timber along the riverbank. They sloped saplings against the wind, building a v-shaped shelter wide and high enough for all of them to sit within. The lieutenant built a warming fire and helped Nicollet remove his wet clothes and hang them to dry on low-hanging branches. Soon the entire expedition was huddled under the lean-to, all of them in their underwear. Finally, the elder scientist stopped trembling, and his skin returned to normal color. "At least there are no mosquitos," he joked, and everyone shared a hearty laugh.

The wind continued to blow until dark, but their protected fire was adequate to cook the remainder of Tip of the Horn's deer from the previous evening. They were famished and ate every morsel. At last, with refilled bellies, they put their dried clothes back on, added logs to the warming fire and laid down to sleep.

Alex awoke during the night. Gradually coming alert, he realized the wind had finally subsided. He crawled forward to look up through the leaves that were barely fluttering. The clouds were breaking up, and a few stars were now visible. He crept back into his bedroll and closed his eyes.

"Stars." Alex heard a quiet voice and opened his eyes. Nicollet was awake and gently shaking Lieutenant Fremont. "The sky is clearing," he whispered. Within minutes, the mapmakers had gathered their instruments and vacated the lean-to. Corporal Whitney was back asleep.

Twisting Trails

* * *

The next morning, when the glowing sun began to inch above the eastern horizon, it glittered across droplets of heavy dew, courtesy of the previous day's moisture. The lean-to, a bulwark against yesterday's western wind, was today's receptacle of sparkling reflected sunlight. A nearly blinding light from the east illuminated the shelter with a radiance that made sleep impossible. The men, however, were eager to rise. Fresh memories of bleak weather made this bright morning especially welcome.

Also anxious to arrive at the pipestone quarry, the team quickly had breakfast and packed for the last several miles to that destination. The short trip to their objective motivated the riders to push their horses into a faster gait. Alex discovered his Morgan gelding was more than willing to stride out. In less than an hour, the column approached a tree-lined stream where they walked their mounts into the water and let them drink.

"Is that the sound of a waterfall?" Alex cupped a hand behind his ear and pointed upstream.

"Winnewissa," replied Broken to Pieces, who turned his pony and led the way toward the melody of falling water.

Alex weaved his way along stream banks strewn with boulders until Winnewissa Falls appeared through the trees. The stream spilled over a stone ledge about two body lengths wide and three high. The spray ricocheted this way and that off the craggy face of the waterfall.

"Beautiful," he declared to no one in particular. At that moment, Justice bobbed his head and snorted as if in agreement. The corporal smiled, patted his mount on the shoulder, and added, "What a privilege to be in this place."

Nicollet walked his horse forward to ask Broken to Pieces, "Where is the red stone?"

The Dakota guide waved his hand as if to say, *follow me* and exited the stream bed to the west. Beyond the creek, a half-mile width of flat prairie opened farther west. On their immediate east, a long perpendicular rock wall rose up from the ground. The rugged wall was thirty feet tall in some places. Its face was still shaded from the morning sun, but Alex could see it was striped with different colored layers of stone—pink, tan, brown and maroon. Over time, frequent jagged vertical cracks split the wall, resulting in a collection of broken rocks at its base. The mapmaker deliberately dismounted and reverently approached the wall. His head swiveled back and forth, up and down, attempting to take it all in.

Over the next several hours, LaFramboise and Renville stayed close to their Native guides while Fremont and Whitney assisted Nicollet. The traders sought to calm the Dakotas' fears that the Frenchman might violate their promise to honor the sacred quarry. However, the scientist's actions were so meticulous and careful that Broken to Pieces and Tip of the Horn soon relaxed. Their conversation turned to the band's buffalo hunt, and that afternoon they divided across the Coteau des Prairies on a scouting mission for bison.

Alex watched Nicollet gently chip away at each layer of the multi-colored wall with a hammer and chisel. Papa Joe sketched pictures of the rocks and wrote notes into a journal. He was still engrossed in this activity when the buffalo scouts returned, empty-handed, late that afternoon. Broken to Pieces approached Nicollet and was surprised to see no pipestone among the collection of rocks the scientist was examining. "No red stone?"

With a sweep of his hand, the Frenchman gestured across the face of the vertical stone. Then he turned up empty palms and shrugged his shoulders.

"Underground," blurted the Dakota guide, pointing at the base of the wall. He picked up a shovel that was lying on the ground and proceeded to dig into the gravelly soil. The rock surface extended straight down. Broken to Pieces repeatedly scraped the shovel blade lower along the rough stone exterior, casting clods of dirt and pebbles over his shoulder. Nicollet and Alex scrambled to get out of the way. Within minutes, the warrior had cleared a cavity that exposed a few more feet of the wall. He dropped to his knees and jabbed the shovel at a spot that made a different sound. Instead of a *clack,* it made a *clunk.* The Native reached with his hand and turned around, clutching a jagged chunk, the dark red color of dried blood.

The scientist received the stone with wonder. He rubbed it with his fingers, scratched a thumbnail on the surface, and lightly hefted it for weight. Then he pivoted and extended the rock toward Fremont at eye level. They both smiled.

Broken to Pieces stepped up out of the cavity and nodded when Nicollet said, "Thank you."

As the Dakota man stepped away, Alex accepted the shovel. He quickly turned to the wall and began to expand the exposure of pipestone. They soon realized that it occupied a horizontal layer between the other various levels of rocks.

"We will remain here overnight," stated Lieutenant Fremont, "so Papa Joe can spend more time examining this pipestone tomorrow. For now, let's make camp and get ready for supper."

After eating, the men enjoyed the relaxing summer evening. Nicollet capitalized on the last hour of daylight to sketch a panorama of the exposed stone wall. From far out on the flat prairie with the setting sun behind him, he had an ideal perspective to view the illuminated layers of colorful rock.

Sometime during the night, he and Fremont climbed atop the cliff with their satchels of instruments. Fortunately, they had a crystal-clear sky to observe the stars from this significant location. Precise measurements were recorded for latitude, longitude and elevation. This pipestone quarry would eventually be properly drawn onto Nicollet's map, by far the most accurate ever drafted for North America's upper Midwest.

By the light of the following day, the excavation and examination of pipestone again engrossed the scientist. With time on their hands, other members of the expedition scattered to pursue their own activities. Fremont concluded that exploration of the greater quarry area would best fulfill his duty to the US Army Corps of Topographical Engineers. Renville rode westward with both Dakota guides, once again in search of a bison herd. Alex and LaFramboise decided to hunt for food in river valleys that meandered to the southeast.

The buffalo proved elusive, but the deer hunters were successful. LaFramboise shot a whitetail buck, which he and Corporal Whitney packed back to the quarry on a spare horse. Approaching near Winnewissa Falls, they were surprised to see a US flag waving from atop a stone column. As they drew closer, the flagpole's location became more of a mystery. The narrow stone pillar was more than twenty feet tall. Every side was vertical, impossible to climb. The sharp-edged top of the spire stood a full body length apart from the nearest bluff.

The fur trader halted his mount and pushed the hat brim back from his perspiring forehead, "How in the world did…"

"Happy Fourth of July!" Lieutenant Fremont appeared up on the ridge. Bounding from somewhere closer to the waterfall, he exclaimed, "Today is our nation's sixtieth birthday."

"Indeed, it is," Alex realized.

"Hey, come on up here!" yelled Fremont as he motioned to a trail leading up and around the face of the cliff.

"I should start butchering this deer," declared Corporal Whitney. "You go see what he wants." Alex took the reins of all three horses and led them to a tree with a low-hanging branch. There he suspended the whitetail buck and began carving away the meat for their evening meal.

Meanwhile, LaFramboise clambered up the trail on foot, "How'd you get that flagpole on top of those rocks?" He was a little winded from the climb.

The lieutenant walked to the edge of the stone-faced bluff. He pointed across five feet of open air to the crown of the jagged spire, "I jumped."

The fur trader stepped tentatively near the brink. He looked down to the rock-strewn ground more than twenty feet below. "Mighty dangerous trick just to plant a flagpole."

"But isn't this a grand spot for the stars and stripes to fly on Independence Day?"

"I'll grant you that."

"Follow me," Fremont pivoted and marched to a point not far from the head of Winnewissa Falls. He stopped beside a huge, oblong boulder that was nearly flat on top. There, the lieutenant pointed his large, sturdy hunting knife at the pink and gray speckled surface of the boulder. Scratched deeply into the slab were the very neat initials, C. F.

Fremont's face was alight with enthusiasm. "Your turn," he offered, extending the knife hilt first to LaFramboise. The fur trader accepted the blade and set to work carving his own initials, J. L. F., into the rock. After their venison supper, the lieutenant led Nicollet and Renville to the boulder where their presence at this historic site was also carved in stone: J. R. and J. N. Nicollet.

* * *

When the expedition departed from Pipestone Quarry, Broken to Pieces and Tip of the Horn led them north. They hoped to rejoin Sleepy Eyes and their band's buffalo hunt. The guides found the trail of their people that afternoon and by nightfall were sleeping inside their families' own tipis.

The next morning, scouts revealed they found some sign of buffalo farther west, but no animals. After breakfast, the Swan Lake band started in pursuit of that evidence.

The explorers said their goodbyes and struck to the northwest, now with Joseph Renville in the lead.

"This wide plateau, the Couteau des Prairies, is my buffalo range," he declared. "All the streams east of this high, rolling country flow into the Minnesota River. Everything west runs off toward the Missouri. But the plateau itself is drained by the Big Sioux. It's up ahead of us, meandering due south. We'll be beside its banks by sunset today."

The amount of water on this prairie surprised Alex. They sloshed through dozens of small streams, and every few miles would reveal a pothole pond or small lake lying in the hollow of a shallow valley. "I was led to believe this territory was dry and flat," he remarked to Renville, "almost a desert."

"Parts of it are flat and dry," responded the Lac qui Parle trader, "moreso as you go north, but it's more a grassland than a desert."

The expedition did reach the Big Sioux River that day. They followed it upstream to a wooded bend and made camp. The remains of LaFramboise's whitetail buck provided a hearty meal for all and full bellies for a restful night's sleep.

The next two sunny July days were nearly replicas. The explorers continued north, parallel with the Big Sioux. The Couteau des Prairies scenery, while beautiful, began to seem monotonous. Sparse meals consisted of small game and a few wild berries, now ripening on summer prairie bushes. The men alternated nighttime guard duty, except for Nicollet, who awoke to take measurements of every starlit sky.

By late morning of the next day, the monotony was broken. Far to the west, across the river, Lieutenant Fremont's sharp eyes spotted a bison herd. More than a mile distant, the buffalo appeared to Alex as nothing more than black specks on a green, sunlit hillside. But a few of the specks were moving!

"We're only two days from Lac Qui Parle," Renville announced. "As soon as we get to the fort, I'll rally my soldiers to come back here and hunt those wooly beasts."

"How 'bout we hunt one of 'em today!" was Fremont's excited suggestion.

Renville looked from man to man and saw unanimously eager faces. "Alright," he granted. "But just one. That will feed us the next two nights, and our three packhorses won't be able to carry the meat from more than one."

They found a place to ford the Big Sioux and splashed across. The bison were out of sight when the riders came out of the river bottom, so Renville pondered a choice of direction.

"We may crest a pair of lower hills between here and the herd," he cautioned. "Don't go charging over the top."

Twisting Trails

They trotted around the first knoll, then slowed their mounts to a walk before ascending the next slope. From that hilltop, some of the buffalo were visible but still beyond another grassy ridge.

When they had ridden halfway up that ridge, Renville stopped and dismounted. He motioned Alex to do likewise and handed over his reins, "Corporal, hold your horse here along with mine, LaFramboise's, and Fremont's. Papa Joe, you get down and hold the pack horses."

Next, he turned to Fremont, "Lieutenant, pull that long rifle out of your saddle scabbard." That done, the Métis trader huddled with the group, "The wind is in our favor, so I don't think they've heard or smelled us. We're gonna get down on our bellies before we peek over this ridge, so they won't see us." Then he crept up the slope with Fremont and LaFramboise behind.

Alex and Nicollet exchanged silent glances. Then they watched while the hunters dropped to hands and knees before lying prone on the ridgetop. A few finger points and head nods preceded long motionless moments. *Boom!* Justice and the other horses jerked at the blast, but none of the men moved right away. Renville was the first to rise. He lifted one knee off the ground and pounded a clap of congratulation onto Fremont's back.

The horse holders decided to move forward. When Corporal Whitney could see beyond into the broad valley, he was astonished. First, because the buffalo herd displayed no general alarm. A few of the beasts skittered away, and others lifted their heads to look toward the men and horses. Alex had expected a stampede after the rifle shot. Instead, the few bison that reacted to the *boom* seemed more curious than afraid.

Another amazement for the corporal was the sheer number of animals. There were hundreds spread through the valley and up the facing hillside. This, however, was apparently only a portion of the entire herd because now he began to see more of them on another slope, beyond another valley! Some appeared almost black, especially about the head and horns. While others seemed shiny bronze in color depending on their angle to the sunlight. A few tawny calves, with no hump at all, displayed some frisky tendencies. The aging bulls, with massive shaggy humps and shoulders, moved with ponderous power.

"Everybody walk alongside your horse to the cow that Fremont shot," Renville advised. "The buffalo won't be spooked by walking horses."

No sooner did they reach the fallen beast than he unsheathed his sturdy hunting knife to begin removing the hide. "This cow is perfect for our purposes," he commented. "Big enough to provide plenty of meat, but young enough so the flesh will be tender."

As the Métis trader butchered this buffalo, his partners carefully wrapped meat within each side of the hide and strapped both bundles onto two packhorses. All the cooking and camp utensils were condensed inside one tarp and balanced onto the third packhorse. By midafternoon, they were walking away. Renville cast a long look over his shoulder, hoping the bison herd was content to remain in this area. He would be back from the fort with his squadron of Dakota hunters in a few days.

* * *

The explorers curved northeast to the shore of Big Stone Lake. Here they made their last trail camp with Joseph Renville and shared the buffalo he had butchered. Come morning, the expedition would follow the Minnesota River downstream to Lac qui Parle.

When Fort Renville came into view, just before the next sunset, a swarm of whooping riders advanced to welcome their leader. Broad smiles on their faces and loud warmhearted greetings made it clear the Métis trader was a popular figure. He traded jovial wisecracks and laughter with the horsemen who provided a loose escort to the fort's main gate.

Approaching the stockade, Corporal Whitney was struck by its similarities and differences with Fort Snelling. This post, like his own, occupied a commanding position at the confluence of two rivers. Acres of surrounding fields and pastures were here to provide the residents with a balanced diet of vegetables and meat. Everyone dismounted outside the gate, where horses were unsaddled and released into a meadow for grazing.

The differences became more noticeable when Alex walked inside the walls of vertical logs—not limestone. Thirty forts of this size would fit inside the perimeter of Fort Snelling, and internal structures were built along just one wall rather than all four. The single centrally located watchtower with one armed sentry took the place of four, one on each corner of the stone citadel. Only now did he notice that all of the busy, non-uniformed residents of this fort had faces of color, not white.

While the race of people performing activities was different, the action was identical. The same tasks—farming, herding, cleaning, hauling—were being done with the same skill and energy. At that hour, a primary task was cooking, and the number of mouths to feed had just grown by five. Anxious faces peered at the hungry explorers from inside a building where smoke curled up from a chimney, and a delicious aroma emerged.

Just then, a teenage girl emerged from that doorway and sprinted to Renville, launching herself into his powerful embrace. "Daddy, we missed you!"

"And I missed you," he laughed, hoisting her over his shoulder like a haversack. "How's your mother?"

The girl squirmed out of her father's grasp but managed to twist herself upon his back, arms about his neck and legs around his waist. "Ha!" she exclaimed. "Mother is making supper."

Alex stopped, frozen in his tracks. Renville's daughter was the image of the Métis girl he remembered from Leech Lake—Angelique—her pretty face and lively voice, the slender body that moved with grace and agility. *I will remember you,* he thought.

"Well, let's go eat while it's hot." Renville's rough response startled the corporal from his recollection. He jumped to rejoin the others and filed into the trader's dining room.

The fort's Dakota inhabitants were politely curious to hear about the expedition and the forthcoming map to be drawn. However, they exploded with excitement when Renville told them about the nearby buffalo herd. "As quickly as we can muster, I will lead our hunters back to the Big Sioux River," he pledged.

"Tomorrow morning!" they shouted. From that moment until after dark, the stockade was alive with activity. People readied guns, powder and ammunition. They sharpened knives and packed provisions. Horses and tack were tended to and travois assembled. At first light of the following morning, Fort Renville was evacuated except for a small, essential crew. The hunting party moved across the Minnesota River and headed for the Coteau des Prairies.

The four remaining explorers exited downriver with nary a goodbye. Their weeklong return to Fort Snelling was over familiar terrain for them all. The last leg of their journey consisted of a quiet routine.

However, the reaction to Nicollet's map was anything but quiet routine. He and Lieutenant Fremont settled into Henry Sibley's new stone house to complete their cartography. The American Fur Company partner proclaimed, "This is the most complete and accurate depiction of frontier territory anywhere in North America. An invaluable tool for the fur trade."

Major Taliaferro declared the combination of Nicollet's map and journal to be a work of art. "The contour lines draw a picture, which is enhanced by your sketches and your written descriptions. I can envision these places, almost as if I had been there with you."

"Actions speak louder than words," Fremont stated, proudly holding a letter from the US Secretary of War. "Secretary Poinsett congratulates Papa Joe on this triumphant map of the Upper Mississippi River basin." Then, lifting the paper higher, "We have been awarded a new commission to begin mapping the Missouri River Valley toward the Canadian border next summer!"

Joseph Nicolas Nicollet (1786–1843)

Joseph Nicolas Nicollet was born in the western Alp region of Savoy in France. A brilliant mathematician and astronomer, he became a professor at the Paris Observatory and won a Legion of Honor medal.[50]

However, he lost favor in tumultuous French politics and lost his fortune in the stock market. Coming to America in search of a fresh start at age forty-six, Nicollet found employment as a mapmaker for the American Fur Company. Using Fort Snelling as a base between 1836 and 1839, he traveled up the Mississippi, St. Croix, Minnesota and Missouri Rivers. With the aid of a compass, telescope, sextant, chronometer, barometer and thermometer, he drew the most beautiful and accurate maps of his day. Nicollet's journals included sketches and notes of plant and animal life, in addition to descriptions of Native American people and culture, augmented the maps.[51]

Michael Barnes

He became a beloved character at Fort Snelling and in the homes of Henry Sibley and Major Lawrence Taliaferro. Cheerful and charming, he was an entertaining violinist and a source of fascinating conversation.[52]

Unfortunately, Nicollet suffered periodic bouts with malaria and other health issues that eventually ended his frontier adventures. He died in Washington, DC, at the age of fifty-seven.[53]

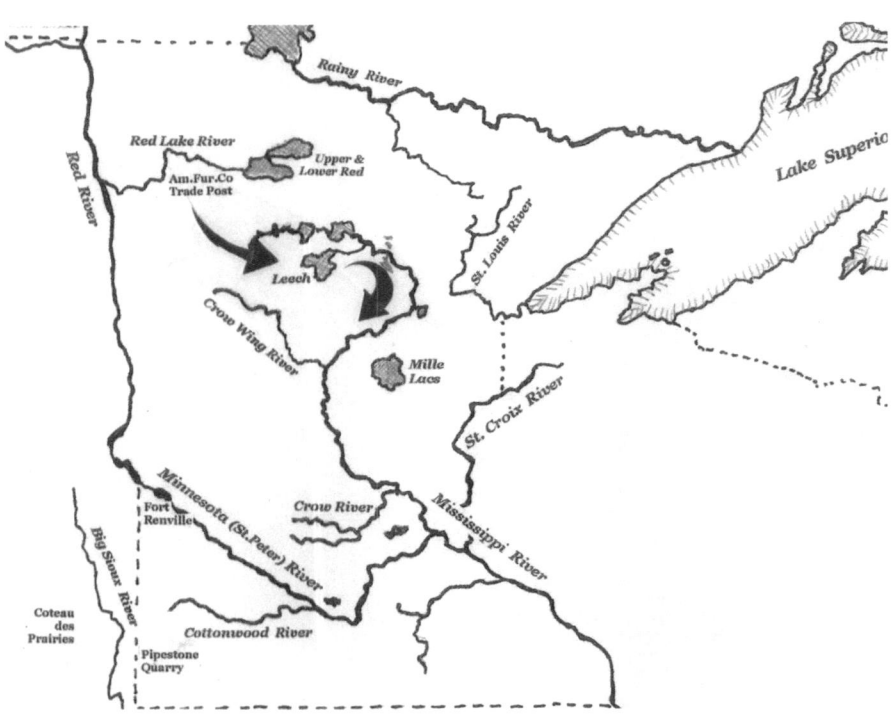

Chapter 13
1837 – The Woods Trail

Angelique's feelings about Pierre Bottineau were mixed. Since his courtship of her the previous summer, she was not sure what to expect from him this summer. Nor was she certain whether she desired his romantic attention or not. The Reaume family's approach to their second annual buffalo hunt had put her into emotional apprehension. However, the entire situation was resolved when they arrived at Pembina to the news that Pierre had taken a wife. Genevieve Larance, a Métis girl from Winnipeg, had become Mrs. Bottineau during the intervening winter.

The hunt was successful, as was her father's trading activity. The family was ready to travel home with a bountiful harvest of bison hides.

"Lucien and I will not take the hides to Fort Renville this year," explained Jean Baptiste. "Travelers up and down the Red River are sharing two pieces of news that will change our strategy."

White Loon's calm, quiet expression told Angelique that husband and wife had already agreed upon a new plan.

"First, we are told that passage on the Red River Trail is not safe. There has been violence between Ojibwe and Dakota warriors. Pierre and Sharlo believe that Métis people are also in danger, so we have acquired two horses and Red River carts from them. We will drive these carts, with our hides and supplies, overland from Pembina to our home on the Red Lake River."

"Is there a trail?" asked Luc.

"The path is old," his father began, "but not heavily traveled. Certainly not by Red River carts. The route will take time and effort, but it will move us away from the Dakota into the land of your mother's people."

White Loon nodded and reached her comforting arm around the shoulders of her younger daughter Gabrielle.

"That brings me to the second part of our plan," continued Jean Baptiste.

"Second part?" Angelique said.

"Yes. The other news is that Ojibwe bands from all of the northern forests are gathering at the soldier fort where the Mississippi and Minnesota rivers meet. The United States government wants to negotiate an agreement that would allow white people to settle on Native land. Your mother's brother, Flat Mouth, will be an important leader at that council."

"What does that have to do with us?" Luc inquired.

"As an American Fur Company trader, I should be there. Such a treaty may have an effect on my business. Speaking of my business," he smiled, "while there, I will sell these bison hides at the trading post beside Fort Snelling. We should get a better price there than we did last year at Fort Renville."

"We?" Lucien's face was bright with anticipation for such a journey.

"We," his father confirmed. "All of us. We will stop at home for a few days to tend our garden, repair any damage that may have been done by weather or critters, and sleep in our own beds."

"We will need the rest," White Loon predicted.

Jean Baptiste continued, "Then we will drive our carts from the *Old Crossing,* through the woods, to the Pillager Band village on Leech Lake. I hope that we will arrive to join Flat Mouth before his delegation has departed. I intend to leave the carts and horses at the village until our return. The buffalo hides can be transferred into canoes for the remainder of our journey to Fort Snelling."

Twisting Trails

Fort Snelling, Angelique remembered. *That is where the young soldier lives...Alex.*

* * *

White Loon was right. The Reaume family needed to rest. So did the horses. It took five days of hard work to travel from Pembina to their home on Red Lake River. The garden was in desperate need of weeding, but they were able to harvest some early-ripened potatoes, carrots and onions. Most of the vegetables were stored in their glaciere of ice blocks. However, some were eaten along with dried meat from the cool cellar. The family enjoyed two days of tasty and nourishing food, as well as two restful nights in their own cabin.

Another journey of several days lay ahead. Children and parents alike were rejuvenated. Occasionally one of them rode on horseback for a few miles, but they also led the animals when fording streams and helped to push the carts through boggy ground. Now into the forest, they encountered some deadfall trees that needed to be chopped or dragged out of their path. In spite of the physical hardships, their family spirit was high, and all regarded the trek as more of an adventure than a burden. At last, they reached the shores of Leech Lake in the early afternoon of the fifth day.

White Loon's family was delighted by their arrival, and Flat Mouth was pleased that Jean Baptiste would accompany the Pillagers to Fort Snelling, "I am glad that a family friend of the Ojibwe will be with us, to better understand the words of the whites."

"Your words of wisdom are better than mine," admitted the voyageur, "but I am a good listener. I will honestly share what I can learn from the fur company leaders and the government officials."

Angelique's grandmother welcomed the Reaume family into her lodge and began to consider how she might feed five additional mouths. But within the hour, a young warrior appeared, with a whitetail doe for their supper. "I, Young Buffalo, offer this deer to feed the family of Angelique Reaume."

Grandmother beckoned the girl out the door of her wigwam, so that she might express gratitude for the gift. He was a powerfully built young man. Short, but standing boldly upright, he held the small doe across both forearms. A bow and quiver of arrows were crisscrossed behind his naked torso. He wore a breechcloth with some quill and beadwork above buckskin leggings and moccasins. "I, Young Buffalo, bring this gift for you and your family."

He stepped forward and extended the deer to Angelique.

"Thank you," was all she could think to say. She awkwardly received the doe into her arms. Young Buffalo pivoted and walked proudly away.

A blank expression was on the girl's face when she turned back to the lodge entrance. Her grandmother burst into a wide grin, which she quickly covered to stifle a giggle. "He is speaking for you."

"What does that mean?"

White Loon appeared at the doorway. "It means that he wants to spend time with you. The gift of this deer is a request for your father and me to grant permission."

"Who is he?"

Grandmother responded, "Young Buffalo is a respected young man. A skillful hunter and already considered a strong warrior." Angelique's gaze shifted to watch the young man walk away.

When Jean Baptiste and Lucien returned from Flat Mouth's lodge, they butchered the deer, and it provided a delicious meal. They gave the hide to Grandmother. "We will not have time to care for this during our trip downriver," reasoned the voyageur.

"The doeskin will make a fine dress for Angelique," the elder woman stated. Then, with a tilt of her gray-haired head, she asked, "What are you going to do about her admirer?"

The father cast a sweeping look for his daughter, stopping instead on White Loon with whom he shared a questioning stare. "We have some time to think about that," he sighed. "Our trip to Fort Snelling will not bring us back here for two or three weeks."

Twisting Trails

Grandmother's eyes twinkled. "Hah!" she laughed. "Young Buffalo is a member of Flat Mouth's war party. He too will attend the treaty council at the whites' army fort."

At breakfast the next morning, the family shared more of the fresh venison. They talked about preparations for the next stage of their journey. Jean Baptiste noticed a young man who carried a birchbark canoe on his shoulders, prompting him to say, "I must make arrangements for someone to provide care for our horses until we return. Then we will need three canoes to carry us, our camp supplies, and these bundles of buffalo hides."

In a few moments, it became evident the canoe carrier was headed their way. He stopped a few steps from the breakfast campfire and lowered the craft smoothly to the ground. Then straightened his tall and slender frame back to full height.

"I am The Big Cloud," he announced. "I offer the gift of this canoe to the Reaume family."

"Your canoe looks strong and fast," Jean Baptiste complimented the young man. "We will be happy to use it for our adventure. We will give it back when we return."

The young man's handsome face wrinkled with hesitation. His eyes darted to Angelique and back to her father, "The canoe is my gift," he insisted. "It would be my pleasure to paddle it downriver with your daughter as my passenger. Flat Mouth has asked me to help defend the Pillager Band on this journey."

Jean Baptiste's eyes widened as he realized the motivation behind The Big Cloud's gift. His daughter had another suitor. "Thank you," he said. Then after a pause, he dodged the young man's suggestion, "I will speak with Flat Mouth about the order of our procession down the Mississippi River."

Again, the warrior's dark eyes moved to Angelique, but this time he did not look away. His admiring focus made her nervous, but she did not look aside. Finally, he smiled, said "goodbye" to her father, and strode away. While watching him depart, she noticed a girl standing just beyond, near the trees. It was Wind on the Water.

She has been watching, thought Angelique.

Is it my imagination, or is she angry? Then her cousin whirled around and marched away.

* * *

Alex was happy to be working with Sergeant Schmid again, if only for a few days. It was time to put new shoes on Fort Snelling's horse herd. A job for more than one blacksmith. Bill was the expert with horses, so he did most of the work with the animals' hooves while Alex handled the iron shoes.

The sergeant wore a set of heavy leather chaps to protect his legs, which looked worn enough to have come from Germany with the old blacksmith. He cradled each hoof between his knees, cleaning and shaving the underside, trimming and filing the edges before nailing on the new or re-shaped shoe. The corporal, half Schmid's age, kept the coals hot in their portable forge. He hammered each iron shoe against the anvil, molding it according to the sergeant's instructions.

They made an excellent team. Both were skillful, hard-working artisans. But their affection for one another made communication easy. Each could anticipate the other's need before a required request, almost like father and son.

They worked outside the blacksmith shop close to the main gate, where a pair of assisting soldiers could walk horses to and from their location with ease. Alex smiled when he saw Justice being led forward. The Morgan knew him from Nicollet's mapping expedition and some shorter jaunts since then. Corporal Whitney took a break from the anvil to greet the chestnut gelding and stroke his neck a few times.

Meanwhile, Sergeant Schmid was struggling to clean the left rear hoof of a nervous black mare. The young horse was agitated, bobbing its head against the halter rope and shifting her three feet on the ground. Suddenly she jerked the elevated leg from between the old blacksmith's knees. He tried to stay on his feet but would have been luckier had he fallen flat on the ground. The mare bucked and kicked both hind feet backward.

Alex turned just in time to see one hoof slam into Schmid's back.

"Bill!" he shouted and rushed forward.

The hoof had struck the sergeant's right rear rib cage and knocked him airborne a few feet, landing on his chest. He slid in the dust, which was still settling when the young corporal knelt by his side, "Bill, are you all right?"

Schmid's eyes were clenched shut in obvious pain. He gasped for a breath and groaned.

Alex twisted around to see one of the assisting soldiers standing frozen with wide eyes. "Private, go get Doc Emerson!" The soldier scrambled toward the fort hospital, which was just around the corner, and Alex bent back over his friend.

Within minutes the doctor came jogging with a small bag of instruments in his hand to the fallen blacksmith. He was followed by the private and a Black man who carried an army stretcher. Doc Emerson asked Alex, "Can you tell me what happened?"

The corporal tried to quickly describe how and where Sergeant Schmid had been struck by the mare's hoof. The doctor gently lifted the older man's shirt to reveal an ugly, hoof-shaped wound. It was deep red in color, but the skin was only slightly torn where the leading edge of the hoof had hit. Doc Emerson placed his stethoscope on Schmid's back, listening to sounds from inside the chest. Then began pressing his fingers onto the blacksmith's ribs. That immediately produced a flinch and a gasp from the prone patient.

"Sergeant Schmid," the doctor communicated, "we're going to move you onto this stretcher and carry you to the hospital." Bill did not speak but gave a slight nod of acknowledgment. The Black man deftly unfolded the stretcher and laid it alongside the sergeant.

"Thanks, Dred," said the Doc. "Now, you and I will get our hands under him from this side while the corporal and the private lift from his other side."

They smoothly transferred the injured blacksmith onto the stretcher. Then each man grabbed one end of a stretcher pole, and they carried Sergeant Schmid to the fort hospital.

Dr. Emerson cut Bill's shirt open and began a more thorough examination. "Corporal Whitney, you can wait in the next room," he directed.

Alex sat down on a stiff wooden chair, but the Black man stayed busy. He folded the stretcher and stood it in a corner. Then grabbed a broom and began sweeping dust toward the door. The corporal asked him, "Did I hear Doc call you Dred?"

"Yes, sir. Dred Scott is my name." The man had a trim physique and a clean-shaven face that seemed full of curiosity.

Recognizing the man was not wearing an army uniform, Alex inquired, "Do you work here?"

"I am Dr. Emerson's slave. I work wherever he takes me. We been to forts in Missouri and Illinois and now here."

"I have never met a slave."

"Well, I never been nuthin' but a slave," Dred replied. "Here, I'm a janitor, a fix-it man. I clean the Doc's medical instruments, run errands, chop firewood. Whatever needs doin'."

Just then, the Black maid, whom Alex remembered from Taliaferro's house, appeared at the doorway. She smiled and presented Dred with a stack of clean and folded laundry. "Thanks, Harriet," Scott offered. "You havin' a good day?"

"I finished cleaning Dr. Emerson's quarters and washed this laundry. Now I'm going to do some housekeeping for Mrs. Taliaferro. I'll see you back home for supper." Then she kissed Dred on the cheek and whisked out the door.

The Black man saw a curious look on Corporal Whitney's face. "Hah!" he laughed. "That's my wife, Harriet."

Alex turned his head to where the young woman had disappeared. Then swiveled back to face Dred Scott. He lifted one eyebrow.

"Yeah," the slave chuckled, "she's fifteen years younger than me." He began stacking the clean hospital laundry onto a shelf. "She was a house slave to the Major and Mrs. Taliaferro when I came here with Doc Emerson. We took a liking to each other, and she agreed to get hitched. The Major, bein' a justice of the peace, he married us and sold Harriet to the Doc so we could be together."

Twisting Trails

Then, the examination room door opened, and Dr. Emerson beckoned, "Corporal Whitney, you can come in." Sergeant Schmid was laying on his back now, with a wrap all the way around his torso. His head was propped up on a pillow, and his eyes were open.

"You could call that black mare a widow maker," Bill offered a weak smile, "exceptin' I'm not married."

Alex was relieved. "You're not dead either!" The jokes provoked the beginning of a laugh from the blacksmith that abruptly ended with a painful cough.

"No, he's not dead," interrupted the doctor with a weary frown. "The sergeant has some cracked ribs that will be painful for a while. He should remain in bed today and refrain from shoeing horses until he gets my permission." Glaring directly at Bill, he warned, "If you cough up any blood, send for me immediately. Otherwise, come back day after tomorrow."

* * *

On their second day from Leech Lake, Angelique's parents had granted permission for her to paddle a canoe with The Big Cloud. His long limbs produced powerful oar strokes, and they gradually pulled in front of the dozen Pillager canoes. He remained relatively quiet during the morning, speaking only about sights along the river and obstacles, rocks and submerged branches that posed a threat to their birchbark hull. Later, when they reached the Grand Rapids, he became more talkative.

The portage trail around the rapids was three and a half miles long. The Big Cloud burdened his back with both big bundles of buffalo hides, asking Angelique to carry only her own provisions. They hoisted the canoe upside down on their shoulders and began the hike.

"What is it like to be the daughter of a trader?" he asked. The question spurred a walking conversation that enabled both of them to share stories about their families.

At the end of the portage, The Big Cloud backtracked with the intention of transporting more Reaume family baggage. However, Young Buffalo had beaten him to the task. He met his rival coming down the path, carrying two packs of bison hides. The other warrior did not speak, but the cocky smile on his face said, *You're too late!* Nonetheless, The Big Cloud ventured farther to lighten the load for White Loon.

Back on the water, they paddled at a more leisurely pace, but Angelique noticed their canoe was steered beyond the hearing distance of Young Buffalo. Her relaxed conversation with The Big Cloud continued, allowing each of them to reveal more of themselves. She thought he was less sure of himself than he portrayed. *Did she like him?*

The flotilla pulled ashore for supper inside a river bend where a sandy beach extended out from the trees to water's edge. No sooner was the meal concluded when Young Buffalo approached the Reaume campfire.

He addressed Jean Baptiste, "With your permission, I would take Angelique for an evening walk."

She would have preferred to rest her weary muscles. But not wishing to insult the young man, she nodded when her father looked to her for an indication of approval.

They ventured along the riverbank. The setting sun still brightly lit the aspens, maples and ash trees on the opposite shore. Their leaves fluttered when exposed to occasional gusts of the western breeze, but only slivers of sunlight filtered through where the young couple walked. The air was still and quiet, making Young Buffalo's silence even more noticeable.

"I brought my bow," he announced after a distance, motioning to the weapon on his back beside a quiver of arrows, "to protect you."

"Thank you." It was evident to Angelique that he was nervous in her company. She sought to lighten the mood, "We might also find some wild game for you to shoot."

The ice was broken. "I'm an excellent hunter," he boasted. "No family of mine will ever go hungry." Then, snatching an arrow from the quiver, he said, "Let me show you." He drew the bow, feather fletch of the arrow beneath his right eye, "See the fungus on the trunk of that aspen?" *Swish. Thunk!* He released the arrow, and it pierced the fungus in the blink of an eye. Young Buffalo bounded the twenty-five-foot distance and wrenched his arrow out of the tree. He proudly spun around and held it aloft for Angelique to see. She smiled and clapped her hands to show appreciation.

The remainder of their evening walk confirmed for Angelique that this was a man of action rather than words. He spoke very little but bent saplings out of her way, gripped her hand up an embankment, and offered to lift her over fallen trees. He was attentive and desperate to impress her but was not a smooth talker. She believed he was a person of good intentions, at times too quick to act and often misunderstood. *Did she understand him?*

The next day, Angelique was happy to be in the bow of her mother's canoe, cruising downstream. Gabrielle was in the front of her father's canoe, and Lucien had joined The Big Cloud. Additional water flow from joining tributaries swelled the Mississippi and provided a more powerful current. Sandy Lake was thirty miles ahead, but they would easily get there by dusk.

Her uncle, Flat Mouth, hoped their Pillager Band would unite with Hole-in-the-Day's Sandy Lake Band at William Aitken's trading post tonight. Perhaps other Ojibwe leaders from Fond du Lac and Red Cedar Lake would be there too.

The attention Angelique received from her two suitors the previous day had worn her out. Both of the young Leech Lake warriors were kind and attentive to her. But their constant attempts to impress her and compete with each other were too much too quickly. She was overwhelmed. White Loon broached the subject between paddle strokes, "What do you think about Young Buffalo and The Big Cloud?"

"They are very different," she replied. "Young Buffalo is impulsive. A strong warrior who will be fierce in battle and work hard to provide for a family. He is not merry and outgoing like father, but I think he has a big heart."

"What about The Big Cloud?"

"He is a thinker. Perhaps a leader," offered Angelique. "He has the handsome face and smooth words for that role. I believe he is more of a peacemaker than a warrior."

"Perhaps it should not matter," began White Loon, "but Grandmother shared with me that The Big Cloud was once expected to marry your cousin, Wind on the Water."

The girl rested her paddle across the gunwales and twisted back to see her mother, "What happened?"

"She did not say."

Angelique remembered the day her cousin was watching when The Big Cloud gave a canoe to Jean Baptiste. *Now it made sense. Wind on the Water was jealous.*

That night when the Ojibwe Bands gathered at Sandy Lake, they held a festive feast.

Two days later, the flotilla grew larger when groups from Mille Lacs and Gull Lake joined near the confluence with the Crow Wing River. Angelique continued to spend time with both her suitors. However, they and her father were increasingly busy with obligations to Flat Mouth. The band leaders held council every night in anticipation of the forthcoming treaty negotiations at Fort Snelling.

* * *

A successful afternoon of fishing had landed a dozen walleye fillets into the frying pan at Henry Sibley's house. He had endured a steady drizzle on the Minnesota River with fellow anglers John Charles Fremont and Alex. However, the fish were biting so well they caught enough for their meal in a couple of hours. Now they were warm and dry in front of a crackling fireplace, seated around Sibley's dining table with Joseph Nicollet.

The French scientist opted out of fishing in the rain, but he had been busy in the kitchen, preparing sliced carrots and green beans, sautéed in butter with onions. Sibley lifted his glass in a toast, "My compliments to the chef!"

"You men did the hard work, fishing in the rain," countered Nicollet. "I am merely your humble servant." He tipped his glass to the others, and they all took a drink.

"Speaking of servants," Corporal Whitney began, "I met a slave last week, Dred Scott. He works for Dr. Emerson in the fort hospital."

Twisting Trails

"Doc Emerson is a southerner," responded Sibley. "Several of the southern officers have brought slaves here to Fort Snelling over the years. Like Major Taliaferro from Virginia, he and his wife have a slave girl at the Indian Agency."

"Yes, Harriet," Alex added. "I met her too. She's married to Dred Scott, and now Doc Emerson owns them both."

Nicollet spoke up, "Help me understand American law," he requested. "We are in a free US territory. How is it legal for anyone to keep a slave whom they have brought here from a slave state?"

"Because slavery is legal in those southern states," Fremont tried to explain. "I grew up in Georgia and Carolina. I never owned a slave and don't intend to, but Major Taliaferro and Doc Emerson bought those slaves in the south. They believe that Dred Scott and his wife are their property, and they've got bills of sale to prove it."

"It's not a settled legal debate," Sibley interjected. "My father is a judge in Michigan, and I've studied some law. I expect a man in Dred Scott's position might someday file a lawsuit to gain his freedom. He could argue that he cannot be a slave in a state or territory where slavery is illegal. A case like that might be appealed all the way to the US Supreme Court."

The men took a few bites in silence before Nicollet spoke up again, "What are your opinions about our Native race of people?"

"My opinion has turned upside-down since coming here," Corporal Whitney admitted. "My father was killed in the War of 1812." He paused, then said, "Tecumseh's federation of Native tribes fought on the side of British troops in that war, against American citizens and the US Army. Folks in Detroit, where I grew up, have not forgotten that. Most have not forgiven that."

"He's right," Sibley agreed. "I'm from Detroit too."

"But since arriving here, I have come to know many Native people—Dakota and Ojibwe, male and female. Almost everyone is a good person. Some are my friends."

Lieutenant Fremont raised a warning, "I'm afraid the majority of Americans are not ready to forget and forgive. Congress passed the Indian Removal Act, and our commander in chief, Andrew

Jackson, signed it into law. Now, our fellow soldiers in the US Army are escorting tribes to Oklahoma Territory from their native lands east of the Mississippi River."

"The Trail of Tears," lamented Nicollet.

"I have heard a rumor which may affect the garrison of troops at Fort Snelling," reported Fremont. "In Florida, the Seminole tribe is refusing to be removed. Their leader Osceola is waging a war of rebellion that, so far, he is winning. Army scuttlebutt says that Colonel Zachary Taylor will be designated to vanquish Osceola the way he did Black Hawk five years ago."

"My father served under Taylor in the War of 1812," revealed Alex, "and he was in command at Fort Snelling when I first arrived here."

"Well, you may get your chance to serve under him again," Fremont suggested. "If he gets that command, word is he'll bring his old regiment, Fort Snelling's first infantry, to do the fighting."

Combat, the corporal thought. *I hope I'm ready.*

After a few more mouthfuls of walleye and vegetables, Nicollet broke the silence again, "Times are changing fast in America," he stated. "Just during my five years on this continent, I have seen a rapid increase of white population into the West."

"And a corresponding rapid decrease of animal population," commented Sibley. "Regretfully, Native hunters and trappers are struggling more and more to find wild game on this frontier. I fear that my years as an American Fur Company trader are coming to an end."

"As are the years for Dakota and Ojibwe people," said the Frenchman, "for life as they know it."

"Well, life as they know it is going to change in a few days," confirmed Sibley. "Leaders from all of the tribal bands in the territory are converging here for treaty talks with Governor Henry Dodge."

"Change how?" Alex asked.

"I hear politicians in Washington, DC, want to buy all their land east of the Mississippi River."

DRED SCOTT (1799–1858)

Dred Scott was born into slavery in Virginia. No exact date for his birth is recorded but believed to be in 1799. The Blow family took him in bondage to other residences in Alabama and Missouri, where he was sold to US Army surgeon Dr. John Emerson.[54]

Scott moved with Dr. Emerson to an assignment in Illinois and then to Fort Snelling in 1837. There, he met his future wife, Harriet Robinson, a slave owned by Major Lawrence Taliaferro, the Indian Agent at Fort Snelling. Taliaferro conducted the marriage ceremony and then sold Harriet to Dr. Emerson so the couple could live together.[55]

The Scott's moved with Emerson to military forts in Louisiana and Missouri. Four children were born to the couple, two daughters and two sons, although both boys died in infancy. After Emerson's death, they attempted to buy the family's freedom, but the doctor's widow denied it. Then in 1846, they filed a lawsuit through the courts, claiming their extended residence in free states and territories made them free.[56]

Michael Barnes

The Dred Scott case moved from Missouri state courts to the US Supreme Court over a period of eleven years. The justices ruled 7-2 against the Scotts, writing in 1857 that African slaves and their descendants did not qualify for US citizenship.[57]

Dr. Emerson's widow remarried an abolitionist who arranged to free the Scott family two months after the Supreme Court's ruling. But the *Dred Scott* decision sparked explosive controversy during the decade that led to the American Civil War.[58]

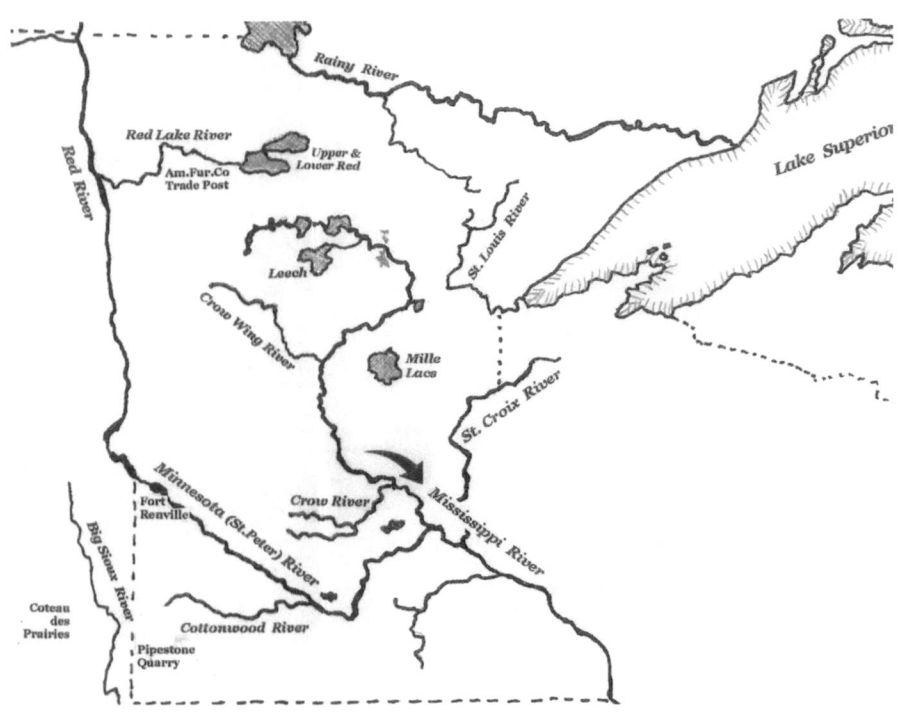

Chapter 14
1837 – Mendota

Knock. Knock. Knock. A rap on the door interrupted the walleye dinner in Henry Sibley's house. The host stood up and crossed to the entry, "Good evening. How can I help you?" Alex could see from the dining table through the doorway a short, muscular, bearded man wearing buckskin clothing.

"Perhaps you do not remember me," greeted the visitor. "I am Jean Baptiste Reaume, an American Fur Company trader from the Red Lake River."

"Of course!" Sibley reacted. "Now I recognize you." He stepped outside to shake the man's hand.

Reaume? Red Lake River? Those names brought back a memory for Alex. *Could this be Angelique's father?* The corporal got up and walked out the door. He heard Sibley's guest talk about buffalo hides, and he saw a teenage boy approaching with a large bundle of hides on his back. It had stopped raining, Alex noticed. A colorful sunset was forming across the river, and a rainbow appeared above. Beneath the rainbow, he saw three females standing beside canoes, drawn up onto the shore. *It's her.*

The fur traders' conversation turned into a muddled murmur to the corporal's ears. He drifted down the path, aware of nothing but the girl in front of him. "I remember you," he said. "Angelique."

Her face broke into a broad smile, "Alex," she remembered. "I wondered if I would see you here." It had been five years. She was pretty as he remembered. But a young woman now, not a girl.

The traders and the teenage boy arrived beside the canoes. Corporal Whitney explained how he had met Angelique with her mother and sister during the Schoolcraft expedition. After a round of introductions, the men proceeded to haul Jean Baptiste's buffalo hides into Sibley's trading post.

"We traveled down the Mississippi with Flat Mouth's Pillager Band to attend the treaty negotiations," explained Reaume. He pointed across the Minnesota River to Pike Island, where Ojibwe tribesmen had gone ashore. "May we camp there, below the fort?"

"They can," Sibley answered, "but you and your family should stay here with me. I have room. And your wife can use my kitchen to prepare meals."

While the two traders agreed on that arrangement, Alex spoke with Angelique. "I would be happy to give you a tour of the area," he proposed.

Receiving her mother's consent, she replied, "I would like that." And they agreed upon the following morning.

* * *

While looking through a window of Sibley's house, Angelique saw Alex paddle a canoe up to the shoreline. She quickly told her mother that the soldier had arrived and hurried out to meet him on the path. He was wearing his army uniform.

"We mustered for assembly this morning," he said, gesturing to his dark blue shirt and light blue trousers, "and then ate breakfast. Have you had anything to eat?"

"Oh yes," she answered. "Mr. Sibley gave us eggs. He and father have already gone to speak with Ojibwe leaders." She pointed across the river to Pike Island.

Then the door opened. White Loon took one step out and waved, "Thank you for washing the dishes."

Her daughter returned the wave and swiveled toward the river, "Let's go." They settled into the canoe and began paddling. It was no more than half a mile around Pike Island, down to the confluence of the two mighty rivers. A steep bluff rose to their left. Angelique's gaze rose higher and higher to Fort Snelling's imposing stone walls almost a hundred feet above.

"I know," spoke the corporal, recognizing her amazement. "It was just as awesome to me when I arrived here six years ago." They swerved ashore near the confluence near a landing marked by evidence of many previous arrivals and departures. Only then did she notice a road that angled upward beneath the fort's sunlit southeastern wall.

As they began hiking up the road, Alex described how the army had built the fort more than a decade earlier, using local limestone blocks. But Angelique was thinking that he looked a little different. Older, of course, and perhaps more muscular. He had the same long limbs and vigorous stride. His face was slightly fuller but just as handsome. And his voice contained the same hint of kindness. *Perhaps,* she thought, *it's the uniform.*

The corporal paused at the top of the road where a wide plateau stretched to the north and west. Pointing across to Major Taliaferro's stone dwelling and the Council House, he stated, "That's the Indian Agency, where I am assigned."

Again, Angelique was barely listening to his words. Instead, she rotated to face the fort's intimidating rocky walls and the symbols of military might above. Sentries with muskets on their shoulders patrolled the ominous stone towers. Menacing cannon barrels were visible above the barricades, and the walls themselves were spaced with narrow openings from which guns could be fired.

Alex sensed her discomfort, "There is some beautiful scenery around here," he commented while sweeping his arm toward the landscape. "Unfortunately, most of those places are too far to walk."

Noticing a pasture of livestock to the north, Angelique inquired, "Could we ride?"

"Horses?" Alex had presumed she could not ride. "I have never seen a horse in an Ojibwe village."

"I am Métis," she stated proudly. "I have ridden with the buffalo hunters!"

"Let's do it!" he exclaimed. Just inside the fort's main entry, the corporal collected saddles and bridles for two mounts. Then they walked to the pasture gate where he beckoned to Justice. The chestnut gelding came trotting to him with a whinny. Alex recognized a dun-colored mare that he knew to be gentle and saddled her for Angelique.

Within minutes, they were cantering westward toward the Indian Agency. Relaxed, on horseback and away from the sinister fort, the girl let loose a shriek of delight. Mrs. Taliaferro greeted their arrival at the agency, "Hi, Alex," she smiled. "You have missed the major. He has gone to welcome the Ojibwe leaders and invite all of them to the Council House tonight."

"Sorry I missed him," expressed the corporal. "Please tell the major I will be back later."

Eliza acknowledged his riding partner with a grin, "Who is this lovely lady?"

"Pardon my manners," he apologized. "This is Angelique Reaume. Her father is an American Fur Company trader from Red Lake River here for the treaty talks. I met her during my travel to Lake Itasca with Schoolcraft."

"Alex is showing me around this area," said Angelique.

"You are a lucky girl," declared the major's wife. "Corporal Whitney is a nice young man. My husband considers him an extremely capable soldier. Potentially an officer."

Both young people blushed modestly. The corporal gave Mrs. Taliaferro a quick salute and tugged the reins to wheel Justice around. As the horses walked away from the house, Alex pointed to the blacksmith shop where he made and repaired metal objects for Native people.

Then, indicating the Council House, he told Angelique her father would meet there later with Major Taliaferro and the Ojibwe leaders.

Angling northwest away from the Agency, the pair propelled their horses into an easy lope. Alex was impressed with Angelique's horsemanship. *She is a graceful rider,* he thought, *as she is at everything else.* Her long black hair fluttered behind as she bounded in rhythm with each stride. They passed a field of crops where a squad of soldiers was busy hoeing weeds, hot work that would get hotter as the July sun arched higher in the sky.

A few miles ahead, they approached Lake Nokomis. Dismounting, they walked their horses along the shore. "You must have seen the Falls of St. Anthony when you canoed down the Mississippi."

"Yes, we stopped to watch the waterfall when we portaged around it," she responded. "Powerful and beautiful."

"I can show you another waterfall. Minnehaha Falls is smaller but just as pretty."

"Let's go."

They remounted and trotted their horses northeast to intersect with the growing stream that flowed out of the lake, toward the Mississippi. Within fifteen minutes, they could begin to hear the sound of rushing water. Alex followed a trail that circled to the right around the waterfall and came back to a bluff below the cascade. Several separate rivulets of water were spilling over the cliff of Minnehaha Falls—some trickling, some gushing. The spilling streams ricocheted down over rocky ledges, splattering into a swirling pool more than thirty feet below.

From there, the creek continued to shoot rapidly away. Water splashed over and around boulders in the brook. It rushed beneath their vantage point and tumbled downhill, out of sight beneath the branches of overhanging trees.

Angelique shouted to be heard over the plunging stream, "It's loud!" But the delighted smile on her face revealed her enjoyment of the noisy spectacle.

"It's less than a mile from here down to the Mississippi," Alex described, "but really steep, with a lot of loose stones. Probably not good for our horses."

They remained on the bluff and beheld the waterfall for quite a while. Finally, Angelique turned away, and they weaved out of the trees. Gradually, the sound of surging water faded behind them. "It's about two miles back to the fort," commented the corporal.

"We'll get a drink for ourselves and our horses about halfway there."

They came to a trail descending toward the Mississippi, down which he reined Justice, "This is Coldwater Spring. The water here is cool and clear." Both of them knelt where the groundwater bubbled from an exposed face of limestone. They scooped handfuls of the refreshing liquid to their lips.

"Ooh! This is good!"

"Water wagons commute between here and the garrison every day," Alex told her. "It's better than water from the fort's well."

After the horses drank from a pool beneath the spring, their riders climbed back aboard and headed up the homeward trail. Alex was reluctant for this scenery tour with Angelique to end, but it was nearly midday.

* * *

The horses were unsaddled at the pasture gate and turned loose to graze. Alex and Angelique strolled to Fort Snelling's main gate, where the corporal entered to return the saddles and bridles. When Alex came back out, the Métis girl was facing away from him. He walked up beside her to find her looking toward a broad open field near the Indian Agency, where a scattered crowd of people shouted and ran across the distant field.

"Lacrosse!" she declared.

The corporal looked to her with a quizzical expression. Before he could ask, "What did you say?" or "What are they doing?" she raced to the field. She was fast! He did not catch up until she came to a halt beside a group of onlookers. Alex recognized that the Major and Mrs. Taliaferro were standing there, as well as Angelique's family and numerous others.

Out on the field, he recognized several Dakota boys and men from local villages. He concluded that many of the others were visiting Ojibwe warriors. In mass, they formed a swarming mob of forty or fifty. A few wore buckskin trousers, but most were nearly naked except for their breechcloths. All of them seemed to be chasing a little ball while carrying sticks three to four feet in length. The body contact among them was violent, and some struck the others with the sticks.

Alex turned to the Métis girl expecting to see a grim look on her face. Instead, he found an expression of delighted excitement. "Go, Lucien!" she shrieked while clapping her hands and bouncing on her feet.

"What is going on?" he shouted.

"It's lacrosse," she proclaimed. "That ball is deer hide stitched tightly around a packing of hair. The players can only touch the ball with their sticks, not hands, and the goal is to knock that ball into their enemies' post." She pointed to a pair of vertical logs planted into opposite ends of the field.

"They're using their hands on each other!" blurted Alex when one powerful warrior bowled over another. Rather than explain, Angelique merely looked at him and burst out laughing.

The girl's mother saw the young soldier's bewilderment. She came alongside him, "Lacrosse is a Native game that our young men play for fun and to ready themselves for actual warfare. This is a contest between Ojibwe and Dakota warriors. The winners will carry away those two deer." White Loon pointed toward a pair of whitetail carcasses laid off to the side.

"How will they know who wins?" the corporal asked.

"They agreed that the first team to score twice will be the winner," she answered, pointing at one of the goal logs. "But so far, neither side has hit a post."

Angelique watched her brother. Lucien was younger and less skilled than most of the competitors, but his enjoyment of the game was evident in the frequent flashes of joy on his face. He was knocked down repeatedly, once so violently that he tumbled a complete somersault. He scrambled to his feet each time and barreled back into the fray.

As the game continued, the Ojibwe scored a point, countered soon after by one for the Dakota. Angelique noticed that her suitor Young Buffalo began to concentrate on defending the Ojibwe

215

post. Though short, he was indeed powerful. Each time a Dakota challenger broke free near their goal, the stout warrior sent him reeling with a shoulder block. Of course, the collisions knocked the ball loose. Usually first to the errant ball, Young Buffalo would swing his stick to whack it toward the field's opposite end. His stick had no pocket in which to carry a ball; it was simply a mallet.

The Big Cloud's stick did have a pocket. The narrower tip of his stick was bent into a circle, held in place by a web of sinew. He could scoop the ball off the ground and run while cradling it in that pocket. Oh, how he could run! Those long slender legs covered a lot of ground with each stride.

Angelique watched as Young Buffalo bashed into another Dakota man. The opponent sprawled in one direction while the ball bounced another. The Ojibwe defender pounced quickly and smacked the ball with a mighty *thwack*! His clout launched the ball into a long high arc, above and beyond the heads of everyone else.

"Yeah!" shouted Angelique, and then she noticed the fastest competitor to react was The Big Cloud. He whirled around and accelerated away from the pack while most were still trying to change direction. His long smooth strides became briefly choppy when he bent to dig the ball from the tall grass. That hesitation allowed one swift pursuer to draw near. The rival reached to grab The Big Cloud's shoulder, but he broke free by flailing that arm. Still a step behind, the Dakota swung his stick, aiming to chop down on the ball-carrying arm. However, the sprinting Ojibwe glanced back to see the swing coming and switched his stick to the other hand. In one final, diving effort the chasing enemy lunged to swipe at the fleet warrior's flying feet. He clipped one heel, causing a stumble, but it was too late. One more faltering stride carried The Big Cloud within falling distance of his foe's goal. He reached his stick forward as he collapsed and stabbed the ball into the post.

Before the hero could lift himself up, jubilant comrades engulfed him. Fifty yards behind, the other hero, Young Buffalo, was also surrounded by teammates. They pointed their sticks at each other. The man who clouted the winning pass lifted his club-headed stick in tribute to the scorer. That scorer turned back to recognize the passer with an aim of his pocket-headed stick.

Together, Ojibwe lacrosse players and onlookers, including the Reaume family, gave a cheer for their worthy Dakota adversaries. Then they converged on the two deer carcasses and started their march down to Pike Island for a victory feast. Angelique remembered to wave goodbye to her tour guide before parading away, flanked by the two heroes.

* * *

Eliza Taliaferro saw Alex standing alone, watching the Ojibwe move away. "Corporal Whitney," she called, "come have supper with the major and me. We have plenty to eat."

He knew that her supper would be far tastier than whatever was being served at the fort. Furthermore, he was expected to be at the Council House that evening when Ojibwe leaders returned to talk about the proposed treaty. "Thank you, ma'am. That will be wonderful."

The corporal asked for a basin of water and washed up before entering the Taliaferro's house. At the dinner table, Eliza gave him a suspicious look and commented,

"That was a pretty girl with you today."

Alex detected that her remark contained not only the statement but also a question.

"She is Métis," he began, explaining that Angelique's mother was Ojibwe and father a French-Canadian fur trader. He described again meeting her at Leech Lake while accompanying the Schoolcraft expedition. After a pause, he agreed, "Yes, she is pretty."

Mrs. Taliaferro revealed a subtle smile and exchanged a sly glance with her husband.

"Colonel Henry Dodge arrived at Fort Snelling today," the major told Alex. "As the territorial Governor, he will speak on behalf of the US Government at tomorrow's treaty talks."

"Will he be here tonight?"

"No, but I spoke with him at Major Bliss's quarters," replied the Indian Agent. "I will be able to share most of our government's proposals with the Ojibwe leaders tonight."

"Will they be happy with those proposals?"

"I doubt it," the major predicted. "*I'm* not happy," he declared. "The American Fur Company is going to get more money out of this treaty than the Ojibwe or Dakota!"

"How is that possible?"

"Well," Taliaferro sighed, "the Native hunters and trappers are indebted to the fur company. Each year, the traders extend them credit to acquire traps and ammunition, and other supplies. Colonel Dodge is prepared to offer around three hundred thousand dollars in exchange for tribal lands. But almost half of that money will go to the fur company to pay off the debts."

"How much land are they talking about?"

"Everything east of the Mississippi River, up to Lake Mille Lacs," reported the major.

"A northern portion from the Ojibwe and a smaller southern slice from the Dakota. The Natives will be allowed to hunt, fish and collect wild rice and maple sap in those areas." He continued to explain, "Whites, however, will begin to settle and buy property there. Plus, lumber companies will venture into those forests to start harvesting trees."

"Things are going to be a lot different around here."

* * *

More Ojibwe men gathered at the agency than the Council House would hold, so a campfire was started outside, around which the leaders seated themselves. Twelve different bands of the tribe attended. Flat Mouth and Hole-in-the-Day had come from the Upper Mississippi. Several more leaders represented bands who lived beside large lakes—Fond du Lac, Gull, Mille Lacs, Red and Red Cedar. Still more lived up the St. Croix River and near Lake Superior—Lac de Flambeau, La Pointe and Lac Courte Oreilles. Many warriors had come with these leaders. They sat with their bands just outside the inner circle.

Corporal Whitney sat beside Major Taliaferro. Nearby was Henry Sibley and a few more American Fur Company men. However, Alex noticed that Jean Baptiste Reaume sat next to Flat Mouth. The Sandy Lake trader, William Aitken, was there too, seated next to Hole-in-the-Day.

The major stood up, and the hubbub of conversation died around the circle. He graciously welcomed the many bandleaders, recognizing most by name. He knew them from previous council meetings during his seventeen years as the Indian Agent at Fort Snelling. Of course, they also knew each other. During the next few minutes, Taliaferro revealed a summary of the US Government's treaty proposals. When he stopped, the hubbub erupted again.

Flat Mouth engaged in animated debate with Reaume, Hole-in-the-Day and the Mille Lacs Band leader First Day. When he stood up, the circle grew quiet in recognition of the Pillager's worthy reputation. "The whites must desperately want access to this land or they would not offer such a grand payment. If they want it so badly, perhaps we should ask for more." He ended with words of caution, "Past experience tells us the Whites are not trustworthy. We must get proof of their promises before we agree."

The Wind leaped to his feet. Not waiting for the growing babble to subside, he shouted, "The Snake River Band says no. The land they want is our home."

Buffalo slowly rose. The great leader from the St. Croix River had earned respect from all, so The Wind reluctantly sat back down. "Tonight, we will talk and think," counseled Buffalo. "Tomorrow, we will choose. Whatever our decision, we must unite. We will show the whites that our Ojibwe nation is a vast and powerful force to be reckoned with."

Talk continued well into the night. It was long after dark before Alex walked back to the fort and fell into his bunk.

* * *

When Alex woke up, the barracks seemed uncommonly busy. Soldiers were bustling about, organizing their equipment more neatly than usual. He caught the eye of Sergeant Schmid, passing by and already dressed. "Bill. What's going on? We expecting an inspection?"

"Haven't you heard?" The old blacksmith straightened uncomfortably and rubbed his rib cage, still sore a week after his injury. "We're movin' out! When the Fifth Infantry gets here, we're goin' to Florida. Gonna fight the Seminoles with Zach Taylor."

"How soon?"

"Don't know," Schmid admitted, "but we've been told to be ready." He grimaced again, "Speakin' of ready, you better roll out. We gotta line up for assembly pretty quick."

Alex got dressed and mustered on the parade ground for the raising of the colors. The officer of the day approached him during roll call. "Whitney, Major Bliss wants to see you. Report to the commander's residence after breakfast."

He ate his morning meal absent-mindedly, preoccupied with anxiety about the forthcoming meeting with Fort Snelling's commanding officer. *What did I do?* he worried. Nervously, Alex approached the square, stone dwelling in the fort's far eastern corner. A guard admitted him into a front room and disappeared to announce his arrival. Shortly, the guard ushered him into an office where Major Bliss sat behind his desk. The major returned his salute but did not bother to stand up, "Corporal Whitney, we received mail yesterday, carried by the convoy that brought Colonel Dodge." Bliss motioned to the territorial governor, seated off to the side. "As everybody has heard, that mail contained orders to transfer our regiment under the command of Colonel Zachary Taylor."

"Yes, sir."

"These orders for you personally accompanied that mail." The major leaned forward, extending an envelope across the desk. It had already been opened. "I have read them," he disclosed.

Alex unfolded a letter from the envelope and silently read its brief contents. It was a promotion! He was going to join Colonel

Taylor's command as a sergeant! Standing back at attention, he was unable to suppress a smile.

"Congratulations, Sergeant," Bliss too was smiling now. Once again, he leaned forward, extending two embroidered patches of sergeant's bars. "Take these to the sutler's store," he commanded, "Have them sewn onto a new shirt."

"Yes, sir."

Now the major stood up and offered a salute with one final word, "Dismissed."

* * *

July 29th, 1837

Dear Mother,

Big news! I have received a promotion to the rank of sergeant. This advancement comes with the transfer of our regiment. First Infantry will leave Fort Snelling soon for reassignment in Florida. I'll be under the command of Col. Zachary Taylor, as father was. We will be expected to enforce the Indian Removal Act and compel rebellious Seminoles to relocate to the Oklahoma Territory.

I wonder if you have had occasion to meet Solomon or Sarah Sibley in Detroit. Mr. Sibley is chief justice of Michigan's Supreme Court. Henry Sibley, their son, has become a close friend of mine. He is a very successful agent of the American Fur Company trading post here beside Fort Snelling.

Thinking of Michigan, I hear you have been awarded statehood. Our national flag will now have twenty-six stars!

I must finish this letter quickly and put it in the mail. My duty with the Indian Agent Maj. Taliaferro requires my presence at peace treaty talks this afternoon. When the treaty conference is finished, I expect the US delegation will leave, and a mail collection will go with them.

I am excited to fulfill my new commission as a sergeant under Col. Taylor. I will miss good friends here at Ft. Snelling, especially Sibley and Taliaferro. Don't know exactly where I'll be when you receive this letter, so await my next mailing before you send a reply.

Hope you are in excellent health, as am I.

Your loving son,

Alexander

* * *

A large canopy now stood on the field where the previous day's lacrosse contest had been played. A table stood under the awning, with papers upon which the Treaty of 1837 would be recorded. Governor Dodge, Major Taliaferro and other US Government officials sat behind the table. Opposite them sat the major leaders of all Ojibwe bands in attendance. Several American Fur Company traders stood off to one side. Beyond the shade of the canopy were dozens of Native warriors standing in the sunlight. A company of soldiers stood farther back. They were armed and in alignment but standing at ease.

Buffalo's directive had been accepted by the Ojibwe. The previous night, they argued all of their disagreements. Now they were united behind one decision, to grudgingly accept the treaty. Game was becoming more scarce east of the Mississippi. They knew the whites would be coming in greater numbers. Nearby Fort Snelling stood as a threatening symbol that their resistance could risk violent confrontation.

The majority of band leaders were silent today, but Flat Mouth stood to declare the honor of the Ojibwe people. He pledged they would remain true to the treaty and challenged government officials to prove lasting trustworthiness by the United States.

Buffalo approached the table to lay an oak leaf beside the treaty papers, a symbol of the forests where the Ojibwe people were promised the continued privileges to hunt and fish, and to harvest maple sap and wild rice.

When it came time to sign the Treaty of 1837, a secretary recorded Native names in English according to their phonetic sounds. Ojibwe leaders' names were recorded along with their warriors, grouped by tribal band. US Government dignitaries to sign included Governor Dodge, Major Taliaferro, Dr. Emerson and Fort Snelling's commander. The French scientist, Joseph Nicollet, also attended and signed, as did American Fur Company trader Henry Sibley.

* * *

With the treaty conference complete, Alex knew the Ojibwe bands would soon depart, and with them, Angelique Reaume. He hurried to the Mendota trading post and Henry Sibley's house. Steering a canoe around Pike Island, he saw warriors preparing to go home. *This paddle across the Minnesota River is an easy one I've made many times,* he thought. *Why is my heart pounding so fast?*

She saw the soldier coming and ran to meet his canoe at the shore. *It was only a short jog,* she thought. *Why am I breathless?* She bent to help pull his canoe up on the bank and greeted, "Hello."

"I wanted to see you again," Alex expressed. He stepped onto the beach to face her.

"Me too."

He half-turned to show the embroidered emblem sewn onto the uniform sleeve of his new shirt, "I got a promotion. I'm a sergeant now."

Angelique smiled, recognizing his pride, but the various military ranks meant nothing to her.

"There is more," he began with hesitation. "All the soldiers from Fort Snelling, including me, are being transferred to Florida."

"Florida?"

"Yes." His jaw tightened in an effort to control his voice. "It is thousands of miles away from here."

That explanation did not give her a tangible understanding of the distance to Florida. From his demeanor, she sensed it was far away. *This handsome boy, who is capable and kind, will soon be gone. I may never see him again.*

Alex ached. *This beautiful girl, with her graceful abilities, will soon be gone. I may never see her again.*

They stood looking at each other without words for a minute. Then Angelique noticed, across the river beyond the shoulder of his army uniform, young Pillager warriors readying to go home to Leech Lake. *Home,* she thought. *Family.* Gradually she realized the most important things in her life were different from the soldier's priorities.

Alex noticed a subtle change in her expression, a distant look. *Distant,* he thought. *My career ambitions and desire for adventures will take me distant from her.* Gradually he realized the most important things in his life were different from the Métis girl's priorities.

"I will remember you," Alex promised.

"And I will remember you," Angelique echoed.

Questions for Readers

Minnesota's Department of Education recommends that students learn "Minnesota Studies" during the middle grades. Learning standards and benchmarks are established for state history, civics, economics, geography, and sociology. Here are five sample questions designed to use *Twisting Trails* as a resource for learning about Minnesota in each of these categories.

1. History: Brief biographies for authentic Minnesota people follow each chapter of *Twisting Trails*. (a) Which of these people is most interesting to you? (b) Why?

2. Civics: In the 1830's, some Native-Americans and African-Americans were not considered U.S. citizens. (a) Can you list examples from Twisting Trails that show inferior rights for these people? (b) How has the U.S. Constitution been changed to guarantee citizenship for racial minorities?

3. Economics: 200 years ago, the fur trade was Minnesota's #1 business. Can you draw a cartoon strip, or story board, or picture map to show the process of the fur trade, from production to consumption.

4. Geography: Each chapter of this book takes place on a different trail — along rivers, across lakes, over prairies, and through forests. (a) Which particular place in the story would you most like to visit? (b) Why?

5. Sociology: The Metis culture of Angelique Reaume's family was a mixture of her dual ancestry — Indigenous and European. (a) Can you cite a pair of family activities, one influenced by her Native heritage and one by White culture? (b) Angelique was raised with certain values and beliefs about religion, family life, and property rights. Can you cite one belief passed down from her mother and another from her father?

About the Author

A resident of Minnesota for more than fifty years, Mike Barnes has enjoyed unique wonders in every corner of the state. An avid outdoorsman, he has fished Minnesota's lakes and rivers, and hunted its fields and forests. He is a married *(Kelly)* father of two *(Greg* and *Andy)* with four granddaughters *(Madison, Claire, Sylvia* and *Lucy)*.

Barnes is now retired from the social studies classroom where he taught history, geography, civics, and economics. His writing is an attempt to provide young adults with an historical fiction adventure that is based on factual Minnesota people, places and events. *Twisting Trails* is a book that parents and teachers can recommend for teen and tween readers who are curious about their state.

Endnotes

1   Rhoda R. Gilman, *The Story of Minnesota's Past* (St. Paul, MN: Minnesota Historical Society Press, 1991).

2   Steve Hall, *Fort Snelling: Colossus of the Wilderness* (St. Paul, MN: Minnesota Historical Society Press, 1987).

3   Evan Jones, *Citadel in the Wilderness: The Story of Fort Snelling and the Northwest Frontier* (New York: Coward-McCann Inc., 1966), (Minneapolis, MN: University of Minnesota Press, 2001).

4   Ibid.

5   Gilman, *The Story of Minnesota's Past*.

6   Duane R. Lund, *Minnesota's Chief Flat Mouth of Leech Lake* (Staples, MN: Nordell Graphic Communications, 1983).

7   Theresa M. Schenck, *William W. Warren: The Life, Letters, and Times of an Ojibwe Leader* (Lincoln, NE: University of Nebraska Press, 2007).

8   Duane R. Lund, *Leech Lake: Yesterday and Today* (Cambridge, MN: AdventureKEEN Publications, 1998).

9   Marybeth Lorbiecki, *Painting the Dakota: Seth Eastman at Fort Snelling* (Afton, MN: Afton Historical

Society Press, 2000).

10 Patricia C. Johnston, "The Artist's Life, The Indian's World," *American History Illustrated* 13, no. 9 (1979): 39–46.

11 Sarah E. Boehme, Christian F. Feest, Patricia C. Johnston, *Seth*

Eastman: A Portfolio of North American Indians (Afton, MN: Afton Historical Society Press, 1995).

12 Lorbiecki, *Painting the Dakota.*

13 William Durbin, "Who Was George Bonga?" *Minnesota Conservation Volunteer*, Nov.–Dec. 2010, 40–51.

14 Ibid.

15 Ibid.

16 Ibid.

17 Lorbiecki, *Painting the Dakota.*

18 *Wakaninajinwin*, www.kouroo.info/kouroo/thumbnails/W/Wakanina-jinwin.pdf.

19 Johnston, "The Artist's Life, The Indian's World."

20 Lorbiecki, *Painting the Dakota.*

21 *Wakaninajinwin.*

22 Philip P. Mason, *Schoolcraft's Expedition to Lake Itasca* (East Lansing, MI: Michigan State University Press, 1993).

23 "Henry Rowe Schoolcraft," https://bit.ly/3Ifcdep.

24 Mason, *Schoolcraft's Expedition to Lake Itasca.*

25 Schoolcraft, https://bit.ly/3Ifcdep.

26 Lawrence Taliaferro, *Autobiography of Major Lawrence Taliaferro* (St. Paul, MN: Minnesota Historical Collections, 1864).

27 Ibid.

28 Evan Jones, *Citadel in the Wilderness: The Story of Fort Snelling and the Northwest Frontier* (New York: Coward-McCann Inc., 1966), (Minneapolis, MN: University of Minnesota Press, 2001).

29 Rena N. Coen, "Eliza Dillon Taliaferro: Portrait of a Frontier Wife," *Minnesota History Magazine* 52, issue 4 (1990): 146–153.

30 Jones, *Citadel in the Wilderness.*

31 Samuel W. Pond, *Dakota Life in the Upper Midwest* (St. Paul, MN:

Minnesota Historical Society Press, 2002).

32   Theodore C. Blegen, *The Pond Brothers* (St. Paul, MN: Minnesota Historical Society Press, 1934).

33   Pond, *Dakota Life in the Upper Midwest*.

34   Blegen, *The Pond Brothers*.

35   Pond, *Dakota Life in the Upper Midwest*.

36   Ted Stone, *The Legend of Pierre Bottineau and the Red River Trail* (Edmonton, Alberta: Eschia Books, 2013).

37   Lawrence J. Barkwell, *Pierre Bottineau, 1816–1895* (Winnipeg, Manitoba: Louis Riel Institute, 2008), www.metismuseum.ca/resource.php/07413.

38   Stone, *The Legend of Pierre Bottineau and the Red River Trail*.

39   Anne Healy and Sherry Kankel, "A History of Red Lake County: Pierre Bottineau" (Red Lake Falls, MN, 1976), http://www.redlakecountyhistory.org/bottineau.htm.

40   Rev. E. D. Neill, *A Sketch of Joseph Renville: A "Bois Brule" and Early Trader of Minnesota* (St. Paul, MN: Minnesota Historical Society Collections, 1872).

41   "The Joseph Renville Story" (2019), https://bit.ly/3DhJIcu.

42   Jon Willand, *Lac qui Parle and the Dakota Mission* (Madison, MN: Lac qui Parle County Historical Society, 1964).

43   Ibid.

44   Rhoda R. Gilman, "Henry H. Sibley (1811–1891)," (St. Paul, MN: Minnesota Historical Society Collection, 2014), https://bit.ly/31df9Z3.

45   Rhoda R. Gilman, *Henry Hastings Sibley: Divided Heart* (St. Paul, MN: Minnesota Historical Society Press, 2004).

46   "Biography: Henry H. Sibley."

47   Gilman, *Henry Hastings Sibley: Divided Heart*.

48   Ibid.

49   "Biography: Henry H. Sibley."

50 Martha Coleman Bray, *The Journals of Joseph N. Nicollet: A Scientist on the Mississippi Headwaters with Notes on Indian Life, 1836–37* (St. Paul, MN: Minnesota Historical Society Press, 1970).

51 Ibid.

52 Martha Coleman Bray, *Joseph N. Nicollet on the Plains and Prairies: The Expeditions of 1938–39 with Journals, Letters, and Notes on the Dakota Indians* (St. Paul, MN: Minnesota Historical Society Press, 1993).

53 David Nevin, *Dream West* (New York: G. P. Putnam Publisher, 1983).

54 Annette Atkins, "Dred and Harriet Scott" (St. Paul, MN: Minnesota Historical Society, 2014), https://www.mnopedia.org/event/dred-and-harriet-scott-minnesota.

55 Lea VanderVelde, *Mrs. Dred Scott: A Life on Slavery's Frontier* (New York: Oxford University Press, 2009).

56 Ibid.

57 Don E. Fehrenbacher, *The Dred Scott Case: Its Significance in American Law and Politics* (New York: Oxford University Press, 2001).

58 Ibid.